From

The Women's Press Ltd
124 Shoreditch High Street, London E1 6JE

The Women's Press
science fiction

This is one of the first titles in a new science fiction series from The Women's Press.

The list will feature new titles by contemporary writers and reprints of classic works by well known authors. Our aim is to publish science fiction by women and about women; to present exciting and provocative feminist images of the future that will offer an alternative vision of science and technology, and challenge male domination of the science fiction tradition itself.

We hope that the series will encourage more women both to read and to write science fiction, and give the traditional science fiction readership a new and stimulating perspective.

SARAH LEFANU

Sarah Lefanu was born in 1953. She taught English in the People's Republic of Mozambique for two years before joining The Women's Press in 1980 where, since the birth of her son, Alexander, she continues to work part-time. Her reviews and articles have appeared in *Spare Rib*, *Time Out*, *City Limits*, *Marxism Today* and *Foundation*. She teaches a course in feminism and science fiction at the City Literary Institute, London. She is co-editor of *Sweeping Statements: Writings from the Women's Liberation Movement* (The Women's Press, 1984).

JEN GREEN

Jen Green was born in 1955. She completed her PhD, an exposé of Christian attitudes to women, in 1982. She has taught literature and science fiction at the University of Sussex and for the Workers' Educational Association, and her writing has appeared in *Spare Rib*. She has been a member of two women's rock bands, *Devils Dykes* (1978–80) and *Bright Girls* (1980–82). She joined The Women's Press in 1983.

DESPATCHES
FROM THE FRONTIERS
OF
THE FEMALE MIND

An Anthology of Original Stories
edited and introduced by
JEN GREEN & SARAH LEFANU

The Women's Press
sf

First published by The Women's Press Ltd 1985
A member of the Namara Group
124 Shoreditch High Street, London E1 6JE

'The Clichés from Outer Space' was first published in *Women's
Studies International Forum*, Vol. 7, No. 2, 1984 © Joanna Russ 1984

Introduction and collection © Jen Green and Sarah Lefanu 1985

British Library Cataloguing in Publication Data

Despatches from the frontiers of the female mind.
  1. Short stories, English—Women authors
  2. English fiction—20th century
  I. Green, Jen   II. Lefanu, Sarah
  823'.01'089287   PR1286.W6

  ISBN 0-7043-3973-0

Typeset by MC Typeset, Chatham, Kent
Reproduced, printed and bound in Great Britain
by Hazell, Watson & Viney Ltd, Aylesbury, Bucks

Contents

JEN GREEN & SARAH LEFANU

Introduction

Over the last twenty years there has been a flowering of women writing science fiction – Ursula LeGuin, Anne McCaffrey and Joanna Russ are perhaps the best known. Despite this, science fiction still bears the heavy imprimatur of male approval: books-by-men-for-men (or boys). When one considers the market, which has always been largely male, and the common themes that run through science fiction, such as technology, pushing back the frontiers of space and combat in various forms, this isn't surprising. Which is not to say that women don't read science fiction, nor, perhaps more importantly, that they aren't interested in technology, or indeed combat (far from it!), but rather that people *think* that women are not interested in such things. All too often, while many writers have been radical and imaginative in technological and social terms, science fiction has maintained an essentially conservative attitude to women and to the relationship between the sexes. Even the inner dream worlds explored by the 'new wave' writers of the sixties tended to be the dream worlds of men.

Changes in the representation of women in science fiction have done little more than reflect the legal and social advances made by women in our society over the past fifteen to twenty years, which affect, for example, the position of women in the workplace or the demands made by women for greater autonomy in sexual choices. Some science fiction, indeed, lags behind even these advances, with writers apparently content to import patriarchal values wholesale into the most unfamiliar of landscapes, creating a trans-temporal and cross-cultural constant out of attitudes that are historically specific to our own times.

Traditionally women have been represented by a series of stereotypical images, such as the perennial wife and mother in her high-tech home, the addle-headed young girl or, if we are allowed to be anything other than passive, the malevolent and power-crazed matriarch. Men have been writing about future possibilities for *them* since the dawn of science fiction. Only rarely does a vision of a brave new world extend its freedoms to women. Joanna Russ has commented (*Vertex*, February 1974) on the extraordinary failure of imagination that allows a world however many years into the future to have as half its population a class of suburban housewives. Her article, 'Images of Women in Science Fiction' argues that, 'There are plenty of images of women in science fiction. There are hardly any women.'

While images of women have changed over the years, it is questionable whether the changes are anything other than superficial. Do these images, in fact, reflect the same underlying anxieties and fantasies about women expressed by the male science fiction writers of the past? The suburban housewife of the 1950's was ousted when sex hit science fiction in the 1960's. Until then, sexual activity had not been seen within the pages of science fiction. The sexual 'revolution' brought single, sexually active women into science fiction, but they formed part of the expanding horizons of the male characters, they were there to show what was now possible for male characters to do. Whatever their sexual role, female characters have always proved convenient as recipients (the listening ear, whether in kitchen or bedroom) for any scientific information that has to be imparted to the reader.

In the wings, rarely centre stage, women have acted essentially as foils to their male counterparts, as enemies, appendages, victims or obscure objects of desire, perennially as the Other. You don't need green skin, a pointed head and two antennae to be treated as deviant by the white middle-class male population in general, and the science fiction establishment in particular. You need merely to be, for example, homosexual, non-white, old, working-class or female. As Ursula Le Guin puts it:

'The question involved here is the question of the Other – the being who is different from yourself. This being can be different from you in its sex; or in its annual income; or in its way of speaking and dressing and doing things; or in the colour of its skin, or the number of its legs and heads. In other words, there is the sexual Alien, and the social Alien, and the cultural Alien, and finally the racial Alien . . .'
('American SF and the Other', *Science Fiction Studies*, No 7, Vol 2, November 1975)

Yet as Pamela Sargent has shown, in her detailed introduction to the *Women of Wonder* anthology (Penguin 1978), there is a well-established tradition of women writing science fiction, starting, indeed, with Mary Shelley and *Frankenstein: or The Modern Prometheus* (1818), which deals with the fearsome implications of scientific knowledge. In the past there has been little encouragement for women to write science fiction; those who did often used male bylines (such as Francis Stevens earlier this century) or ones that were not gender specific (such as C L Moore and Leigh Brackett) to overcome prejudice from editors and readers. Many women, writing under their own or assumed names, have followed the tradition of science fiction in featuring male rather than female protagonists, thus perpetuating the peripheral status accorded to women in science fiction. Some, like Joanna Russ, have found the transition to writing novels based around a central heroine difficult:

'Long before I became a feminist in any explicit way, I had turned from writing love stories about women in which women were losers, and adventure stories about men in which men were winners, to writing adventure stories about a woman in which the woman won. It was one of the hardest things I ever did in my life . . .'
(Unpublished letter)

Given all this, why is it, then, that science fiction is so attractive to women writers? Certainly it provides the perfect arena for speculative visions of the future, for realising and exploring a whole range of political and personal possibilities. It provides, too, an opportunity to imagine oneself standing outside patriarchal culture and thus to name and question its components. Science fiction allows us to see beyond the restricted roles that are prescribed for women; it allows us, as Suzy McKee Charnas has said, to write our dreams as well as our nightmares (*Khatru* 3 and 4, November 1975).

Science fiction also allows us to take the present position of women and use the metaphors of science fiction to illuminate it. We may be writing *about* the future, but we are writing *in* the present. Can we *not* now, for example, write about women as housewives because 'housewife' is a stereotype of a woman? But the majority of women do housework, whether they are married, or single with children, or caring for elderly parents. To deny this aspect of women's lives is as distorting as to present us as housewives and housewives only. Pamela Zoline's marvellous short story, 'Heat Death of the Universe' (*New Women of Wonder*, Vintage 1978), is about Sarah Boyle, housewife; the entropy of the universe enters her house and chaos cracks open the fictive order of her life. To be a housewife is indeed a serious business. There is a world of difference between what women can do and what society says they should be doing but the two are also linked in a number of ways. One of the tasks of a feminist politics is to investigate this interrelationship, and the task of a feminist writer is to reflect its complexity.

This potential has been realised by women writers such as Joanna Russ, Vonda McIntyre, Marge Piercy, Ursula Le Guin, Suzette Haden Elgin, James Tiptree Jr (Raccoona Sheldon), Chelsea Quinn Yarbro, Naomi Mitchison, Sally Miller Gearhart and Suzy McKee Charnas.

We see this anthology as continuing in this tradition by extending imaginatively the possibilities for women and thus challenging the norms of traditional science fiction writing. Here women are depicted as active and capable and as central to the narrative. The stories reflect the importance of a new perspective, rooted in a feminist awareness, which questions the seemingly changeless nature of the dynamic between women and men in science fiction.

This collection goes beyond the depiction of women as

amazing amazons, brilliant businesswomen, all as hot for sex as any lusty hero. It is not a collection of women of wonder, pace Pamela Sargent, whose three anthologies paved the way for this one, and heaven knows we do still need and want women of wonder to dream about. Although these stories include fantastical elements they are based in the everyday experience of contemporary women and reflect the dilemmas that women face within a patriarchal culture. In this collection 'Long Shift', for example, set in a woman-centred urban community, presents an unexceptional protagonist who has to confront the problems and stresses of her job.

Feminism has taught us what women can do; it has given us a basis from which to project our visions of the future, but it has also taught us how far we still have to go. Thus some of the stories provide us with visions of a future where sexism is non-existent, dealing, as Mary Gentle says, 'with feminism by taking a feminist background for granted, and going on from there'. Others are concerned with the present, in other words with the actual tactics and mechanics of liberation.

Women and work emerges as an important theme within this, and our stories present a varied series of positive images of women as workers. Many of our writers stress the importance for women of developing a full and independent role within the workplace; others show, however, that the need to earn a living can make women vulnerable to sexual exploitation.

The themes of birth and reproduction have a special and central place within the collection. Years of seeing women presented in science fiction as baby machines and full-time nurturers has made many women writers fight shy of depicting women as mothers in their stories at all; they preferred to write stories about women as amazons and adventurers, doing anything in fact but bearing or rearing children. The advent of sex into science fiction in the sixties saw the emergence of the 'exotic means of getting pregnant' story, with its hidden sadistic elements, satirised here by Joanna Russ in 'Clichés from Outer Space'. These kinds of stories did little to endear feminists to the theme of reproduction.

Feminism allows us to reclaim the importance of bearing children on our own terms, allowing us to return to this much-abused theme and expose its radical meaning and potential. In many of the stories reproduction is shown as an important and political phenomenon that shapes and conditions the relationship between women and men, and thus affects the whole structure of society. For the woman who sees the child emerge from her own body, connection with and control over her offspring is instantaneous and irrefutable, but for the man the link is assured recognition through the institution of marriage. Many of the stories here explore this fundamental link between biology and culture, between the innate and the constructed. Some reflect on the implications of genetic engineering and recent developments, such as test tube babies, which represent man's attempts to appropriate the reproductive process for himself and thus gain power over the future. In 'Love Alters' on the other hand Tanith Lee shows us a society in which reproduction is separated from the biology of female and male, and in which two people of the same sex can produce a child together; here, interestingly enough, there is no struggle for predominance between women and men.

Penny Casdagli's 'Mab' transforms the myth of parthenogenesis into a powerful symbol of autonomy; she overturns the man-made myths of male creativity, in which men, in reversal of biological reality, give birth to women (Adam to Eve, Zeus to Minerva) and exposes them as a 'monstrous usurping of the mother-rite', and the mother-right, which ensues. In general throughout the collection the potential of myth-making is recognised, and the dual capacity of myth to oppress or liberate explored.

Technology has an important part to play in many of the visions which follow. Some stories are cautionary in their approach, dealing with the dangers of the pursuit of the unknowable. Others treat the importance of taking responsibility for the changes that technical advance may bring about. If women tend to view technological advance in a negative light, it is not because they are necessarily anti-technology per se, but because feminism offers us a particular critique of science and technology. And it is equally important to seek out its radical potential, to envisage women appropriating and using it as a force for positive change. It seems important that rather than take refuge in the conservative genres of magic and fantasy we look to science fiction and to the integration of technology into our imagined futures.

The threat of the devastation of the planet by nuclear war casts its shadow over many of the stories. Zoë Fairbairns in 'Relics' weaves a story around life at Greenham Common, mocking the men who bring war about and the men who survive. In her story, birth is an act of defiance, a new direction. In 'Instructions for Exiting this Building in Case of Fire' Pamela Zoline presents women as a kind of universal motherhood allied against the potentially destructive forces of nationalism.

Another theme common to many of the stories is the repressive State, in which women so frequently end up at the bottom of the hierarchy. Many stories offer a fine moral vision, not because women are innately more moral than men, but, traditionally at least, as underdogs we are in a good position to understand the consequences and implications of laws made for rather than by us. Our stories range from the bleak to the hopeful to the transcendent. Overall, though, a kind of optimism is felt, a belief in the strength and efficacy of women, both isolated and together, to combat, outwit, subvert or at least chip away at the repressive institutions that seem all too frequently to inhabit our dreams of the future.

JOSEPHINE SAXTON

Big Operation on Altair Three

Josephine Saxton was born in Halifax in 1935. She left school aged fifteen, became an art student, was married twice, has four children and two grandchildren. She 'wanted to be famous writer/painter/dancer since tiny child, still working on it. Happily divorced now studying traditional Chinese acupuncture for licentiate, writing novels, short stories and flippant articles.' Her works include The Hieros Gamos of Sam and An Smith, Vector for Seven, Group Feast, The Travails of Jane Saint *and numerous short stories. Her new novel,* Queen of the States, *is forthcoming from The Women's Press.*

She says of 'Big Operation on Altair Three', 'The idea came from an American advertisement for a car which made reference to a circumcision done on the back seat. I was reminded of sculptures lifesize (name forgotten famous modern artist) of sex in back seat of a Ford in the Fifties, so took it from there.'

I'm looking for another career, but at my age this isn't easy. I'm in perfect health and as full of drive as ever, of course, but as we women of Altair are finally noticing, this is not an easy time or place for us to live in; the prime posts go to men. Back on Earth there has been total equality of opportunity for hundreds of years; I took it for granted that on Altair the situation was similar. It took me a while to wake up to this, but when I spoke with my friend who's in social history, she illuminated me somewhat as to why.

'What's happening here in the twenty-third century is what happened during the Industrial Revolution back on Earth. A double-bind. Cheap female labour but the sole role of motherhood imprint. Patriarchy syndrome. More kids to work the pits and so on—you know!'

Well, I suppose I had known, from school, but history wasn't my strong point and all that stuff was—well, history. I am in advertising, I work in holograds. Part of my job is finding the 'stars' and persuading them to do the stunts for the ads—I was the one who got the guy to do the tranks ad—the one where he is surrounded by poisonous lizards and just purrs at them, grinning. (*Stay calm in the stickiest situations*—one of them almost got him but he just laughed. I mean, he was risking his life but that's largely what makes holograds sell things, people get a real buzz out of knowing we don't fudge any of the events, with holograds you *can't* fudge.) I have to arrange the insurance, the hospital standby—sort of continuity and stage manager's aide. It's interesting, but I'm beginning to have moral qualms, something I cannot afford.

I come from pioneering stock, and pioneers don't have moral qualms and, as you know, there's no moral issues about settling a place, raping it for all it's got and then moving on. Anyone questioning the system gets hospitalised along with the Lords of the Universe nutters who try to tell you there's a race of evil immortals who are influencing humanity and running the show for their own ends. My pal in social history says there has always been a whipping-post for people's deep anxieties. It used to be the Gnomes of Zurich, international bankers, Freemasons (whatever these are). No, I don't subscribe to that stuff, but I do feel maybe Altair isn't for me any more. But where else could I go? It is the same everywhere, men and younger women succeed. It's crazy really: we are brought up to stay healthful, live longer and then: 'move over Granma, we don't need you.'

I think what made all this begin to get to me was Alison Kesla's ad for the Airborn car last year. I didn't actually work on that job much, but it was our firm that did it all and I was around when it was being made. I've worked on ads for things I knew were rubbish, thought bad and plain bad value for money, but this, well, now perhaps I should be doing something else.

There's so much I enjoy about my job, I'm good at it, there's plenty to sell on Altair, it's a long way off exhausted and with millions of untouched planets to go at, who cares about a bit of smoke? Apparently ecology was necessary on Earth before Stardrive but now we have all the energy we need. An infinite boom. I'm a little nervous about putting down on paper these hints of moral issues, it would go against me if it got back to the firm; moral issues are not compatible with the economy. Still, how could I want to return to the chaos of democracy—things run so smoothly from a central government, nobody is short of anything—or are they?

You know Alison Kesla, of course. She starred as the Ice Cream girl, very beautiful with her reddish-gold hair and freckles and green eyes and perfectly-shaped ivory body. But the dark thing got hyped, people were getting bored with Alison's type and she was beginning to worry. Like me now, perhaps she wondered, what and where next?

So we had this commission for the car ad. The Airborn isn't really airborne of course, a hover-type is totally unsuitable for the dust here, but it is a very flash super-speedy, stable, hyper-sprung version of the family hatch-back but bigger in the back for weekend exploration trips. Not being able to make and keep good roads here what with the small earthquakes all the time, the temperature changes, dust and the two-hour cactus problem not yet having been solved, well, the stability of cars is a major seller. One guaranteed to stay upright and smooth over all terrain is the one people want and the Airborn is the latest ultimate.

You've probably got one now. Most people have. It was a successful holograd. I think it is a clever car with its vacuum-cleaner-type outside air-conditioner, the way it grabs the dust and compresses it into little pellets and shoots them out the back. I cracked up laughing the first time I saw one, it looked like an armoured anjotan had eaten too many glean-beans, with sound-effects. You can shut that function off for city work because nobody needs peppering with miniature bricks, but in cross-country, it is unbeatable for maintaining good vision at high speed. And, you know, the reason the suspension is so perfect is that the shock absorbers are built on exactly the same principle as the human spinal vertebrae; fibrous sacks of gel capable of expanding and compressing, and the discs don't break open even under any amount of pressure like human discs because on rebound, another perfectly compressed disc slides into place ready to take the rebound shock while the volume equalises. Result, not a tremble in the inner compartment which is suspended separately inside the outer car. The gel in those discs is a secret formula. Some people said it actually was gel from human spinal discs but of course that's just a sick joke. You could be in a sitting-room but you'd be travelling at up to five hundred miles an hour and not feel a tremble. Very, very expensive. Aimed initially at the professional classes with a potential female market, those with the money. Was there an angle which would get both markets? Not a sex angle because that would annoy the husbands. There's a bed-seat in the back of course, for the hitch-hiker—even in the middle of the Altairian desert, fantasies hold out.

So, the line was not sex but it had to be women. Female bodies sell everything to anyone, but we needed something a little different, to get the scientists, artists, doctors—It was doctors which got it started but before that somebody came up with a tired idea of a glass of red wine standing on the front seat and the driver pulls up in about five yards at a cliff edge in an earthquake and there isn't a drop spilled; the goof who brought that up got some scornful glances, the drink-drive maximum being a lobotomy! Besides, the upholstery is white suede from some rare goat-like creature somewhere on the edge of the galaxy, and in setting up the scene it only needed one drop spilled and the whole car would be ruined. Laughter.

I suppose it was red marks on white upholstery that sparked off the final idea in somebody's subconscious, along with the mention of doctors. A guy said, 'We could do a surgical operation on the back seat, something tricky that requires precision.'

'Yeah, a lobotomy on you!' snapped the chief, but a moment later his expression had changed, something had clicked.

As you know, hysterectomy is very fashionable as the ultimate contraceptive, any woman who has had one stands a better chance for a job, those few days a month more of maximum output impress a male boss. Very lucrative for surgeons. We liaised with the clinic circuit and got excited about this bizarre super-hype, and the search for the surgeon and the model began. We got Marlin Drafe who was famous in both cosmetics and gynae, he had been on the line of 'if the difference is biological, ladies, it can be fixed'.

I wondered at first about Alison Kesla but they told me in the Art department that it was her creamy colouring on the white background and things like that which you expect from Arts, and I supposed that Alison must be glad of the chance to get this big scene for her faltering career. The new Ice Cream lady was a fabulous black girl who let the stuff melt a little and drip down her body. Sales have gone way up apparently.

The ad is beautiful, the Arts lot were good. Her make-up was lightly gilded, her reddish hair perfect, her expression dreamy on pre-med tranks, her green eyes calm and far away, and the shot of her long legs as she got into the car and slid back on the white satin sheets (over plastic, they were serious about the upholstery) and then the way she drifted off to sleep as the driver went from 0–500 in something a little longer than the car itself. We'd rehearsed the camera-work several times a day for nearly a week so we could get every shot perfect at that speed, the beams had to reach target and stay there throughout the run, there had to be no break at all or the public would say we had filled in from studio work. But our technics people are great, really great.

Drafe baulked at first at having to work kneeling, but money overcomes such problems, and considering the relatively small space, with the oxygen and the tray of instruments (they put this in a magnetised tray to calm the surgeon's mind; he didn't have faith in the stability of the car and he was worried he might not be able to put his hand to something if they shot around) he did a perfect job without assistance. You get this wonderful purple glow from the mountains outside the car, the red splashes, the first incision was very slow on purpose (Arts again) and then when he has finished he slowly takes off his gloves and gives just a gentle stroke to her body! Then when she wakes with a smile on her face she murmurs, 'When do we start?'. I should think that alone gets women making the decision, for both op and car in some cases.

I'll never know how she managed that sleepy smile. After the ad, recovering in hospital, she cracked up completely. The bit that wasn't visible in the ad was her pregnancy. She wanted that child. The father was important in the firm. If she'd refused the job she'd never work again she'd been told.

Alison is working—the ad put her right back at the top. She seems okay. But she wanted a child, and so do I. The time off won't do me any good in my career. But I'd like to get out of advertising anyway. Secretly, I feel it goes too far sometimes. But how else can I survive now, here, on Altair Three? Or anywhere. I need to think. I need to think a lot.

MARGARET ELPHINSTONE

Spinning the Green

*Margaret Elphinstone lives in Scotland with her two daughters,
and spends most of her time writing and gardening. Her stories
and poems have appeared in* Writing Women *and* Scotia
Review. *She is co-author of a forthcoming book on gardening,*
The Holistic Gardener *(Turnstone Press, 1986) and has recently
finished her first novel,* Crying for the Moon.

*She says of her story, ' "Spinning the Green" was conceived
on a bus between Dumfries and London, the result of six hours'
thinking about feminism, the peace movement, my trips to
Greenham and the English countryside. For a long time I have
had strong feelings about the way traditional fairy stories have
come down to us, especially as my children, like many others,
insisted on having the Ladybird versions read to them again and
again, a process from which I have never recovered. I am very
interested in fantasy and science fiction. They can be powerful
genres for feminists to use, since with a few notable exceptions
they have been dominated until now by patriarchal attitudes.'*

Once upon a time there lived a rich merchant. He had three
daughters called Elsie, Lacie and Tilly, and they lived on the
profits of a treacle mine. Elsie and Lacie were not clearly
differentiated in the minds of anybody, they were just elder
sisters, and from that you can draw your own conclusions. Tilly
was as kind as she was good, and as good as she was beautiful,
and as beautiful as she was kind. And if that doesn't tell you
what you want to know, swallow your subversive curiosity and
read on.

Now the merchant had been worried for some time, for

shares in treacle had been falling rapidly, as a result of a cruel government campaign which forced him to add Treacle Rots Your Teeth in letters no less than one millimetre high on every billboard advertising treacle. Also, the matter of spoil heaps had recently become a sticky issue in the environmentalist press. So the merchant saddled his horse one day, and called his daughters to kiss him goodbye and wish him well, for he was setting out to an international convention to establish the future secure foundations of the treacle industry.

Before he set spurs to his horse, however, he turned to his daughters and said, 'Is there any little gift you would like me to bring you when I come home again?'

'Diamonds,' said Elsie, her eyes gleaming. 'Diamonds, gold, pineapples, peaches, oranges and sherry, and two tickets to a cricket match.'

'Coffee,' said Lacie, smiling sweetly. 'Coffee, chocolate, tobacco, soya, nuts, beef and a tract of primeval forest.'

'And Tilly my dear,' said the merchant fondly. 'What about you?'

And Tilly, for reasons of her own which will become apparent later, replied, 'A red rose, Papa, if you please.'

The convention was moderately successful. The merchant was not entirely happy. He had an obscure feeling that he was being duped by his partners from across the Western Sea, and he wasn't keen on the new policy of exporting guns hidden at the bottom of the treacle barrels. So he rode home slowly with a slack rein, passing unseeing through the perilous tracks of the Wild Forest, while little graphs flashed across the grey screens of his mind, and square green digits bleeped continuously through his thoughts.

The horse had other ideas. (It is important to remember that, because the world does not change by chance).

When the merchant looked up again, he found himself in a part of the forest he had never seen before, a wild perilous growing place, where the trees crowded so thickly that the dead trunks were held up by their living neighbours. Strange matted creepers hung from branches far above, while curious rustlings and calls echoed through the undergrowth. The merchant found it wild, and shuddered. He was utterly lost.

'We are utterly lost,' he said to his horse, who naturally did not contradict him.

At that moment an arrow embedded itself in the merchant's saddle-bow.

Yes, an arrow.

The merchant registered a faint thud, and saw it quivering, inches from his hand. His eyes widened, and slowly he raised his arms above his head, hoping that was the correct thing to do under these unusual circumstances. The arrow was a yard long and had a green feather. The horse took a step forward and began to crop the long sweet grass.

'How do you do?' called the merchant quaveringly, when the silence grew too intense.

As soon as he spoke two figures appeared, swinging lightly from low branches that overhung the path. They stood, arrows notched, one behind him and one before, so that there was no way left to turn. They were both clad from head to foot in garb of Lincoln green.

'I have no money,' gasped the merchant, 'and even if I had it would be against my principles to acquiesce in so subversive an activity as the redistribution of wealth. I have always paid my taxes, and if you don't believe me I will vouchsafe to you my national insurance number, so that you can dial the police computer and check that I am a responsible citizen, and find out everything you wish to know about me and a great deal more which you would be a fool to believe anyway. Please do not threaten me with violence. I have a place in a fallout shelter which cost me a great deal, and it would be most unfortunate if it were wasted. Will you let me go now if I offer to send you a consignment of treacle?'

They ignored this speech completely. The one in front of him lowered her bow and came near enough for the horse to nuzzle her face. 'We have come to invite you to dinner,' she said.

They blindfolded him and led him to their camp by many secret ways. The dinner was excellent, though the merchant could have eaten something a little more substantial than fresh fruits and herbs of the forest. He reckoned there must be at least two score of the women in green. There was no trace of any man among them, and yet they totally ignored him. Their children joined in the feast without hindrance, running freely round the clearing, returning to help themselves from high piled dishes, disappearing under the trees so that shrill laughter rang from the shadows. Above the merchant's head the green canopy of branches appeared to dance and flicker in the firelight. Between the leaves he saw the still cold points of stars looking indifferently down upon him. His horse was gone.

Only the two women who had captured him took notice of him. They treated him well, bringing him food and drink, and even condescending to talk to him a little. They asked nothing of him, and threatened him not at all, but that in itself made him uneasy. Finally he raised the subject that troubled him. 'Do you wish me to pay the bill?'

'There is no bill.'

A few minutes later he tried again, under the guise of light conversation. 'Am I right in thinking that your organisation is dedicated to the recirculation of capital?'

'There is no organisation.'

Apparently they insisted upon direct speech. 'Presumably you want my money?'

'We want no money.'

Incredulous, he tried to understand. 'Then what do you want?'

'Nothing you cannot give.'

Was that a threat? Trembling, he said, 'Then don't torture me. If you will let me go free, I will give whatever you ask.'

'You have no need to fear. What we want from you, no woman ever took from man by force.'

After that they left him, and fearful thoughts troubled him.

He began to grow strangely sleepy. The voices of the women and the interlacing branches above him seemed to weave together into bizarre patterns. The children were silent, or departed, and the women were sitting in a wide circle. Their voices rose and fell, and their hands were busy. Across the firelight he saw that they were spinning, spinning green threads, green thread twining together, spindles growing heavy with green. He watched neat fingers twisting the thread, and then weaving it, a green web woven, the circle of spinners become a circle of weavers. They spun the thread and wove the web, and the merchant's eyes grew sleepier, his head heavier, and he could watch the weaving of the web no longer. Only the voices drifted on into his dreams, weaving words to and fro across the circle:

'Who else is there now
Can spin the green
To cover the earth anew?'

Languorous sleep engulfed him, there was a scent like wild thyme in the air. He dreamed he was on a bank soft with oxslips, strewn with violets, and over his head musk roses shone palely in the moonlight, and around their stems grew a matted canopy of eglantine. He slept.

He woke in the cold light of dawn, and the shreds of wild sensuous dreams fled before his rising consciousness. Regretfully he sat up and rubbed his eyes. He was sitting in the place where the archers had ambushed him, and beside him lay his pack, untouched, with his cloak and saddle and bridle. No horse. Stiffly he got to his feet, aware now of a slight ache in his loins, but of no other hurt at all. In fact he felt curiously light, more relaxed in his body than usual. Yet his plight could hardly be worse. He was lost and far from home and his horse was gone.

He sighed and picked up his saddlebags. They were depressingly heavy; Elsie and Lacie's presents were not light. That made him think affectionately of his youngest daughter, and at the same moment a mass of tangled briars caught his eye, studded all over with delicate wild roses. Red roses. The merchant reached up painfully under the weight of his pack, pulled down a branch, and, ignoring the thorns that tore at his fingers, he picked a stem heavy with bright flowers.

There were enraged shouts and footsteps behind him. He turned to see the two women, their bows once more bent against him.

'I beg your pardon,' he stammered, and the roses trembled on the stem clutched in his hand.

'How dare you?' Their wrath was terrifying. 'How dare you, after we have treated you well and let you leave unharmed. How dare you pick the roses? Must you destroy every living thing that you find growing freely? How dare you do such a thing here?'

'I beg your pardon,' he said again. 'I meant no harm. The roses were for my daughter, Tilly. She asked me to bring her back a rose. Really, it wasn't my idea at all.'

'We are very angry,' said the other. 'You have no right to pick the roses.'

'Please do not kill me.' The merchant fell to his knees, his head bowed, and so failed to see the glance that passed between the women. 'It was my daughter's wish. I never meant to anger you. My other daughters have all that they asked for here in my pack. Tilly asked only for a rose. What can I do to save my life?'

'There is only one thing you can do now.' Her voice was scornful. 'You can send your daughter here in your place. If you can persuade her to do that, and bring her back within thirteen cycles of the moon, then we will not pursue you, but will let you live as you will in your own place for ever. But if she does not come, you can be very sure that you will be sent for, and there will be no further escape. So be warned!'

'Very well,' gabbled the merchant. 'I promise you I can persuade her. She will come if I explain it to her. I will see to it that she comes.'

The women said no more, and when the merchant dared to glance up they were gone. Trembling, he shouldered his pack once more, and set out to find his way home.

Tilly was the first to see her father returning. She was weeding the front garden, while her sisters were indoors reading romances and eating liquorice allsorts. Tilly dropped her fork and called to them. 'It's Papa home, and he's lost his horse.'

'Lost his horse? How dreadful! I wonder if he has our presents then?' Elsie and Lacie hurried out to see.

Soon the three sisters surrounded the weary merchant, begging him to tell them what had happened, how had he lost his horse, what misadventures had befallen him.

The merchant mentally reviewed his story. It did not sound particularly heroic, especially as there was still a slight numbness in his balls which suggested that something terribly embarrassing had happened to him. He cleared his throat, thinking fast, and told his story.

'Alas, alas, dear daughters,' he began. 'I was wending my weary way home, thinking only of you, my loved ones, when by mischance I lost myself in the Wild Forest. Exhausted and afraid though I was, I pressed ever onward, knowing that therein lay my only hope of returning to comfort my beloved children. Then suddenly . . .' Here he paused and looked around wildly for inspiration. 'Suddenly I heard an unearthly roaring behind me. The ground shook, the birds took to the air in clamorous terror, the very flowers by the wayside wilted and drooped their heads. There sprang out in front of me a hideous Beast, an image more vile than anything I had beheld in wildest nightmare, a loathsome brute of indescribable ugliness. With a fearful roar he seized me . . .' He saw his daughters looking curiously at his unscarred form clad with customary neatness. 'However, his grip was astonishingly gentle. He took me to his palace in the heart of the wood, and vanished from my sight.'

'How very odd,' said Tilly thoughtfully.

'How simply dreadful, Papa,' cried Elsie and Lacie. 'How noble and brave you are. No one else would dare to go where you have gone. What happened then?'

The merchant began to perceive a flaw in this re-telling of his tale. He gave Tilly an appraising glance and changed his tone a little. 'The palace in the forest was strange and beautiful, a place of enchantment. Invisible hands fed me with ambrosial delicacies, invisible guides led me to a luxurious bedroom. I had but to wish for any mortal thing and it was brought to me: exotic fruits and wines, fresh linen clothes, a colour television with six channels, and mysteriously scented chemicals to put in the sunken bath. Even the toilet seat was lined with white fur.'

'Good gracious!'

'The next morning I found myself alone. My breakfast was neatly laid, so that I only had to plug in the coffee pot and put the sliced bread in the toaster. I ate my fill, and left a note of thanks by the emerald-studded telephone. I found my way out through delightful gardens, between beds filled with the brightest flowers I ever beheld. At the gate I chanced upon a bush covered with red roses. At once I remembered you, dear

Tilly. I reached up and picked a spray of roses.' The merchant paused dramatically.

'What happened to your horse?' asked Tilly.

Her sisters silenced her at once. 'How can you be so unfeeling? See what our poor father has suffered, and you ask about a horse! Go on, dear Papa, go on.' Their eyes were hopefully fixed upon his pack.

'Immediately I heard again that terrible roaring. Again the ground shook, and the Beast appeared before me, more hideous than ever in the clear light of day. I confess I quailed before him. He towered over me, threatening me with huge talons and growling furiously. "I will kill you at once," he shrieked. "For I have treated you well and in return you have dared to pick my roses. For this you must die! I will tear you limb from limb forthwith!"

' "Oh please don't," I said as bravely as I could. "I have three daughters waiting for me at home, and if you eat me, whatever is to become of them? They will starve in the gutter, or somewhere similar, and there will be no one to succour them in their distress!" '

'And did he listen?'

The merchant brushed away a tear. 'Alas, dear Tilly, how am I to tell you this? He said he would let me go on one condition: that I bring you back within thirteen cycles of the moon, in my place.' He glanced at Tilly again. 'He said you could live in luxury in his palace, waited on hand and foot, and that he would provide you with anything you desired. But go there you must, and stay there at his pleasure.'

'So I should think,' said Elsie. 'After all, it was her that wanted the rose.'

'It doesn't sound a bad life to me,' said Lacie. 'And you could always try kissing him. He might turn into a handsome prince.'

'I'd rather he turned into a frog,' said Tilly. 'Papa, did he kill the horse?'

'My brave girl,' said the merchant, embracing her fondly. 'I knew you would never fail me. Let us be happy together while we still may. What have you prepared for dinner?'

A year later.

Tilly waited patiently by the rose bush. Her father had bidden her a fond but hasty farewell, and now she was sitting quietly on the ground, a little puzzled that there was no trace of any garden or palace, but not particularly afraid. Birds called through the wood, and a couple of green dragonflies fluttered in the sunshine. Tall trees towered around her, and narrow paths disappeared into tangled undergrowth. A warm inhabited place, but not tamed. She did not feel far from her own kind, but there was no trace of man. Then who?

She thought about the Beast, and frowned. This strange offer of a life of luxury, tainted by the threat of violence. A Beast that wanted her, who would provide her with her heart's desire, yet force her to his will. Whose anger was turned against her, because she had wanted a gift innocently gained. Who said that even the flowers of the forest belonged to him, and who could have her delivered into his power by mere command. Such a creature must be incredible, had she not learned its nature from her own father. Tilly shrugged, and went on waiting.

She couldn't remember falling asleep, but when she opened her eyes, women in green stood around her, their bows slung across their backs. She stared, and silently they stared back.

'I'm Tilly,' she said at last. 'I am my father's ransom.'

They nodded, as if they had expected her, and signed to her to follow them.

They took her to the clearing in the forest, and brought her food and water, and gave her a bed of fern to lie on, sheltered under green branches. They were silent, but not invisible. Tilly supposed the enchantment was done differently for her, and waited for the Beast to come. But he did not come, not that day, or the next, or the next.

At night she had dreams.

She would fall asleep looking at the patterns woven by leaves over her head, and her dreams were of green threads spinning, and a green web woven around her by many hands; a circle of spinners invisible under the stars, a circle of weavers with the green web stretched vibrant between their hands. Voices twined through her dreams, the singing of the spinners. And out of the weaving of words she caught a few lines circling, which wove their way through to her waking thoughts, so that she remembered them in the morning:

> 'Who else is there now
> Can spin the green
> To cover the earth anew?'

She woke thinking of a place her father owned where the wind blew across scarred soil until red rock showed, where once a forest stood. She thought of the red rose she had asked for, which had brought her to this place. When the women came with her breakfast she was waiting for them.

'Where is the Beast?' she asked.

For the first time one of the women spoke to her.

'The Beast has gone home,' she said quietly, and left.

The next day Tilly tried again. 'Where is the Beast?' she asked.

This time another woman answered.

'We are the Beast,' she said, and went away.

That was no help, but Tilly was ready to try again. 'Where is the Beast?' she asked on the third day.

'The Beast is in your head,' said the third woman, and departed.

Tilly sat with her hands pressed to her head and thought. Why had her father not told her the truth? To save himself embarrassment? If that were more important to him than the fate of his daughter then things she had taken for granted all her life must be considered again. Clear anger began to grow in her, welling up like cold water out of the earth, sweeping away the dust of lies and obligations which had so long engulfed her. She leapt to her feet and strode out into the deserted clearing, and called with all her strength into the silent hidden forest.

'There is no Beast,' she shouted, and the leaves stirred above her in the sun. 'THERE IS NO BEAST.'

The women came.

They ran from the dimness under the trees and surrounded her, spoke to her with friendly voices, looked at her with understanding eyes. If there ever were enchantment, she had broken it. And if anything were real, it was as she saw it, for the power of any man's nightmare is gone when there is no one left to believe in it.

As the women led her to their camp, she heard in the distance the thud of unshod hooves, and the neighing of wild horses.

The seasons passed, and Tilly learned what it was she needed from the forest, and she learned also what the forest needed from her. She found out who she was, but that cannot be told outside the wood, not yet. Her clothes were now woven of green cloth, for she too became a Spinner. And in the spinning she came to know her companions, as herself.

The roses were flowering again on the briar bushes, and Tilly thought again of her father. She asked the women how she might get news of him, and they directed her to a well of seeing.

The first thing she saw was her sisters. They had strayed into the fringes of the forest, and stumbling on the edges of another world had fortuitously ended up in the arms of two young men, Lysander and Demetrius. Rather than come face to face with the unknown they had married them forthwith, almost before the two couples had had time to tell one another apart. She saw her father, relieved, at the double wedding. If her sisters had encountered subversive passions in the Wild Forest, they were neatly tied up now, and any sense of wistfulness could be projected on to Lysander, or Demetrius, or anywhere else where the grass looked greener.

As for her father, he went home alone, and fell prey to various undiagnosed complaints. His doctor wrote him off in his file as depressed, possibly neurotic, and prescribed tranquillisers. The merchant began to drink too much, and was soon in a bad way, as Tilly saw in the well of seeing.

So she went to visit him. The night before she left the women warned her, 'Don't stay past one cycle of the moon, or you too will change, and maybe never come back at all.'

Tilly heard their warning, but when she got home she found life more absorbing than she had expected. Her father cheered up wonderfully, and she helped him sort out his affairs and plan an early retirement. This included booking a round-the-world cruise avoiding winter everywhere, and building a new swimming pool in the garden. Her sisters also required her sympathy on the problems of relating to men and married life. She knew it was her duty to listen to them, as her freedom was so obviously painful to them. All in all, nearly two months had gone by when there came a night of storm which blew the late summer leaves from the trees. The sound of the wind penetrated Tilly's sleep. She dreamed of things dying and forgotten, and in the centre of nightmare she saw a green web broken, and a world where there were no more trees.

First thing next morning she went to the well and said a spell of seeing. She saw no visions and heard no pleas. But a voice came from the depths, cool and clear, asking for nothing:

'Sister, the choice is yours.'

Within the hour she had said farewell to her father and sisters. She told her father she would come again when he really needed her. She told her sisters that if ever they wished they were free to come and find her. Then she left them, and was soon lost to sight, a woman in green among green trees.

JOANNA RUSS

The Clichés from Outer Space

Joanna Russ is the Nebula and Hugo award-winning author of
many short stories and novels, including Extra(Ordinary)
People, The Female Man, The Adventures of Alyx *(all from*
The Women's Press, 1985), And Chaos Died, The Two of
Them, On Strike Against God. *She is Associate Professor of*
English at the University of Washington, Seattle. Her critical
works include How To Suppress Women's Writing *(The*
Women's Press, 1984) and numerous articles on feminism and
science fiction.

I have a friend who has put together an anthology of feminist
science fiction stories. Actually I have several friends who have
done so, but the friend I am referring to here is an imaginary
one, so I shall call her Ermintrude.

Ermintrude is keen of eye, brilliant of brain, intolerant of
nonsense, and has surprisingly powerful forearms. (Editors
develop these by screaming and tearing their hair a lot.) So
powerful are her forearms, in fact, that it is possible for
Ermintrude—even when overworked, underpaid and suffering
from schlockfever (this is a disease editors get from reading too
many stories submitted by the general public) to carry up to
ten-and-a-half pounds of vividly purple prose in her arms at any
one time. However, a pile of manuscripts does tend to be
unstable, and upon visiting Ermintrude recently I found her
supine on her living-room rug and up to her frontal sinuses in
vast quantities of rejected fiction. The stuff had slipped and
fallen, as usual, and out of sheer discouragement (I think) she
had followed. Anyway, she lay sullenly upon the (really rather

aesthetically interesting) pattern of rejected manuscripts and pronounced, in a voice I shall never forget:

'If I get *one more story* about weird ways of becoming pregnant. . .'

'Oh come on,' I said. 'It can't be as bad as all that. I know there are men who can't imagine women having any other adventures than biological ones, which is why they write such guff, but. . .'

'Read one,' said Ermintrude.

Well, after I had, and had helped Ermintrude up, and we had kicked the manuscripts about a bit to relieve our feelings. I went home, Ermintrude got out her anthology, and I thought I'd heard the last of the business. But that pile of rejected mss must have been the vehicle for a curse, or *geas*, or malevolent principle, or at any rate some kind of filterable virus which had clung to me, saturated my clothing, or otherwise affected my person. The whole business was *not* over. How do I know?

I began to write trash.

No, not the kind I usually write, a different kind. Actually I was not the active agent in the writing of the stuff at all. To this day I don't know who— or what—is. I began to have strange and horrible dreams in which the boundaries of history and logic disappeared, fulgous luminescence streamed from old copies of *Conquer Absolutely Everything* and *The Sexist From Canopus*, and teenaged, male science-fiction readers vanished screaming into geometrically impossible bull-sessions located in the fourth dimension. A certain obscure invocation ('male bonding ritual' is the closest I can get to actually pronouncing the phrase) recurred constantly and throughout my dreams there grew a frightful din, an alien, rugose drumming, horrible, mind-blasting and obscene, which finally roused me one night from the worst (and last) dream to discover that—

My typewriter was typing all by itself!

Mind you, I don't say 'writing', for after I left a sheet of paper in the machine the next night (if not to satisfy the alien intelligence which had obviously travelled from Ermintrude's rejected mss to the sort of tacky metabolism—a Sears Electric—which suited it best, at least to mute the noise) the creature stopped, as if panicked by the actual sight of its own words. Then slowly it attempted a few scattered phrases like 'mighty-thewed' or 'her swelling globes'. Lately it has got more enthusiastic and its efforts have begun to bear a definite resemblance to conventional prose narratives of the science-fictional kind. In the forlorn hope of satisfying the damned thing (otherwise there will be nothing left but exorcism, and I don't *want* to type all five hundred and twelve pages of *Sexual Politics* on the machine—think of the time involved, let alone the increasing cost of typing paper!) I am attempting to have the following—well, fragments—published. Maybe this will content the Thing in the Typewriter. I have had to read all sorts of fiction in my career as a teacher and so has Ermintrude (as an editor) but nothing—nothing!—could be as abominable, as mind-destroying, as abyssal, and as dull, really, as the following collection of:

Clichés from Outer Space

The Weird-Ways-Of-Getting-Pregnant Story

'*Eegh! Argh! Argh! Eegh!*' cried Sheila Sue Hateman in uncontrollable ecstasy as the giant alien male orchid arched over her, pollinating her every orifice. She—yes, she—she, Sheila Sue Hateman, who had always been frigid nasty and unresponsive! She remembered how at parties she had avoided men who were attracted by her bee-stung, pouting, red mouth, long, honey-coloured hair, luscious behind and proud, up-thrusting breasts (they were a nuisance, those breasts, they sometimes got so proud and thrust up so far that they knocked her in the chin. She always pushed them down again). How she hated and avoided men! Sometimes she had hidden under sofas. She had stood behind open doors for hours on end. Often she had wrapped herself in the window curtains, hoping to be mistaken for a swatch of fabric.

But this was . . . different.

Ecstasy pounded through her every nerve. How she had wanted this! Now she could have children. Would they have tendrils? Roots? Would they emerge as a bushel of seeds? A tangle of leaves? Would one of her toes fall and root itself in the ground? It didn't matter. Whatever her son would be like (and she knew, somewhere deep inside her, that she would have a son) she would love it because it would be His.

Realisation poured through her: *She really loved men!*

She had loved them all along. But she had been afraid. Afraid of their strength, their attractiveness, their gentleness, their cute way of coming up to her in the street and saying, 'Hey honey, that's a great pair of boobs you got there,' which had set her heart racing.

She remembered Boris's direct, strong gaze, and the crushing power of his beautiful arms as he had attempted to rip off her clothes.

She remembered Ngaio's twinkly, humorous politeness as he said, 'The reason that you keep disagreeing with my intellectual conclusions, Sheila, is that you're a bitch.'

She remembered José's tender, masculine protectiveness as he had said, 'We can't hire you, Sheila, because this is a man's job. It's too difficult for a woman.'

She really loved men.

'*Eegh! Argh! Oh! Oh! Argh! Eegh!*' cried Sheila Sue, convulsing all over the place.

The giant orchid tenderly wrapped its fronds . . .

(to be continued—unfortunately)

The Talking-About-It Story

'Oh my, how I do love to live in an equal society,' said Irving the physicist, looking about with pride at the living-room of their conapt, which Adrienne, his wife, had decorated the interior of with her brilliantly intuitive flair for interior decoration. Adrienne had been a plant geneticist, but had decided that what she really wanted was to stay at home, have eight children, interior decorate, garden, cook organically, grow herbs in the windowsill (it did seem to be rotting the wood a little), and go barefoot. She was very close to the earth. There was nothing feminine about that; it just happened to be that way. It was her decision so Irving respected it.

'Yes, wouldn't it have been awful to have lived in the old,

unequal society?' said Adrienne. She went into the kitchen to see how the alfalfa soufflé was getting on.

'Yes, living in a sexually egalitarian society is absolutely the best thing there is,' said Joyce, the laser technologist who was taking twenty years off from her career to raise four children because that was what she really and truly wanted to do. 'Just imagine how horrible things must have been in the old days!'

Her husband, George, an IBM executive who made six billion new dollars a year, smiled fondly at Joyce. 'Yes,' he said, 'now that men and women are equal, things are so much better. I hate to think of what they used to be like!' He loved and respected Joyce and had built her a little workshop in the basement where she could practise laser technology in her spare time.

Their Black maid, Glorietta, came in and announced . . . (to be dealt with—severely)

The Noble Separatist Story

'Tell me, Mommy,' said Jeanie Joan, snuggling up to her beautiful, strong, powerful, gentle, wise, loving, eight-foot-tall Mommy who was President of the United States, 'why aren't there Daddies any more?'

'Well, Jeanie Joan,' said her Mommy, 'once there were lots and lots of Daddies. Daddies were nasty, vicious men who went away to something important called "jobs" while Mommies and babies lived in little prisons called "homes" and pined away for lack of healthy exercise, intellectual freedom, and the ability to earn their own livings. Daddies weren't brutal (usually) and didn't (always) beat up Mommies and babies with baseball bats. Mostly they just passed a lot of laws saying that Mommies weren't equal and had silly thoughts and raging hormones and couldn't work or think properly except for taking care of "homes", and babies. So the Daddies had all the nice things to themselves.'

'What nasty Daddies!' said pretty little Jeanie Joan.

'Yes, weren't they all?' said her Mommy, carefully pushing off her left knee *Moll Flanders, Das Kapital*, Engels on the family, John Stuart Mill's *On the Subjection of Women*, and the complete works of George Bernard Shaw. Jeanie Joan might misinterpret them. She could study them when she was older.

'And then what happened?' said Jeanie Joan, well on her way to becoming a beautiful, strong, powerful, gentle, all-wise, loving, eight-foot-tall, completely perfect Mommy herself who would never swat anything in anger, not even a mosquito.

'Well, dear, after a while all the Mommies got together and they saw how silly everything was. And they passed a lot of new laws saying that people were equal no matter whether they were Mommies or Daddies or whatever colour they were, and after that everybody loved everybody and there was no more war or poverty or racial discrimination or greed or selfishness.'

'But the *Daddies*—!' said Jeanie Joan, kicking her Mommy gently in the ankle.

'Well, Jeanie Joan,' said her Mommy, 'the reason everything got so wonderful was that the Daddies just couldn't stand a world without war, poverty, racial discrimination, greed, selfishness or hate. They weren't really human at all, you see. So they committed suicide, every one of them, within three weeks. And so did the little boy babies. We call that "raging testosterone" or "constitutional inferiority" or sometimes just "discouragement".'

'What big words!' said little Jeanie Joan thoughtfully.

'Yes,' said her Mommy, carefully removing from her right knee Marabel Morgan's *The Total Woman*, a biography of Phyllis Schlafly, Queen Victoria's denunciation of women's rights, and six thousand copies of *Vogue*.

They might accidentally fall on little Jeanie Joan's head and bruise it. She could read them later, too.

'Tell me, Mommy,' said Jeanie Joan (she was a talky little thing), 'why . . .'

(to be avoided—at all costs)

The Turnabout Story
or
I always knew what they wanted to do to me because

*I've been doing it to them for years, especially in the
movies*

Four ravaging, man-hating, vicious, hulking, Lesbian, sadistic,
fetishistic Women's Libbers motorcycled down the highway to
where George was hiding behind a bush. Each was dressed in
black leather, spike-heeled boots, and carried both a tommygun
and a whip, as well as knives between their teeth. Some had cut
off their breasts. Their names were Dirty Sandra, Hairy
Harriet, Vicious Vivian, and Positively Ruthless Ruth. They
dragged George (a little sandy-haired fellow with spectacles,
but with a keen mind and an iron will) from behind the bush he
was hiding in. Then they beat him. Then they reduced him to
flinders. Then they squashed the flinders to slime. Then they
jumped up and down on the slime.

'Women are better than men!' cried Dirty Sandra.

'Lick my boots!' cried Hairy Harriet.

'Drop your pants; I'm going to rape you!' cried Vicious
Vivian in her gravelly bass voice.

Ruthless Ruth said nothing (she never did; it was rumoured
among the gang that she had never learned to talk) but only
chewed her cigar and flicked open an eight-inch-long, honed-
steel, poisoned, barbed, glittering knife! Growling, she moved
towards George.

And these women are financially supported by their husbands!
thought George. *Those poor, terrified males fastened to the
bedroom door by diabolically constructed chain-link thongs,
which only let them loose to make money!*

Our hero thought his end had come. But suddenly Ruthless
Ruth turned green, smoke came pouring out of her ears, her
facial expression changed, and she fell to the ground, writhing.

It was that time of the month!

Dirty Sandra and Hairy Harriet likewise turned green, lost
their judgement, dithered, turned six or seven colours, and
groaned, wallowing on the ground and clutching their sto-
machs. They were in no condition to do anything to anybody
now.

That left Vicious Vivian. In mid-snarl she changed, too, but
differently; she slank towards George, her mouth pouting, her

body inviting, her large, moist eyes pleading with him to give her what she needed.

It was the other time of the month for her.

'Tell me, Vicious Vivian,' said small, sandy-haired, iron-willed, bespectacled, heroic George; 'Where is your centre of command, who is your leader, and what are your battle plans?'

'I will tell you everything,' sobbed Vicious Vivian in a gentle soprano, melting to her knees and embracing George's calves in the extremity of her biological need. 'I adore you. I want you. I need you. I can't help it.' And she told him everything, nibbling at his knees and sighing between-whiles. 'Oh, take me with you!' she cried; 'I love you and I have betrayed The Cause!'

'You couldn't help it,' said George compassionately, and stealing her motorcycle, he rode off into the sunset. He must get his secret to the Humane Instruments of Monumentality in Sausalito. Now he knew why female factory productivity only reached the norm four days out of every month. Now he knew why female scientific brains only worked in the rare few days between that time of the month and the other time of the month. Once the HIMS had this information (and a calendar) they could use it to take the world back from Women's Liberation and build a truly free and equalitarian society for everyone, not just men but women, too (taking into account their special physical needs, of course).

George's bad back, stuffed sinuses, flat feet, trick knee, migraine headache, hayfever, bladder infection, and angina pectoris began to . . .

(to be burned—with tongs)

GWYNETH JONES

The Intersection

Gwyneth Jones was born in Manchester in 1952. Her publications include six novels for children. Her first adult science fiction novel, Divine Endurance *(George Allen & Unwin), was published in 1984. Her new science fiction novel,* Escape Plans *(George Allen & Unwin), will be published in Spring 1986. 'The Intersection', she says, 'is not an extract from* Escape Plans *but might be taken as a preview.'*

She says about her story, 'I wanted to describe a Dystopia that would have enough guilty attraction to make my character ALIC's belief that she lives in the best of all possible worlds disturbing. Knowing that sensible readers would not be tempted or impressed by riches beyond the dreams of avarice, etc. just on their own, I turned the Space people's earth—the underworld— into an exercise in vindictive conservation, on the grounds that if I ruled the world I might be sorely tempted to tidy the bulk of the human population into hygienic confinement, prevent all kinds of pollution and destruction by force, and so on. And I would never go to parties.'

I said, 'I'm going into the Trojan Camp.'

'What have you got?'

'Two naked singularities and a monopole.'

SETI came over and put the other headset on. 'You can't hold it,' she commented briefly.

'I know, I just feel like letting rip a little divine wind.'

SETI studied the map. I saw her black eyes narrow in amusement. 'You have an arrangement with Farside, don't you.'

'That would be telling.' I grinned an indiscreet grin. Tactical discussion with non-players is a shocking crime in a war-game. But I like to live dangerously. Besides, the chance of one of my co-players accessing my underworld holiday in detail seemed remote. My monopole moved in among the asteroids, breeding free energy (for my operations) at a furious rate. The presence of the other two arguments was indicated. We don't go into petty details like laser troopers zapping each other nowadays. The fighting's all done in power equations of cataclysmic absurdity. I accessed Maria, present holder of the Sub-Jovian region, but she did not deign to comment. All I could see of her was her station and a portion of tasteful living-room. She might be out, or off-line, or just off line of sight, sitting there getting very annoyed. She'd been representing the earthside face of the moon for so long (we'd been playing for two years) I couldn't remember her real name without checking. Hence my rash excursion. A game that goes on for ever is no game at all.

I pushed my chair away and left the station. If any other player wanted a conference they could talk to my desk in our usual way. I only felt bound to make myself available to the immediate victim. It was a pity, I thought, that the underworld couldn't learn civilised amenities like talking to an empty screen. Personal privacy, which does not and cannot exist in any real sense, is the most indispensable convention for social comfort. SERVE sees all, SERVE records all. Anyone who wants to can pull anyone else out of the directory, if they feel like taking the trouble, and very little of life is classified access. But that's all the more reason why we like to live alone, meeting physically (or even eye to eye) only to make love; to share moments of real warmth. On the underworld, the indigenous population seems to spend all its time trying to clamber into one room, for an endless orgy of jabbering and staring. It's so abrasive.

It's not that I don't like reality. I enjoy my station games, but there's a limit to what a *deeby* (direct brain access) headset can give you while you're sitting in a console chair. At home I would be at the stadium, running around in person in a whole vicarious scenario. On the underworld they have Vic stadiums, but we're not allowed to use them because (MEDIC says) we would keep breaking our arms and legs in the massive gravity. The facilities would need conversion anyway. Those indigs who are on a level to understand games don't play any of the kinds we know. They don't play in person at all. They have a special class out of their own masses for the physical part. It's a version of vicarious experience that has its own bizarre appeal. Except that instead of staying at home hooked up in comfortable privacy, we have to gather in a 'Pavilion' by the stadium and stand around in our headsets with glazed expressions. Between events, we chat. What can you find to say, while still trying to savour the sensation of miscalculating the water-jump and having a fragment of broken bone suddenly pop out of your shin? Absurd.

I wandered across the bare floor of my capin and stood in the wraparound looking out. Mist gathered among the deodars and pines, melting into the pearl-grey sky; and below me dark glistening undergrowth fell away, splashed with a few scarlet flowers. The underworld has its compensations.

I was staying in the Subcontinental Habitat Area Control Threshold Installation: in acronymic, SHACTI. The indigs called it 'Shacti'. They never could learn our language. It is difficult—the shifting contextual rules about when to pronounce an acronym and when to elide it; when to use lower case for an abbreviation, derogation, conflation and so on. To make matters worse, I am ALIC, and I know the second two are 'integrated circuit' but the original significance of the AL is lost in the mists of time. SETI means Search for Extra Terrestial Intelligence, but who remembers that? It's just a personal name, I explain. Like yours. So they call me 'Alice' which always irritates me. Poor indigs!

I'd escaped the 'high-class hotels' on the Ridge itself. Being the home of Mission Command for the whole Subcontinent SHACTI was always packed with enabled indigs. But I had discovered I'd once been to school, briefly, with one of the Rangers. Rangers are always starved for new civilised company, so that accessed me a unit in the LECM. Local Environment Contained Modules; a handful of capsule installations landscaped into a cloud-drowned hillside. It was meant to be used by underworld personnel in transit. The Rangers call these places *pits* but I loved it. One empty room, a shelf at the back for my bedroll, a galley and a minute bathroom both bolted onto the walls, and nothing else but the wraparound full of trees. There was a leanto where an anonymous number something or other attended to the cap's inner needs. I could have done it myself, but local protocols insisted, and she didn't bother me.

Fortunately, when SETI and I actually met again we found we quite liked each other.

She set out to join me in the wrap, and immediately fell over Pia.

'Shit, ALIC. I wish you wouldn't move your furniture around.'

She is blind. She was conceived that way: it was a trade-off for some other wonderful quality—one of those peculiar bargains our executive ancestry lines make with PRENAT from time to time, just to prove they love excellence more than common sense. She wears a prosthesis, a little thing she puts in her eye that stimulates the proper area of her brain, mimicking the optic nerve she hasn't got. But she takes it out whenever she can. No system in the system could make her take a permanent generation. She has a real experience, she says, of *alienness* at her fingertips. Better than the world's best Vic. I wonder which she means. The dark world, or the one I call normal?

Pia howled, and retired to her corner, where she had a home nest of underworldly cushions. Sulks.

'Don't cry Pia—'

'I'm not furniture!'

We laughed. She stuck her tongue out at us.

She's not. She's a sweet child, and sensual and loving, my companion for this holiday. But she doesn't like being laughed at. I leased her, now I dream of taking her home. I know I won't do it, but it's going to be a wrench to send her back.

SETI had work to do and appropriated my games station. A Ranger's life isn't all parties at the Pavilion. The Subcontinent was showing signs of restlessness as usual. I communed with my cedars. Pia crept out and came and laid her head on my knees. I rubbed my hand over the black velvet: not bare, it didn't look right on her. It's not natural for an indig to be depilated. I pulled the tag in her ear affectionately.

'*You're* not unruly, are you Pia?'

'No.'

'Why can't the silly numbers stay quiet in their centres, and leave our poor Rangers in peace.'

SETI gave a sigh. My station was released from the august internal embrace of SERVE-in-SHACTI Mission, its contact with the great processes returning to a more modest level.

'D'you want to come and see an anomaly, ALIC?'

I was deeply flattered. Ranger business is not generally accessible to idle globetrotters.

Some people won't even consider visiting the underworld. The gravity well terrifies them, and admittedly it is not a comfortable journey. There are also various gruesome stories about the indig masses. It's the sheer size of the numbers that appals, as much as anything they might do. But after all, if you trip up and tear your clothes on a rock in a Martian wilderness park, you could be dead.

'I'd love to.'

We wore soft suits. It was regulations for SETI to be formally dressed, and Mission Command expected visitors to conform at least around official installations. But in fact although the underworld is the only place in our whole world (in the known universe!) where you can walk out of controlled environment with no protection—tourists don't. Rationally, you know you're safe. But it's just impossible to relax, without a little irrational reassurance. The anomaly was quite a way out in the SHACTI hills, a long day's walk for the indigs on the ground. We took a flier from the Mission pool: a luxury for me. There was an air grid immediately around the Ridge, but outside of that mere civilians had to make do with hiring ancient sold-off Rovers, locally maintained and, like all Rovers, totally bemused by trees.

We parked discreetly. I took pride in moving almost as easily as SETI. If you come to the underworld it's worth the effort of doing some weight-training beforehand. The differences from home EG may be small, but you do feel it. The worst thing is falling. Poorly-prepared holidaymakers get covered in wonderful blue and purple bruises. And then, feeling mortified, they eschew MEDIC aid so the Mission monitors won't know: and go around indoors covered up from neck to ankle. The Rangers think it's a great joke, whenever some hapless tourist pretends she's taken a fancy to indig dress.

The crowd was gathered on a tongue of flat land between two ridges, a floor of green turf set with stately pines. At the apex, the tip of the tongue, the ground dropped steeply in the usual SHACTI way: empty air with a distant backdrop of wilderness and cloud. SETI and I stood in the trees on the side of one of the ridges, looking down. We had our helmets on, but faceplates open and air supplies retracted. The air wasn't warm. The people were shivering and wrapping their arms around themselves.

'It's periodic,' murmured SETI.

The indig masses live in environmentally controlled centres, some of them very large objects housing three or six millions. SHACTI centre is comparatively tiny, a scarp extension sealed onto the slope under the Ridge: population about AB,000. There's some mysterious force, especially active on the Subcontinent, that drags part of the mass in a centre outside, at random intervals. One explanation is that they're trying to get away from UBIQ surveillance. Every centre has an incident quantifier system, and the masses fear and resent it. It is an odd sort of fear, because, of course, we are all watched all the time by SERVE, and often by any amount of other systems that protect us and keep us alive. But the masses seem to feel that UBIQ is different for some reason.

SETI explained this to me quietly. We talked on suit radio. She had her onboard (her suit was a Ranger's and full of sophisticated gadgetry) enhance the significant bits of the exterior sound. She pointed out to me that there were more women than men. This was disquieting for SETI, indicating that the event might be serious, but I didn't mind it at all. The indigs themselves have a distaste for their collective male. Incapable of sustained steady concentration, the men are useless for the kind of work the masses do. They roam around the passageways in their centres, attacking each other and vandalising whatever fittings they can reach. We both observed several private air cars half hidden in the trees at the back of the crowd. So some of SHACTI's enabled were present: members of that small fraction of indigs who have one way or other climbed out of the mass. They are the ruling class of the underworld, and many of them have (hence the name) access to standard facilities.

'It's like watching something on a slide—'

The crowd squirmed like a weird virus, magnified outrageously and projected on the landscape. The woman who was the cause of it all—SETI's 'anomaly'—was up in front, standing against the cloudy sky. She had grown her hair long: this was *de rigeur*, I knew, for an indig anomaly.

It has already happened, but it hasn't arrived yet. Before I speak to you today, it will happen . . .

A wave of motion passed over her audience. A mass of round and oval globules turned up to the stars, through the branches of the pines. The reference was obvious. She was talking about the chronic paradox, the one we all know. There was once a serious lobby against the CONMAG drive. It would scramble people's brains! leaving home and reaching Mars a small fraction of a second *before they ought to*. It was a nice idea. Pity you lose it all on the deceleration. A lot of the indigs have not grasped this. They think the reason we look so young to them is because we travel a lot. I'm not an expert, maybe there is some residual effect. But it can only be on a barely measurable level—more philosophy than physics. I can safely say asymmetric ageing has yet to become a grave social problem.

However, the ship the indig was talking about wouldn't be coming from Mars. It wouldn't be coming from anywhere in the local group, it wouldn't be coming from Virgo. We know that. Nor even farther still. We know too much altogether really, about the likelihood of such a visitation. The more we seek the less we find. I wished I was an indig and could turn my face and look at the sky, hopefully. Anomaly spoke with passion, about the starry messenger who was just about (paradoxically) to arrive, and *explain everything*. Alien visitors are always going to do that. And the crowd sighed with longing.

We must be equal to the challenge!

She wants us to start building starships again, so we'll be eligible to join the galactic federation when we're finally invited.

Still looking at the sky. Don't they realise that at the very least the NET would pick it up approaching as far out as anyone can imagine. Might possibly register such an event rather before this long-haired object. . . .But of course it's going faster than light, so Near-space Event Tracking can't catch it. Ingenious anomaly!

Up til now, FUNCTION had given our instructions in light. But now there is something more than light—

'What's "FUNCTION"?' I asked SETI. 'Is that an acronym?'

'Not exactly. It's the Sub term for SERVE.'

'Oh, yes. I remember.'

SERVE does indeed give its instructions in soliton packets of light. Our Missions also operate in photonics. Hmm, I thought. The idea that there's something more important than our mode of command sounds ominous.

SETI didn't react. I lost track of the declamation looking at the crowd. They were so small and cold, huddled under the open sky in their thin clothes and little plastic slippers. What kind of hunger drove them to come out here, to brave the penalties they'd suffer for leaving the centre without process, to endure an environment that must seem hostile, frightening, alien? I felt a kind of admiration . . .

'ALIC—'

SETI spoke quietly, but with a hint of warning. I wondered why, then suddenly realised that the crowd had noticed us. Quite a few of the globules were now pointing in our direction. I looked for a lead from the Ranger. She smiled faintly. There were about two thousand indigs. She was armed, in accordance with normal practice, with a handgun that would fire one small clip of tranquillising pellets: and couldn't recharge in less than twenty seconds.

'Seal your face.'

We sealed our faces—I'm not sure whether it was to inspire awe or in case they started chucking rocks—and quietly retired.

'That was exhilarating!' I said.

'For a moment, yes.'

* * *

Then I hired a Rover in fairly reasonable repair and an Olympus support tent, and Pia and I went over the alt. wall. We wandered in the beautiful empty places where SERVE only knows how the border runs between Northern Two, Panasia and the Sub. I was glad, after the first day, that we weren't taking that so-called support anywhere near its brand-name, but it kept us warm and dry and more or less fed. We saw goats and marmots and bearded vultures and a hundred other kinds of bird; and once a real live wild woman wrapped in weird garments: tag gleaming in one ear, a lump of raw mineral dangling from the other. She came to our camp. The Rover was sitting in a corrie of ice-shattered granite in the side of a high valley, with brilliant flowered turf below and white giants standing all around.

I was outside the support in my softsuit, watching the sunset. I hardly dared breathe. Trailing behind her was a young man, her husband or her son. My *ulaux* (underworld local auxiliary: a convenience SHACTI Mission had thrust on me)—jumped out at her officiously, but to my delight the woman stood her ground. The young man had in his shoulder, under a thick greasy layer of clothing and another, ditto, of pure filth, an incredibly deep puncture wound. It obviously went right through, as obviously it had been produced by a laser beam in the hands of someone who had never learned a lasarm is not a projectile weapon. It oozed nastily. I gave her some antibiotic powder. My *ulaux* told me the 'wild number' would probably eat it herself, or keep the sealed pack as an ornament. She wanted us to leave immediately, but I banished her to the Rover's cab and settled down, hoping for more custom. What fun, I thought, to be a Ranger and spend your whole tour ministering to this unique place and its creatures. One of the all-time certified goodies, like an elf or an angel in a fantasy game.

Modern firearms are not manufactured anywhere in the underworld, CHTHON—Combined Holding for the Terrestrial Habitats Operational Network—doesn't allow it. I felt quite outraged to think of someone from home trading in deadly weapons with the wild indigs. I almost called up SHACTI, but realised in time I was being naive. The Mission must know.

They knew when to interfere and when to leave things to SERVE. So I called up tourist information instead and learned with some chagrin the actual altitude of my camp and the heights of the majestic snow peaks that surrounded us, in standard feet as well as local metres. We use base 12, because of its useful factors and fertile relationships with machinecode bases, but the indigs can't be persuaded to give up their decimal scales. Alas, the underworld never sounds as impressive as it looks. However, I thought, I defy anyone to top my wild woman. I had her recorded, of course. In strict manners I should have offered her a copy, as we could hardly exchange access addresses. I wondered if she'd have eaten that. Lucky for my poor *ulaux* I didn't think of it. She'd have had hysterics.

6B40 feet below the plains of the Sub lay seething under a hot soupy blanket, patterned with indig centres and the intensive ADAPT plant to feed and support them. It was the same in every bloc. When CHTHON was first enabled there was hardly anything left of the ecosphere except for a few high marginal lands. So here we installed our Missions, on the Threshold where air pressure was the same as we kept it at home, and the underworld still had some natural beauty. It was different now that the indigs were contained. Forests had been replanted, the seas were coming back to life. But still no one went down into the depths much, except Rangers on duty.

My perfect valley rolled slowly out of sunlight. The snows and sky slipped from crimson to magenta to deep indigo, and I waited in vain for more patients. I found myself thinking again of that odd phenomenon outside SHACTI. A huddle of faces turned up to the sky, a shivering blot of ever-hopeful humanity . . . So many of them tucked up in SHACTI centre, but still they longed for company. A new face, a friendly greeting. Or even a hostile greeting, let's not be fussy. Are human beings always lonely?

I suddenly felt oppressed. I decided perhaps I'd had enough empty scenery.

We crossed the transwall plateau, and stopped off at one of the sealed leisure complexes to watch the enabled at play: a fascinating sight. The more hostile the outside environment the more prestigious the resort, so long as one has no contact with it whatsoever. While Pia and I were there everything was bathed in a peculiar orange glow, from the food to the swimming pools. I think we were pretending to be on Titan.

* * *

Late one night I ran my desk, a chore I'd been putting off since I returned to SHACTI. Anything urgent would have got to me. SETI lay back in my bedroll alcove with Pia, smoking her pipe (a dashing Ranger affectation I'd have liked to acquire myself, but I didn't want to seem too callow). I'm always disappointed by my in-tray whenever I get back from anywhere. There seems to be such a nice little heap, but when you start opening the files there's never anything interesting. I was using the keyscreen so I could talk to SETI at the same time.

'Any more exciting confrontations with the indigenous fauna?'

''Fraid not. Things have been very quiet.'

'So what became of the anomaly?'

'Oh, she was killed.'

Killed!

That is not a word we use for accidental death (which doesn't really exist). Or for an event duly processed by the systems.

'The —er—Sub-President's in residence at the moment. She had the woman arrested. A few days later there was a party and our poor anomaly ended up as part of the live entertainment.'

I was shocked into silence for a minute or two. No human being, no human *agency* ought to have the power to take another's life.

'How revolting. What did you do about it?'

'Nothing. Sorry, ALIC. You know we never interfere with the tame indigs unless we have to. That's CHTHON's orders.'

I found I had erased half my last quarter's air and water bill. Not a bad idea, but the systems always get you in the end. I began to recover it. What an awful thing. Ridiculously I felt personally wounded. I had been *thinking* about that woman. And now she was gone—just gone. Funny, I thought, how CHTHON's 'non-interference' gets adapted to protect a fancy-titled enabled who probably has friends at home. But I wouldn't argue about it. No doubt most systems are a little corrupted from time to time. No doubt SERVE evens things out in the end.

I asked casually, 'And did anything happen? Anything going blip in the night?'

SETI laughed.

It was very quiet: that curious hollow stillness of the underworld. No whisper of the autonomics, no sub-audible feeling of traffic racing in the lightlines underfoot, overhead. I flipped through a three-year-old magazine, abandoned in the capin's memory by some previous visitor.

Pia got up. She trotted into the wrap and knelt there, gazing earnestly.

'What is it Pia?'

'I don't know. Maybe I saw it—'

I went over, touching the wall on my way so the curtain field came on. Pia and I looked out of our cove of shadow into transparent night.

'There's nothing there but darkness, Pia.'

'Perhaps I should come and look,' remarked SETI dryly from behind the curtain.

Beyond a clear-cut frieze of cedar branches the small blurred stars lay set in deepest sapphire. The moon was out of sight, likewise that scrap of silver webbing following four hours behind, which I call home. I spotted a few earth orbiters. No strangers.

The libration of earth's masses is certainly a great achievement. It's hard to contemplate the incredible complexity of the balancing forces involved. So many systems, so many conflicting interests: only SERVE knows how it's done. SERVE, the mind within all systems, here or at home. Zero variation process controller, that which closes the loop. We sometimes say we wrote it, but no one wrote SERVE. It wrote itself, out of its own accumulated data. . . .Advanced analysis aside though, the libration works. They are all fed, they are all sheltered. There's no pollution, there's no war: and only the occasional nasty little murder. I suppose that must be all right too, if SERVE allows it.

A great achievement, but it's not the one we wanted. When

we left home, we never meant to come back. Not even to look after the aged parent. Do I really envy SETI? We had such plans. Long ago we sent out our travelling jewellery to all the local stars that seemed to have planetary systems. Human crews followed, in CONMAG2 probes. In every case the result was barren disaster. We thought we'd wait to send out multigeneration ships until the information got better. It got better and better, but we never sent our ships. There's nowhere for them to go. Nowhere. We have enough barc rocks and gasballs in our own back yard to keep us occupied until the sun runs down, so why waste money?

Comfort yourselves children. One day Mars will be green.

But that's no answer. The bad thing is that we are alone. We've been listening out in deep space for a thousand years. We've never intercepted so much as a single sigh. Who could have thought this universe, which seemed so big and bright, could turn into a locked and empty room? We can cry and cry, no one will ever come.

And yet, who knows. That indig might have caught some pulse, some intimation on the world lines. She seemed very sure. The stranger might even be coming in tonight.

I sent Pia back to bed, but I sat there for a long time staring into the dark: trying to count the stars and hoping I could get the number wrong.

BEVERLEY IRELAND

Long Shift

Beverley Ireland has worked as a teacher and a professional performer/songwriter. She now lives in South London and works as a freelance journalist. Her first short story was published in Spare Rib *in August 1984 and she has also contributed poems to the anthology* No Holds Barred, *edited by the Raving Beauties (The Women's Press, 1985). In 1984 she was closely involved with the occupation-campaign to save the South London Women's Hospital from closure.*

'Long Shift,' she says, 'started as a series of notes on the future of London as a place for women to live and work, and is dedicated to my sister, Alison, in thanks for her love and support.'

Bee Baxter eased her Elektra Cruiser into the nearest vacant parkbox and slipped the ignition into three-hour hold. Already, a fierce blue sky bounced a far away promise of scorching sand and mild sea onto the concrete plaza of City Women's Industrial Co-op. Bee shrugged as if to shake off the irritation she was feeling at the prospect of her long shift.

Her housegroup would be on the road for the Marina by now, she thought, remembering their excited forays into freezer and cupboard as she'd hunted round for her casefile and keys.

'Dammit,' she muttered, her face screwed up against the sun and at her own disappointment at missing a day out in it. She was rather pleased when the parkbox failed to give back her cardlock, necessitating the much-satirised remedy for the unreliability of this latest showpiece of anti-theft, anti-vandal technology: a swift kick to the controls. The blow delivered, her cardlock slid from the console, and the heavy up-and-over door of the parkbox thudded down into place.

'Lovely day, Bee,' smiled Syreeta from the security desk.

'Too bloody right,' murmured Bee as she passed. Then, realising she had been offhand with the older woman, she turned. 'You getting off soon?' she asked, leaning her heavy casefile on the fine old wooden desk that was the security workspace. 'Going to take in a bit of sun?'

Syreeta let out a long, ironic bark of laughter.

'Some chance! Got my final assessment in just over a month and they're still throwing new work at us at evening class.'

'I don't know how you do it, with this job as well,' Bee said, suddenly chastened. Her own shift over, she would be free to do whatever she liked. Why, there was nothing to stop her driving out to meet the others at the Marina in time for the afternoon autosurf. Swinging her casefile across her shoulder, Bee flashed an encouraging smile at Syreeta and headed for the lift.

City Women's Co-op suffered all the disadvantages of older, non-purpose-built industrial premises. It had been thrown up in the eighties by some corporate architectural pool, and seemed to consist of a series of afterthoughts and compromises that suited it for neither office nor workshop function. Cable-space and direct access were limited, and had been time-consuming and costly to improvise. There was no ground floor workroom, and the Co-op had sectioned off a large part of the reception area for crêche and mainframe facilities. Heavier operations had been set up in a group of prefabricated workshops behind the main tower, which jutted the maximum ten storeys high. Bee's workspace was on the top floor, pleasantly close to the roof garden, and with a sweeping view out over the dockland farms.

As she stepped out of the lift, Bee felt that discomforting, dry stress that was the building's main drawback as far as she and her departmental colleagues were concerned: static. The Premises Committee had done what they could, having replaced the old, plyfibre carpeting with shaved cork, laminated the metal window frames with anti-stat sealant and put in a humidity filter. But in this type of building, you could never get rid of the problem entirely. All Kinotelergists tended to be particularly sensitive to even the lowest stat presence: Bee even got dizzy from background levels in thundery weather.

Over the door marked Kinotelergy Operations, the green light was on, so Bee went straight in. Fanushi was sitting near the centre of the workspace, the gold and green of her sari glowing in the light from the corridor. Although she sat very erect and poised, Bee knew how tired she was from the slightly rounded silhouette of the clay-brown shoulders.

'Oh, Bee, I'm utterly vaped. What a bloody shift. Turn off the curtains, will you?' yawned the tiny, silk-clad figure.

Bee hit a button on the desk console and the smoked glass of the four plate windows cleared and became transparent. The workspace filled with hard, cobalt-blue daylight, and instantly became dully hot enough to bring out a prickling line of sweat on Bee's upper lip. She punched out the air-filter code, and the machine rattled to a low, steady hum, pouring out a delicious, chilled breeze.

Fanushi yawned again and stretched her thin, muscular arms in an extravagant arc behind her. Bee noticed she had chosen a new spot to work from, slightly west of her usual focal point and almost facing the door.

Fanushi noticed her staring at the chair and said nonchalantly, 'It was just an experiment. Probably why I'm so wiped out. Think I'll stick to the old spot from now on.'

Bee grinned, acknowledging Fanushi's grudging attempt at shifting her focal point. It had been Bee who had presented the KT Society meeting with a paper calling for a more adventurous, experimental approach to focal point positioning. Fanushi hadn't seemed particularly interested in Bee's research at the time, so it was good to see she'd taken it in, and was willing to give the idea a chance.

Bee moved behind Fanushi's chair and started to massage the taut, tense area below the ridge of her colleague's skull. It always got you there: the effort and muscular tension of a long shift seemed to concentrate in a tightly-bunched knot that could result in a searing headache if not soothed away. As her large, blunt fingers kneaded and pinched in a steady rhythm, she felt Fanushi's shoulders relax back into their usual, graceful line.

'Terrific—I feel human again,' she sighed, rising slowly from her chair and moving over to the desk console. Squinting a little against the blank glare from outside, she fed in the details of her shift, bringing her caseload up to date.

As a medical and veterinary specialist, Fanushi had to be painstaking about her work schedule: her subjects had to be focused at the exact times on her jobsheet. Even the most skilled KT Op had not quite cracked a method of focusing a moving subject, and the onsite supervision of subject positioning and restraint was itself a skilled piece of work. This was usually done by trainees, and before she had specialised, Bee had spent several months on a dairy unit, ensuring that ailing and recalcitrant milk cows were strapped down in focus to deadline.

Bee's own speciality was mineral and hardcore engineering. She had always liked the good, solid magnetism of metal and rock. Because of the stationary nature of her subjects, her work could progress at a more leisurely pace than the medics': she had never suffered the shock of dislocation when a subject accidentally moved out of focus.

Once, a child in the South Sector had slipped her straps when Fanushi had been working on her. She had been focusing really deep, investigating some cystic genes the child had inherited. The KT trainee hadn't been watching, and the child had just wriggled off the bed, out of focus. Fanushi had been found sprawled on the floor, hardly conscious, her lips blue and mottled. The force of snapping back, like a burst of high-frequency feedback through a shorted headset, had sent her reeling across the workspace. It had been eight months before she'd worked again.

Her datafeed complete, Fanushi made to go. 'All yours,' she told Bee. 'Think of me up to my eyebrows in mud and runny noses,' she added, in mock agony.

Bee remembered it was Fanushi's turn to take her house-group's children on a camp-out. It was one of the shared jobs all housegroups with children spread among themselves: once a month during the good weather, three adults and as many as ten children would set out for a few days at the campgrounds. The more sophisticated among the adults would claim to dread this concentrated exposure to parenting, but it was usually enjoyable, with the edge of novelty to enhance the sense of outdoor adventure.

'Come off it, Fanushi, you'll have a terrific time. You know you love tenting,' Bee said somewhat ruefully, thinking of sun slanting through the huge old trees up at the campgrounds.

'It's the nightfires I really like,' said Fanushi, her dark eyes brightening at the thought of the hundreds of nocturnal beacons scattered across the hillside camp. She picked up her things. 'See you then, Bee. Happy hunting,' she said, and left in a shimmer of gold and green.

Bee sighed, kicked off her sandals, and sat down heavily in front of the desk console. She punched in her codes and jobsheet numbers. The job in hand was a demolition order and it was going well on schedule.

Bee loved demolition work. It gave her an immense sense of achievement to focus deep inside a huge, seemingly-solid edifice, to ferret out the weakest parts, then wear away at them gently, insistently. With just the right combination of calculus and instinct, you could bring almost anything down when and where you wanted it.

In her time at the Co-op, Bee had felled two cooling-towers within five hundred metres of housing communities, with not a single window broken. Her pleasure at the moment of their perfect, concertina-like collapse often returned to her: like twin stacks of playing cards, they had caved in sweetly upon their own foundations, wreathed round with a halo of fine, red dust.

The console rattled up a series of figures beside which a small point of yellow light flashed the priority signal. Bee called up the jobsheet, which informed her that the area Planning Committee had commissioned a subsidence survey on a sector designated for new housing.

'Shit,' Bee said aloud. The rush job would take the better part of her shift, leaving little time for her demolition project. For nearly two weeks now, she'd been working on a long-disused housing tower, already weakened by years of neglect and its own lack of structural logic. She'd found herself absorbed by the challenge of getting the building down upon itself, plotting the lines of least resistance to contain and direct its eventual collapse away from the new housing communities which flanked it. She'd been looking forward to getting back inside it: focusing spiral-wise up the pillars that formed one side of the concrete-clad steel frame, taking crucial, bite-size pieces out of each central core. Now it seemed she'd be spending her shift deep underground, routinely cataloguing her findings beneath the tangle of service ducts and the thin, aqueous clay layer that formed the city's bed.

Bee called up the City Basin geodata, and while the computer ran through search, she went over to the automat in the corner and fetched herself fruit tea. The warm, scented liquid cleared her throat as she settled down to check her focus scope. The figures ran across the screen, accompanied by 3-D sections of the South Sector. She was familiar with the data, which charted an area encompassing the river and the fault that rippled below it in a series of small, monoclinal fractures. The instability pattern was minor, but repeated, and the Planning Committee were duty-bound to check on any proposed housing site within its range. Over the years, repeated drainage of the clay layer had left the bedrock dried out and weakened, so that any slight shift of the South East fault could, in theory, lead to fairly dramatic subsidence. Bee vaguely remembered that several years previously, an underground tremor had registered II on the Mercalli Scale, but it had been isolated, and generally regarded as a one-off.

'What a day to go underground,' Bee thought, with a last glance at the burning day outside before she snapped on the curtains and killed the air-filter.

In the gloom of the silent workspace, Bee felt for her spot, and pulled over a chair. Her KT teachers wouldn't have approved of her doing this without first sealing the door, for even the preliminary stages of focusing are meant to take place in isolated space. But like most KT Ops, Bee had evolved her own variations of focusing procedure. Having positioned her chair, she activated the door seal, which turned on the red no-entry light and jammed the handle. This automatically cut out all the deskphones: only in case of fire or other emergency would she be disturbed now. With the cassette recorder round her neck, Bee started the breathing. Deep mouthfuls resounded in her chest, flowing outwards in a rounded, musical sigh. Gradually, the pitch of the sound came lower, and, lulled gently into the first stage of relaxing, Bee let her mind slip into the positive awareness techniques she'd been so thoroughly schooled in.

Listen to yourself.

She began with her housegroup's day at the Marina, remembering the flash of bright water and the crisp tang of the estuary from her last visit there. Sprawling lazily on the sand with Nadia, her old friend, strong and loving companion of many years, now out on a desert farm, greening much hotter sand with sweat and technology.

Listen to your body.

A high chimney, belching out a greenish, billowing spume of choking sulphur, overlooked her grandmother's house, blackening the garden, calking the old woman's lungs. Her grandmother's laboured breathing just before the end was like the grinding of a crippled machine, tearing itself from within.

No, not that way.

Steady the breathing back to a slow, regular flow. Slow and steady like the straight, dipping strokes of a swimmer rising on the line of autosurf. Lupita, the gentle, serious student, had showed her how to swim like that. On land, her myopic clumsiness had made her movements awkward and selfconscious, but in the water, Lupita, glasses taped to her nose, cut the surface as effortlessly as a dolphin. Go with your breathing, she had said, let it feed your body till you feel yourself sliding in an unbroken curve.

Sense your body.

Hesitating, the oiled fingers flutter against the curve of her thigh, then come to rest, warm and firm stroking her till she sleeps, as she sleeps, long after she is awake, early before day.

Bee was not afraid of this dark. Focusing, for all its visual terminology, was not a function of sight. The kind of disembodiment that followed the sleeping phase meant that any impression of darkness was an anachronistic illusion: without eyes there could be no blindness.

Sense yourself.

Bee's physical awareness was now limited to a small area at

the base of her tongue, too vague to define, but vivid enough to allow her bodied self to record impressions in speech. Once it had shocked her to play back the slurred, monotonous voice on the cassette player, but nowadays she sent her tapes straight through for transcription without worrying how she sounded.

But if Bee had little consciousness of her body, her sense of place was heightened. She was where she was, not where she wanted to be. With the agony of displacement felt by a homing pigeon, she craved reunion with a place she couldn't name, a set of coordinates that tugged at her urgently. Sharp yearning mounted into a kind of directionless panic, no less a shock because she'd been through this stage hundreds of times before. Experience told her to ride it out, seek her centre, find the stillpoint.

She concentrated on her distant body's receding, rhythmic pulse, and gradually the sense of whirling and tumbling slowed, halted. Calm. She had a hold of her focus.

The clear energy that was now the working part of Bee rode like a drop of water on a thread, propelled by its own weight, meeting only the resistance of its own magnetism. Gathering momentum as the pull of the focus reeled her in, Bee slipped through the branches of a tree, through a foraging ant's thorax, down among earth and stones, sewage, bones and clay. The pull became lateral, and she slowed, knowing she was close.

The urgency evaporated, and in its place was nothing. She suddenly felt light and steady, aware of her surroundings as if she were standing on a hill on a clear, bright day. She was in focus.

Testing the distant muscle, she felt it respond, like a kite at the end of a long wire.

'Okay. Let's see what we have here.'

She moved across the folds and fissures, noting the depth and stability of the marine sediments with their packed layers of eocene fossils suspended in mild, gastropod surprise as the sea was taken from them some seventy million years before. Following a half kilometre rent in the pitted mudstone, she came to a shatterscape of radial cracks, each no more than a metre long.

'Minor shear stress,' she recorded. 'Local and stable.'

Methodically, she moved on, marking and evaluating clay drainage and damage, skipping over the buried sea bed, racing along a bentonite seam. Some part of her was subdued by the great age of the rocks pressed around her, and the voice back in the workspace became low and reverential under the weight of all that time hardened into stone.

She worked on. Then, zipping to the eastern edge of the faultline, her litany of observations pouring fast and fluent into the cassette recorder, she passed the last of the checkpoints which marked out her focus scope. From the charts, she knew that the fault began to peter out here, and she felt for the narrowing, her signal to wind up the focus.

Another twenty metres and the fissure gaped as wide as ever.

'Damn,' said Bee into the machine. 'Somebody's buggered up on the fault coordinates. Doesn't stop where it's marked. Hang on, and I'll plot the tail-off, get the maps up to date.'

Swerving left and right, she followed the fault around its topsy-turvy course, unable to find its end.

'Shit . . . NO!' The voice struggled out of its flat intonation, shocked from routine. 'I can't believe this. It's a space, and it's huge. Someone's really messed up on this fault projection— there must've been a massive new movement down here.'

Bouncing from wall to wall of the giant, ragged crack, she focused along the fresh fissure, taking measurements, temperature and pressure readings as she sought to assess the full extent of the new damage. She was unaware of damp shale and débris passing through her, and dropping to the bottom of the fault, far below.

'I've covered 2.37 kilometres north-north-east. The thing's sort of turned back on itself, and the gap's as big as ever. No, bigger. Widens out into another kind of cavern, radiating out at several points. Lots of sediment, toprock buckled. Shit,' the voice paused, '. . .I can feel the clay!'

Fear at this last realisation overrode the distance between Bee and her throat, and the voice burst out, high and angry. 'How come this has been left till now? With the clay layer in this condition, I'm recommending priority halt on all building work within a 2-kilometre radius of this mess. Just hope you've got all your high-rise down along this line . . .' The voice faltered as

Bee came to a halt just inside the mudstone wall of the split. She rechecked her coordinates, then moved off along one of the points of the fault-star. Tracing the devastated layers of rock and clay, she advanced, propelled by a disturbing thought. The tower! When she'd left it, the week before, it was weakened but stable, its foundation-columns jutting sturdily down into solid ground. That had been before all this unforeseen fault activity had undermined her careful calculations. If shock waves from the fault seam had spread much further east, there could be repercussions within the tower's foundations, and a high wind might then mean trouble. In this weather, it was an outside chance, but enough to offend the professional perfectionist. Best to check it out.

As she headed for the tower's coordinates, she met yet another cavernous angle of the new fissure.

'It's really shot up in here,' she recorded as she moved on. 'Seems to be a load of concrete waste or something.'

She stopped dead, silenced by what she had found. Around her, the crushed, shattered tips of old concrete pile foundations lay at odd angles among the bedrock. She was directly beneath the tower.

She sensed the damage even before she reached it. Veinous cracks had leached up into the concrete piles, spreading complex, nightmare patterns of instability into the blockwork.

'Trouble,' the voice said, wearily. 'I'm leaving the fault and going up to have a look.'

Extending a focus, either in terms of time or space, was something Bee knew to be dangerous. But risk-evaluation had always been one of her strong points, and it was clear what needed to be done.

Moving up into the service shaft level, Bee felt the deep tugging that signalled she was straying out of her vertical coordinate range. It was like climbing with weights attached to her, and the effort brought out little runnels of sweat on her distant body, which Bee registered as a dryness and stiffening at the base of her tongue.

Step by step, she monitored the state of the metal skeleton of the tower. Deep inside the concrete pillars on one side of the building, she had left precise, uniform nicks in each hardened steel core: the first stage of undermining the tower's stability. Now she noted how her neat sections gaped raggedly, how the metal was buckled and torn. The voice back in the workspace was silent: she needed all her energies to mount the twenty-three storeys rearing above her. Beneath the ninth and tenth floors, she rested in a knot of twisted steel reinforcement, ignoring the drag of her focus range urging her back down towards the ground.

There was no doubt. Damage to the tower was acute and critical. Left to itself, it could come down at any time, severely jeopardising the two housing communities on either side.

She could wind up the focus and put out an evacuation warning.

No time. The tower could go random any moment. Too much risk. Have to bring it down.

She sought and located the most obvious areas of weakness, and set to work redressing the tolerance between tension and compression, only dimly aware of the time her body was passing through, of the energy flowing out of her, somewhere else. Working opposite the greatest concentrations of stress, she hurried to correct and coax the angle of descent back to where she had intended.

As well as the rational sense of danger, something else spurred her efforts: the need of the professional to protect and nurse her project through a crisis; to impose calm and rightness on her domain; to triumph over the merely accidental.

The metal bowed and gave slightly as Bee etched away at it, methodically, insistently.

Listen to your body its needs are your own.

Far below, on either side, housemates were sunning themselves in the garden squares, preparing meals, moving to and from their places of work.

Listen to your body.

The many, separate bodies down there reached her with a louder voice. She was answering with an alternative to flattened houses, crushed limbs and lives: a mere dustcloud which would blot out the sun for the short space of an afternoon.

Listen.

She knew that her body had slid from its chair. Only a minor correction was needed to adjust her focus, hardly a pause in her work.

Outside the KT workspace, Leah, arriving for the next shift, waited, uneasy at the continued red light over the door.

Deep within the body of the tower, a momentary shudder signalled stress imbalance. Windows popped from their frames as Bee raced to the other side to justify the load.

The ring of splintering glass silenced the garden squares below. Heads turned towards the tower, which seemed to sway under the glare of the sun pressed hard on its flat top.

The women had gathered from all parts of the Co-op, and now milled round Leah, who waited anxiously by the security desk. 'I'll need the crêche clearing, and fast,' Leah told them. 'I'll have to focus on the KT workspace, see what's wrong.'

Perched high up near the top of the tower, Bee sounded out the vibrations running up through the frame.

Not much more, then down she sits. Rock-a-bye baby, down we'll go, she crooned, unaware that she was no longer joined by voice to her body. The link was gone; she was too far away.

Rubbing her neck, Leah told the waiting women: 'Doesn't look good, her pulse is weak. Better get up there right away.' Immediately, two women carrying aid-packs dashed for the lift. Leah shrugged her shoulders, drooping after the effort of the impromptu focus. A woman offered her arm for support. 'Just couldn't find her,' Leah said, quiet and perplexed. 'Checked her focus scope and followed her right in, but I couldn't get a hold.'

On the flat, bleached roof of the tower, Bee felt the long, yielding sigh of broken resistance, the inner shattering of metal bones, as the giant sagged to its knees, wire sinews flailing. Down she rode it, guiding the blind head into the grave she had prepared, marked only by the ruin of its beautifully broken body. At the last moment, she joined the rising dustcloud, juggling playfully with flying fragments of earth, rock and sun. Swirling on the bursting air, she caught up the clamorous, metallic peal from below, wove it into a silvery fugue, and danced along it.

TANITH LEE

Love Alters

*Tanith Lee was born in 1947 in north London. She has to date
thirty books in print, including work for young children and
young adults and around twenty science fiction and fantasy
novels for adults. She has also written TV scripts and had four
radio plays broadcast. She has recently completed her first
historical novel, which concerns the French Revolution.*

*'The idea for this one has been waiting in the wings for some
years, springing out when it, not necessarily I, was ready, which
happened to be in time for this collection. Like a lot of the
speculative-science fiction I've written, it pivots on the principle
of a reverse image. It isn't only the future that's on trial here, but
the present. After all, yesterday, today was tomorrow.'*

I had been married to Jenny for two whole years, when I fell in
love with a man.

It happened in October. (The leaves were yellow.) I didn't
know what was going on—and if that sounds coy, I can't help it.
It wasn't like any emotion I'd ever experienced before, or it
didn't seem to be. I thought at first it was anger, or autumn.
Then one morning I walked out of the apartment and down the
stairs, and along the Avenue, under those topaz trees, and I
knew. It made me sick, physically nauseated. It disgusted me as
much as I may now be disgusting you, telling you. But I *knew*.
There was no going back.

Worse than everything, I felt there had never been any
warning. Nothing. I was quite normal, I was like everybody
else. Reasonably ambitious, quite talented, capable of happiness, and grief. And as for Jenny—well, I was envied Jenny.

And there were plenty of times, even after three years together, when I wondered how I'd been so lucky as to find her, and to be loved by her.

When I was at college, I had made some mistakes in relationships. In a funny way, I'd virtually been pushed into picking the wrong ones, because everybody was so sure I ought to like the boyish rangey sort of girl, the kind you see in adverts for certain soaps, with one shallow breast bared, a bow in her slender tan hand, and a lean hunting dog at her side. Or else the big pushy type, who would 'Take care of' me. All that because I'm just the opposite. And I let myself be convinced. My God, both my mothers joined in. They'd bring the daughters of friends into the house, flat-chested, golden athletes, or older women who never wore a dress. I had a few affairs, not all bad. But I can be a bitch, and I got bitchy, and I did a lot of harm to women who never deserved it of me. I began to think that was the only scenario: a hopeful attempt, followed by protesting too much that this was great, followed by boredom and slight panic, and going for the throat. All affairs ended that way, didn't they? Slinging plates, slamming doors—

One winter morning, on the river bus, I saw Jenny. She was little, and she had beautiful hair like softly gilded ash, and her eyes were full of soft clear winter sunshine. We started to talk, and the grey river went by, and I thought: Damn, damn, why does the trip only take twenty-five minutes? But it was as if we'd talked to each other a lot already, known each other, lived next door, played in the garden as children—a slight mysterious gap in time, and now we had met again. And I thought, she can't possibly feel the same as I do. When we got to the Central Jetty, I asked her if she had seen the new three-screen movie at the National View. She would say, Yes. Or she'd say, No, I loathe that sort of film. Or she'd go red and freeze me with her gentle eyes. Or she'd say, I'm going tonight with my girlfriend. And then I'd drown myself in the bloody river. But actually she said, 'If you're asking if I'll go and see it with you, I'd like that. But I'm free for lunch today, too, if you are.'

To start with, when people saw us together, they assumed it was merely a friendship, the kind you might have with a man—or a sister, perhaps. My elder mother (Eleanor had been dead only eighteen months, and sometimes we still both cried about it), had some notion Jenny was a sort of crazy substitute for Eleanor, who had been that feminine, dulcet kind of woman, too. But Jenny was no substitute, and though she was my friend, it wasn't that either.

We decided to live together after five weeks. It caused more upset than when we married a year later. I remember a girl at Computer-Eyes, whom I'd once dated, and who came up to me and said, 'Listen, you're making a big mistake.' As if all the mistakes before, of which she had been one of the messiest, hadn't told me at last Jenny was right, was perfect.

There has been universally so much of this opposites attract rubbish. Friends now even said to me that Jenny and I looked wrong together, because we were physically alike, not in colouring, of course, but both being small, 'curvaceous'—as some are pleased to call it—very feminine in appearance. To my mind, since I started growing up, this cult for a 'masculine' or 'feminine' divide in partners is the depths of idiocy. Jenny and I could swop clothes, and could buy lingerie for each other, which was both useful and amusing. Both of us without shoes, she was just one inch shorter than me. We wore our hair the same length.

I recollect very clearly, she once said to me, 'But all that is finished with. I don't understand why everyone still has to pretend to be women and *men*.'

But it was the general rule. The male staff at C–E, even friends of mine, conformed to this standard. There were the male men, and the female men. I'd more or less accepted it in men. With women, it had always vaguely annoyed me, especially when it seemed to be ruining my life. After I'd met Jenny, I found I could tolerate it less and less with my own sex. A woman was a woman, wasn't she?

As for Jenny, she never had a lover before me. She was so gentle, she didn't want to hurt them, the types she didn't want. She used to say she'd been waiting for me. She knew somehow one day we would meet. I used to love her saying that.

We got married in the summer of '85. My mother, Lin, wanted us to have a great big showy wedding, so we did it to make her happy. It was a lot of fun, in its way. Lin also wanted granddaughters, and she'd begun to think she would never see any. 'One dark little girl for you,' she said to me, while the champagne flowed, and Jenny laughed with a white rose and silver confetti in her hair, 'and a blonde for Jennifer.'

'Oh, why stop at two,' I said. 'Let's make it a round dozen. And you can look after them, mother mine, because Jenny and I will be out working one week after we collect the brats from the baby-bank.'

'Now don't call it that,' said my mother.

'You would prefer the five-mile-long technical name? Anyway, I don't like babies. Ghastly things. I used to be one, and I know.'

But Jenny smiled at Lin, who loves her madly, and Jenny said, 'In a year or two, it would be nice.'

'I hate hospitals,' I moaned on. 'And it's a day off work, sometimes two.'

'What nonsense,' said Lin. 'When Eleanor and I started you, it was ten minutes each. I wasn't even sore. We used to go to see you once every week, all through the seven months you were growing. Eleanor used to cry. She thought you were beautiful even when you were just a little curled up embryo.'

I was afraid Lin was going to cry herself, but she cheered up and only gave us a lecture on how easy it all was for women, because obviously the X chromosomes make girls automatically. ('Gosh, Mum. Do they *really*?' I said.)

The clever part is, of course, to make the eggs fertilise each other, and the sperms do likewise in the case of a male partnership that wants a son. There you need, too, the Y to show up in order to concoct the right mix with the X. I have never grasped the mechanics, and had no wish to at my wedding. Marco, whom I had known and worked for for years, then broke the lecture up by telling a very bawdy version of his experiences while he and Alex got their boy.

'Dear girls,' said Marco, with his long fair hair trailing in the wine, 'I just couldn't—I could *not*—I got sent home in disgrace three times. And then they discreetly trundled in this machine with rubber hands. I *ask* you—'

'Do you truly,' I said to Jenny, hours after, when we were alone, 'want children?'

'Isn't that the best reason for getting married?'

'No. The best reason is to grapple you to my soul with hoops of steel.'

'Silly,' said Jenny lovingly. 'We'll make pretty daughters.'

Three months later, Marco came up to me and apologised for telling That Story.

'What story?'

'God. You know. About the hand-job for the baby. Alex has been on at me for weeks to say I'm sorry.'

'Well, when I remember, I'll let you know if I forgive you.'

'Did I ever tell you,' said Marco, stirring his cherry-flavour caffeine drink, 'I knew a guy once who wanted to have a daughter.'

'Nobody does that. I suppose it might be possible, if the Y got left out, which it never would. Isn't it illegal? The only case I ever heard of, which is doubtless a lie, it was a female birth with a Y added in. The women kidnapped the boy and drove off somewhere in the mountains. But they couldn't cope. Eventually he was abused, beaten, locked in cupboards, that sort of stuff, poor little kid—'

'You are so *intense*,' said Marco. 'Lord, I was only joking. Look, there's someone I want you to meet. You're going to be working with him on the *Magenta Dream* contract. He's some whizzo genius Alex was at college with. OK?'

But being Marco, the contract hovered, and I didn't meet the whizzo genius for another twelve months. His name was Druse, and I disliked him instantly. The look of him, his manner, his way of speaking. We disagreed on everything. The layouts, the promotion, the packaging, the choice of models. Even the computer terminals waxed partisan. My personal console would give Druse nippy little electric shocks. When I had to feed into his board, it would block. Many times the repair team had to come in, with their black box and their friendly scowls.

Druse (I hated his name, too. Why did I have to work with a man who sounded as if he should be a mutant breakfast fruit?) was unattached. He had been living with a man in Springs, but the relationship fell through. All his relationships, according to Alex, did this. Druse had a tall, coordinated runner's body, and dark red hair I wished cheerfully to pluck with red-hot pincers.

He was the *male*-type male. The firm's freelance girl-boys tended to haunt him. Druse took no notice except sometimes to be pretty cutting, and that didn't endear him to me either.

I became so angry all the time, I began to have migraine headaches, which hadn't happened to me since my adolescence. The medical Jenny made me take returned a verdict of stress. It prescribed homeopathic pills, and mooted a holiday.

'The remedy should have been,' I said 'a strong poison to slip in that monster's midday caffeine.'

'Surely he's not so bad,' said Jenny. 'He's clever, and he needs to work with people, but they make him uncomfortable. Then again, he hates being alone.'

'He doesn't have to be.'

'He doesn't know what he wants.'

'Let's hope he discovers, and it turns out to be to jump from a sixtieth-floor window.'

Jenny had met Druse in my company once or twice at C–E social events, and there had been an occasion when she came to meet me from work. They stood and talked quietly, as I finished off a rush piece of copy. I didn't do it very well, I was keeping an eye on him. But Jenny is Jenny, she seemed to have calmed him down. He even laughed once.

Next day he said to me, 'You have a lovely wife. That makes two of you. Two beautiful girls.'

And he looked at me, a long long look, out of his dark auburn eyes that burned. My impulse was to sling something sharp and heavy at him.

'Don't,' I said, 'try to get around me. I know I have a beautiful wife. I know what I look like. And I know you think I have the wits of a four-day-old soufflé. Which opinion, my friend, is mutual.'

'Jesus,' he said. And gave me the normal look again, contemptuous, cold, miles off and glad to be so.

'Marco says,' I said, 'we should try to finish this project together. So let's try. You try not to insult me, and I'll try not to murder *you*. How about it?'

'Stop shooting your mouth off,' he said. 'I know you have a brain. You just forget to use it all the time.'

'You wouldn't know what a brain is if you found one on your

in-tray.'

'You act like a child,' he said loudly.

'You act like a moron!' I shouted. 'Why are you here? You should be on some desert island. You hate human beings.'

'Then that lets you off the list,' he said.

'Listen, Druse,' I said. 'I don't know why it is, but the moment we met, you and I, we took an instant dislike. Let's be adult. We can go to Marco now, and have ourselves reassigned. The contract is going to slip this way. We're making a mess of it.'

Then he exploded. He went white and he came at me and I thought there was going to be a fight, and every fighter's hold I know came whipping into my mind, all ready for him. (It shames me, that. In or out of context. I might have killed him. He'd never learned those moves.)

'Don't you bloody throw this project down the drain because your damned stupid ego won't take any competition. *You* are the fly in this jam.'

'For Christ's sake,' I yelled at him. 'Why don't you go and fuck someone and get it over with, and then you can go fuck yourself!'

And I slammed the switch down on my console.

Instead of shutting off, it shorted out. And instead of giving Druse a shock, it flung me five feet across the room.

I heard myself scream, like some heroine of long ago in those ancient movies, which now, through their all-pervasive heterosexual content, are mostly banned as objectionable. The scream hung in the air, and I heard it fade and sink and die.

I lay on the plush. I thought: I'm lying on the plush. Then I opened my eyes. Druse was kneeling by me, checking my pulse. He looked at me. 'Don't move,' he said.

'I don't think I could,' I said.

'I've pressed the emergency bell,' he said. 'Someone's coming. You're going to be fine.'

Suddenly I started to cry. I lay there with the tears running down into my hair. Reduced to infancy, I was sobbing, 'I want Jenny. I want Jenny.' I could hear myself, like the scream, and dispassionately my mind remarked to me, Oh, you are making such a fool of yourself.

But Druse held my hand, and he stroked away the tears and the hair and he said, 'The moment someone comes, I'll call her. It's going to be all right.'

His hands were warm and kind, strong but not harsh, not brash. He's got beautiful eyes, I thought. They remind me of Eleanor's eyes. He could be her son, only women never have sons, or brothers, or fathers, any more. Just the way a boy never has a mother, a sister, a daughter. Because now it's as it was always meant to be. Once birth and the continuance of the species ceased to rely on the function of a woman's womb, the impact of a man's semen, the pleasure-drive they used to call 'sex' reverted to something more natural and fundamental: The recognition of one's own self in another. They say it took only twenty years for that to happen, and another twenty for humanity to face up to it, agree, relax. And twenty more, maybe, to see the other method the way we see it now, as stupid, uncouth, clownish. In fact, before the mechanics of progeniture had altered things, there had been plenty of men, and large numbers of women, who preferred to seek pleasure with those of their own gender, and could accept love in no other way. It was simply biological function that held the process up so long. The natural bodily urge was male–female, but the natural intellectual, spiritual *truthful* urge ran always in opposition. You see, I have read the books . . . But there are ethnic primitives still, who practise the old formula, who even carry their offspring physically to term. And there are perverts who *want* it. Men who want to sleep with women, and women who—

I sat up, and Druse grabbed me. 'Keep still,' he said. But he held me. I lay against him. I felt safe. *Safe!*

Before the C–E medic arrived, I fainted, and woke up in the firm's clinic, all expenses paid. They kept me in a day or so, but, as he had promised me, I was fine.

Oh, I was fine.

And then I had the holiday that check-up had suggested, and found in any event the electric shock had cured my migraines. It seemed to me I never thought so clearly in my life.

Jenny managed to get leave too, and we went to Paradise Beach. We had a good time. The late September, early October sun was almost tropical, and the blue palms swept the earth. We ate pineapples, and danced to music under stars large as the great golden shells you find in the sand. I'd never loved her more. I used to go to sleep in her arms with a sense of utter peace. We didn't make love, not once. She never reproached me, or tried to persuade beyond the mildest limit. I was tired, wasn't I. I'd nearly been killed. I'd had a bad year. Yes, Jenny, be kind, be thoughtful.

Let me not, to the marriage of true minds, admit impediments. Love alters not when that it alteration finds, nor moves with the remover to remove. . . . He wrote all those sonnets to boys, Shakespeare, centuries ago. (All to boys. The other version surely isn't credible.)

Jenny, not altering. Sweet Jenny, under the palms, in her beach costume, smiling, sea colour in her eyes, and unalterable love shining.

When we arrived home, I made a joke about going back to the grind of work. I made jokes about Druse. And when I realised I was making them too often, I controlled myself and stopped. I didn't know, not consciously, even then. I thought I was ashamed. The autumn season had affected me. I'd have to be polite to him, too, since he'd held my hand.

The leaves had changed. The leaves were yellow.

I went out one morning, down the stairs, on to the Avenue, on my legitimate way to return to legitimate work and, as I walked among the topaz trees, I knew.

I wanted to bolt back to the apartment, and to hide. The people who passed me on the street, some of whom I knew, greeted me. But I had a notice pinned to my back, and branded on my forehead: the word *pervert*.

Coming to the East Jetty, I caught the river bus. I had met my wife on this bus, over three years ago. I'd thought, If she won't come out with me, I'll drown myself. And for Druse, what would I do?

I tried to imagine, cruelly, how it would be, if he had any feeling for me, to touch, to hold, to kiss, to make love—and finally I had to go down into the bus lavatories. I vomited. I vomited because when I had thought of making love with Druse, a tide of sexual desire had gone through me, as strong as—*stronger* than—any pleasure-lust I had ever felt for Jenny.

When I reached Computer-Eyes, I was trembling. Somehow I got up to my floor and found my space, and sat down before my console which was sparkling new. Marco had tied a bow around it, and there was a label: *Trust me. I won't shock you.* I smiled, since I ought to, as I took off the bow. As I was doing that, Druse came into the room. It's a large room, and there were other people there, and going in and out, and there was no reason I should know it was Druse, but I did know; and it was. He started to walk towards me. I seemed to freeze, but I froze with heat. I was burning alive. No escape.

'Hallo,' he said.

I didn't look at him. I looked at the bow off the console as I tore it in small bits.

'Druse, I'm sorry, I can't work with you.'

'That's okay,' he said, very quietly. 'The project was finished while you were away. Marco is supposed to have let you know. So, we're all on fresh contracts now. But I just came over to say, I'm glad you're all right. Welcome back.'

I looked up at him. And once I began to look at him, I felt I could never look away. He met my gaze and returned it. Was it the same for him? There was something in his eyes, there always had been, something I never saw before in the eyes of any man.

'I have to talk to you,' I heard myself say.

'Yes,' he said. 'When do you want to?'

'Now,' I said. My hand shook so hard I could no longer even rip the paper bow. 'I'll go out. Up to the Glass Garden. This time of day, it should be empty. Will you—?'

'I'll meet you there. Give me five minutes to make it look good.'

The Glass Garden runs around C–E's twentieth floor, a ballooning window-walk full of plants and little fountains splashing glassily in glass basins. Hardly anybody was about, except the girls on the soft-drink stand, and the automatic ice-cream vendor getting itself ready for the mid-morning break.

He wouldn't follow me. Or he'd want to, and something would prevent him. And when he got here, what would I say?

And if I was able to say anything, and if he said anything in return, what then? Our society has no place for the kind of people we'd be. (Was it this that drove him out of Springs? The knowledge he was potentially a misfit.) No, of course it isn't illegal. Heterosexuality is merely—offensive. Or risible. There are even a few dirty jokes about it. It's the untidy ignorant thing we did, when we were animals tied to procreative functioning. Funny. And now, if he and I were to be the subject of that kind of humour, what? Leave our jobs. Go away somewhere. Pretend to be good friends, oh such good friends. And date girls, and date men, to sustain appearances. Invent wives and lovers elsewhere. And in the dark, in the shadow under the stone of convention, *couple*, make love—no, we couldn't call it that—screw, *do* it—and it was so alien, could I even bear to let him. *Could* I? But I wanted him. I wanted it. I didn't care how alien it was. *Wanted*.

And Jenny, where was Jenny in all this nightmare, this fire-shot blackness beneath the potted trees?

Druse stepped between the leaves and sat down beside me.

'I told them I'm taking the key for the *Tiger Light* project up to twenty-one. That gives me about twenty minutes before I need to do it for real.'

'Druse,' I said.

'I'm here.'

I stared into his face again. He was very serious now. He looked vulnerable, and sad.

He knows. He's been seeing it all, the way I have. We're in the dark together, and we don't know each other.

'Why,' I said.

'Why what? I know it's sticky,' he said. 'But let's talk it through. I don't object. Come on.'

'Why did you leave Springs?'

'Why do you think I left?'

'To get away from a man.'

'That's right,' Druse said. 'To get away. And, as you see, I got away and straight into something much worse. Didn't I?'

'Did you?'

He couldn't hear me. I couldn't breathe, and so had no breath to speak. I wanted him to hold me. I wanted not to have to talk about it after all. I wanted the world to be different.

'Look, kid,' he said to me with such tenderness, 'this hasn't been kind on you. I'm not saying it's been terrific for me either, but that doesn't matter now. I've given it some thought. I wasn't sure you—that you realised. But you did, you do. You know. So when I've taken this damned rubbish up to twenty-one, I'll go find Marco and see about a transfer out of here. Get out of town. Leave you in peace, the two of you.'

I started to say, to try to say, I didn't want that, but the words wouldn't come. He shook his head at me and smiled. His eyes were bleak. You couldn't look into them any more. Their doors of sombre amber were fast shut.

'For God's sake,' he said, 'one thing you have to know. I only saw her twice. Yes, I engineered the meetings, but they were both in public places. And she—she didn't know. Well, I think she knew why, the second time, she knew why. But not that it would happen, that we'd meet. And I guess she never did tell you, but that was to protect you. Not any sort of subterfuge. Because there really was nothing. She loves you. You're the only one she'll ever love. The other thing—that just isn't in her, to be that way. And I should have accepted that straight off. It never could be that way, with her. Please don't ever have a second thought on that.'

I found I was breathing again. Breathing was easy. It was being alive that was difficult.

'What are you telling me?' I said. '*Who*?'

'Jenny,' he said. 'Your Jenny, who loves you. Who'll never love anybody else. No woman. No man. Your Jenny that I wanted. Your Jenny, the one I—but you know all that.'

My Jenny. My sweet Jenny. Ash-blonde gilded hair, eyes shining with sea-shimmer and love. Jenny, my Jenny, who loved only me. And that he loved.

I closed my eyes.

'I'll leave you now,' he said. 'I'm sorry. You're a nice lady. We should have got along better. Be happy, please, if only for her sake.'

After he was gone, I sat alone in the Glass Garden until the mid-morning break, when the area began to fill with people, music and noise.

Then I went down through the building and out on the street, and I walked somewhere. And in the end, I came to a View, and went inside. They were featuring contemporary films, the *Romeo and Julio* whose doomed lovers are both male, and the *Julia-Juliet* where they are both girls of fourteen. But there was a tiny notice in the foyer, such as you sometimes find in this part of the city, that later in the day there would be an adult limited performance of an older print, one of the man–woman versions over a hundred years old.

I watched the two straight films. Then I bought a ticket for the freak-show.

The audience laughed a lot, some of it hysterical embarrassed guffaws, and some frank laughter, genuinely helplessly tickled at the spectacle.

There was even a moment when he is in bed with her and they are naked. He kisses her breasts, he does it with excitement and with ecstatic love, and she responds to him. At this moment, even the laughter fell silent. From disgust or astonishment, or, as in my own case, out of a sort of *dread*?

I came from the View and immediately called Marco, and lied. Then I called Jenny, and I lied. I called my mother last, and went over, and sat in her bedroom because she had a cold. She's got a girlfriend now who even looks slightly like Eleanor, and the girlfriend, who wants me not to mind her, was extra tactful and left us alone.

But I couldn't talk to Lin. And indeed, what was there now to say?

About midnight, I reached home, and Jenny.

She said, 'Druse called me today.'

'It's all right,' I said. 'I know. I know it wasn't anything.'

'I was only,' she said, 'so sorry for him.' She came to me, and held me in her arms. And I held Jenny and kissed her hair. No one would have laughed to see me do it, or recoiled in revulsion. But my heart was cold. And cold it has remained.

The leaves fell, and the days fell, and winter came, and I worked hard at C–E, and Jenny worked hard. We're saving up now, since more and more Lin keeps hinting about granddaughters. And I believe Jenny believes it will heal our marriage, this peculiar stillness which has settled over it, like snow.

Druse, I heard, went north, and is working for a branch of C–E near the ocean.

Darling Jenny, if only I could tell you. If only I could trust you, the way Druse trusted you, with the secret of difference. This bruises you, you think it's your fault. That I don't love you now because I think you're a traitor, or a tease.

Jenny, I'll always love you. But not the way I did. I can't. I wasn't waiting for you, after all. No, I was waiting for him. And he—*he* was waiting for you.

It'll be spring soon. The bare trees on the Avenue will spin green floss about themselves, and the grey river brighten. Everything is always changing. Seasons, weather, time. So why not the climate of love? Why not?

Oh, Jenny, why not?

LANNAH BATTLEY

Cyclops

Lannah Battley lives in a Northamptonshire village with her husband and fourteen-year-old daughter and works in the medical records department of a psychiatric hospital. She has been, amongst other things, a laboratory assistant, an actress and stage manager, an interviewer and a librarian.

The central idea for this story was sparked off, over fifteen years ago, by 'those famous live television pictures of Neil Armstrong and Buzz Aldrin bounding slowly on the moon's surface.'

I was relaxing in my favourite spot in the bar on Space Station 40 when I first saw Nella Nelby. I was sitting at the end of the great seamless window with a cool drink and a magnificent view of the cosmos when she entered the Travellers' Lounge.

Nella was tall, slim, dark and beautiful. She should have strode to the bar, head erect, careless of the rabble around her. Instead, she sidled in looking worried and glancing nervously over her shoulder. She still drew a few admiring glances for all that.

It was inevitable that such a magnificent creature, once served her drink, should choose to share my table and show me up as short, pudgy, pale and as plain as a pixel.

Having sat, she became no more relaxed. She perched her travel bag on her knee and hugged it to her as if it might grow rotors and hover away. She sipped her drink diffidently and tried to take in the people around her, myself included, without meeting anybody's eye. And I was trying to assess her without too obviously staring and making her the more embarrassed.

Strictly speaking one should never open conversations in Space Station bars but just occasionally I do.

Thinking that she might feel less tense with somebody to talk to, with astounding originality I asked, 'Travelling far?'

She jumped slightly and gasped, 'Earth.'

'It's a fascinating place so I've heard, but isn't it a little primitive?'

'No. I love it. It's beautiful. You've never been there?'

'It's not on my run,' I said.

'That's a pity. It's lovely. Still very wild in places.'

'You like wild places?'

'Yes.'

'You're having a holiday there, I guess.'

'No. Work. I love my work too.'

'So do I, though it gets rather routine at times.'

She must have been well aware of my occupation as I wore a pilot leisure-suit with shoulder insignia. I had nothing else to wear as a matter of fact, because my luggage had inadvertently been rerouted through Sandergate Phi.

'What do you do?' I asked.

'I'm a linguist and translator,' she said. 'I work in conjunction with the Planetary Archaeological Service.'

'So you often visit Earth then?'

'I've been twice before.'

'And you must specialise in Earth languages.'

'That's right. I'm also a specialist in Vectis, Palladic and Porteran.'

I was suitably impressed, and said so. She in turn said that she was impressed by my being a pilot. Female crew probably outnumber male these days but there are not that many women captains.

She introduced herself then, and I told her my name. She had visibly relaxed once she began talking about her work so I asked her to tell me some more about it.

'At the moment I'm concentrating on Latin and Greek, particularly Ancient Greek.'

'I thought all those languages were ancient.'

She smiled and said, 'Some are more ancient than others. They are excavating a site on—on an island in the Mediterranean. That is the land-locked sea which, if you remember your Earthian studies, was where many civilisations flourished. Our project is to finally prove that Earth was the cradle of humanity.'

'I didn't think there was any doubt.'

'Certainly it's a very common belief, but it's almost impossible to prove conclusively. Carbon-dating works on Vectis in much the same way as on Earth and that is proved to have a much more recent civilisation than any Earthian culture. As to the rest, nobody can tell. One can only compare their cultures with the various Earth civilisations. Some academics will consider that a particular comparison is irrefutable proof, others that it's fantasy.' Her face became pained. 'But now I have the proof in here.'

She indicated the bag still perched on her knee.

'In there? I thought you said it was almost impossible to prove.'

'Almost. But this isn't proof that Earth was the cradle of humanity.'

'I'm sorry, I thought you said it was.'

'This is proof that it wasn't.' Her face seemed to collapse in despair. 'Professor Beck is furious and has hinted that my sources are spurious.'

'Well it rhymes,' I said.

She looked puzzled.

'Furious, spurious,' I said.

'Oh, I see.'

'And are your sources spurious?'

'No. Certainly not.' Her hands hovered over the bag. She seemed in two minds about opening it, then pulled a wry face and shrugged. 'Look, this is one part of the proof,' she said, undoing the bag and bringing out a folder which she handed to me. 'It's only a facsimile, of course, but the source is impeccable, believe me.'

'You're not revealing your source?'

'Not to a complete stranger, no.'

'I can't say I blame you,' I said, riffling through the file. 'On the other hand, I can't think why you are telling me, a complete stranger, so much about it.'

'I suppose it's that I'm choked at Professor Beck's reaction. I've just got to tell somebody and get it off my chest.'

The folder contained the print-out of a spaceship logbook. Basically it was the same as the one kept on my trans-planet run, and on any other ship for that matter. But there was something about this one that was different. The typeface looked as if it had been produced by one of the earliest computerised systems, and there were settlement names that were similar to some I knew but not quite the same.

'Is this very old?' I asked.

'The original is about three thousand years old,' she replied.

'Standard years?'

'Yes. I cannot date it accurately because Professor Beck is refusing me access to the necessary facilities.'

'That man sounds a real abort-system,' I said. 'He's jealous, I suppose. He was in charge so he wants all the glory.'

'He is a she,' said Nella, 'and there's no glory. I've proved just the opposite of what we hoped to establish.'

'The truth will out,' I said, and settled to read the evidence.

I scanned the readings, the navigational detail which seemed quite meaningless to a modern pilot, and the crew rotas. There seemed little of interest to be gleaned from these so I moved swiftly to the Captain's Remarks section.

At first the trip was uneventful and the captain could afford to be mean with words. Most entries read, 'All systems functioning normally. All personnel in good health.' There was the occasional excitement of 'Emergency Stations Drill, 004 hours.'

That was until they encountered the meteoroids and the Emergency Stations became the real thing.

There was ample warning and avoiding action was taken but it was a particularly dense and deep mass. The captain was either exceedingly skilful or incredibly lucky, for the ship managed to zig-zag more than halfway through the vast band before it was hit. A large mass pierced their hull and demolished two of the stern holds. The adjacent holds resealed automatically, preserving oxygen and life.

The other damage was much less spectacular but caused havoc. Small fragments peppered the hull and many penetrated to places where there was no automatic seal operation and the result was death and destruction. All bulkheads have automatic seal these days, I'm glad to say.

As suddenly as the meteoroids came they were gone. The ship remained at Emergency until every alarm had been dealt with and calm was restored.

'Our crew has been decimated in the strictest sense of the word,' wrote the Captain. 'Four are dead out of a total muster of forty. We committed their bodies to the wide during the first watch. Of the remainder, nine sustained injuries of some kind. Some damage to the computers occurred, but fortunately the navigational functions are intact. There is also damage to steering and engines, added to which, all emergency and repair equipment was lost in the after holds. Our position could have been infinitely worse. As it is, we can make our way, albeit slowly, to the nearest planet, BK3, under auxiliary solar power.'

The captain and crew learnt from the computer information bank that BK3 had been superficially explored three or four generations before and was then sparsely populated by primitive tribes of hunters and gatherers. A more advanced group was living by an inland sea and inhabiting its many islands. They had developed agriculture and probably trade for there were water-craft and seaport settlements. Their dwellings were strongly built and permanent. There were some fine structures built of stone which appeared to be public buildings. The planet was rich in a variety of minerals which were largely unexploited by the indigenous population.

'But will it provide suitable constituents for us to meld into pliable, unsnappable plasticite for steering guides and a tough enough steelite for the main engine?' the captain fretted in the record.

Once arrived, the ship went into orbit while information about the planet's surface was monitored. They encountered a very basic problem which they were not expecting. The atmosphere was unbreathable. The reports of the earlier expedition had not included this fact. The captain had presumed that the surface was compatible with human life because if it were not it created such practical problems as to merit some small mention.

'The meteoroid damage to the computer could explain this discrepancy,' the logbook read. 'Although I would expect a hit to delete a whole tape not a part of one, it is possible that an impact removed the information regarding atmosphere on BK3 from the computer store. Alternatively, it could mean that the surface is perfectly healthy and the computers are at present giving a faulty reading. In the interests of safety I must ignore this possibility. All personnel are instructed to wear suits and helmets on the surface while readings are adverse.'

A scout car was sent to the surface, piloted by the second in command, Polson, who was accompanied by three crew members, Grant, Vectan and Kirilli.

The mother ship continued to orbit the planet and its log would have returned to the mundane except that at the end of each day the captain included the following reports from the scout car.

Day 1: We have landed in an area where a large expanse of water swirls against a jagged mainland fringed by promontories and rocky inlets. This sea is dotted with mountainous land masses which made touchdown a delicate business, but we managed a safe and uneventful landing on one of the larger islands. This gives good readings for minerals suitable for steelite.

So far as we can tell, the population is small and well spread, a tribe of herders. We have seen their animals, which have thick curly coats above four spindly legs and give weird guttural calls.

We feel certain that we were not observed when landing and have used the cragginess and a natural cave as part of our camouflage which is as near perfect as I have ever seen. The most orthodox programmer on landfall cover could find nothing to criticise.

So far so good, but the readings for the atmosphere outside remain at high danger level making our task more difficult. We began drilling inside the cave at once and extraction began. Plenty of suitable steelite material but nothing suitable so far for steer-guides.

Day 2: We have seen many more quadrupeds and also had a closer view of their keepers. They have not seen us. The herders seem to be small in stature but undeniably humanoid. It is hard to believe that these are not oxygen-breathing mammals like ourselves, but the readings continue to indicate insufficient oxygen and also a dangerously high radiation level. Outside the scout car we continue to wear suits and helmets. They make the physical effort of mining hot, laborious and slow. We have still found nothing suitable to meld into plasticite for steer-guides and, more worrying, the readings do not show anything suitable in the vicinity. We would be grateful for the nearest location from the mother ship readings to save time when we are ready to move on.

Day 3: Drilling in suits and helmets in a high surface temperature makes for slow tiring work. All the same, we are making good progress. In two more days we shall have enough steelite and to spare for the main engine.

We are surrounded by grazing animals today and also saw a humanoid much closer; small, slender, thin-limbed and clad in a short tunic.

Captain's eyes only: Code 448321967: I note your confidential remarks about no readings on planet for minerals suitable for plasticite manufacture. When we have finished the steelite mineral extraction in two standard days we shall make a minimum altitude scan to search for low-level plasticite deposits not detectable from orbit height, as instructed.

Day 4: The mouth of the cave is board and one of the quadrupeds strayed in today. Kirilli jokingly said that she would measure the creature for plasticite readings and turned the gauge upon it. To our amazement there was a low reading. Grant and Vectan were astounded when I said to bring the creature aboard for further tests. Kirilli thought it was a huge joke and chased it around the cave. When it looked to escape the way it had come I ran to the opening and frantically waved it back. The others thought I was mad so I felt obliged to explain that there was no record of any minerals suitable for plasticite manufacture detectable from orbit.

The animal was brought into the scout car for analysis. The smell was appalling. The extractors are going full blast. We may have to wear suits and helmets inside the car if this stench does not abate. The plasticite reading was given off by a long, tough, stringy tendon which is part of the interior workings of the creature. To extract sufficient for our purposes will be a laborious, messy, stinking and horrendous task but I shall await your instructions.

Day 5: The humanoids do not appear to be searching for the missing animal. Their tending of the creatures seems to be extremely haphazard. We caught two more quadrupeds close to the cave mouth and extracted the required part inside the car. I have decided that in future we shall wear suits and helmets and do the work in the cave.

Later we herded six animals into the cave. Although we are improving with practice at our task we could not deal with them all at once and rolled boulders across the cave entrance to stop those creatures not being dealt with from wandering off.

Day 6: Two herders were searching for stock today. We, in fact, had several of their creatures in the cave. The animals were making a terrible din with their hoarse calls until stunned, but they remained undiscovered. Grant has manufactured some camouflaged fencing to put across the mouth of the cave.

Vectan suggested that as there seem to be very few herders and they are, in any case, primitive and without weapons it would be a good idea to set up a whole series of fences outside the cave. If we could manage to herd a hundred or so creatures within this corral we could effect a quicker and more efficient system of extracting the plasticite based on our present routine. This will make our presence very apparent to any observers on the surface and I feel the need to ask permission to put the plan into operation.

Day 7: The scheme is working well. We fenced round about fifty animals today and could have encircled more if extra fencing units had been ready. We saw two small humanoids on the sky-line for a brief period.

Day 8: All goes well. More fence units have been erected. We managed to cram the increased area with creatures, Kirilli and I chasing, coaxing and manoeuvring the wayward beasts inside the circle. We must have looked very ridiculous at times in the course of our duties. While we were leaping about like maniacs Grant and Vectan were working steadily. We are incinerating the unwanted remains of the creatures.

Day 9: Vectan reported two small humanoids peering over the fencing today. As soon as he saw them they were off and away over the rough terrain with the speed and dexterity of mountain animals.

I fear that they will report our activities and bring back herders in great numbers, perhaps armed. I have ordered that if the intruders appear again they must be stunned and detained to prevent this but already it may be too late. We need three more standard days to complete our task.

Day 10: No herders have come to interrupt our work nor have the two humanoids who were spying upon us been seen again. The work progresses well.

Day 11: Grant caught one of the spies actually right inside the cave. She stunned the humanoid immediately and tethered it to a fence unit within the cave. Vectan is certain that this is one of the two which he observed on Day 9.

Day 12: We live in fear of massed herders coming to look for their own, but so far nothing has happened. We would like to communicate with this small being now that it is conscious but it is impossible. We cannot remove our helmets outside the scout car and we cannot take the humanoid inside for fear of contamination. We believe that it has not yet reached full stature but that even fully grown would be quite small compared to us. The work goes well and if, by good fortune, we have no interruption will be completed tomorrow.

Day 13: The work is completed. The humanoid was released and driven over the ridge. Kirilli remained on the peak to make sure it did not return to see the scout take off. Grant, Vectan and I cleared the site and so far as possible removed all trace of our temporary occupation.

Kirilli has returned to the scout and we are now about to take off and look forward to docking with the mother ship.

There the record ended.

I looked up at Nella who was sipping her second drink.

'It makes fascinating reading,' I said. 'But I just don't see what it proves.'

'BK3 is the Earth, of course, and if an expedition visited it while the indigenous population were primitive herders then Earth was not the cradle of humanity.'

'But there's nothing here to prove that BK3 is the Earth. In fact, it seems unlikely. It has no oxygen and is irradiated.'

'It has low oxygen and is irradiated,' Nella corrected. 'But I suspect that their computer was at fault after the battering they received. I think they probably wore suits and helmets on the surface quite unnecessarily. The fact that the figure 3 appears in their classification of the planet is interesting, don't you think? Earth, after all, is the third planet out from the sun within its solar system.'

'But that's hardly conclusive,' I replied. 'In essence, there's very little to go on. There's nothing to indicate the name of the ship, its route, its destination or when the journey was made.'

'There are place names mentioned there,' Nella replied, 'though, as you said, the spellings are weird. They could fit in with the ship having to make an emergency landing on Earth but that's just by the way. What really clinches it is the manuscript which ties in with the ship's record or, more properly, with the scout car's reports.'

She began to reach into her travel bag, but then thought better of it.

'The original of this, against all the odds, was preserved by a freak of nature on the planet Earth. I can't afford to lose it because I have no other copy. I honestly think Professor Beck would have me killed to get it back. I'm pretty certain I've been followed half across the galaxy anyway.'

She looked up and glanced around the bar and then froze, staring with horrified eyes at the main entrance to the bar.

'Oh no,' she whispered.

'What is it?' I asked and looked round at the person who had just entered.

The man was vast. He was also the ugliest human I had ever seen. His overall shape was pyramidal and the top of his triangular head spread out and down to jowly folds of skin around his collar.

'It's Doctor Roskopf, Professor Beck's assistant,' gasped Nella. 'If only there were some way out of here without him seeing me.'

'But there is,' I said, pointing my thumb over my shoulder. We decamped through the female urination facility, breathing sighs of relief that there was still sexual segregation in some things. With my knowledge of the Space Station's lay-out it was a simple matter for me to lead Nella down firechutes, up emergency stairs, through air-lock cavities and even along cable ducts. Not only was Doctor Roskopf unlikely to know the way but he would also be hampered by his bulk. Even so, once arrived at the twenty-second staging I suggested that Nella kept out of view while I checked that there was nobody about.

We entered my apartment unobserved, and locked ourselves in. After a slight hesitation Nella handed me the document which seemed to be the cause of our tortuous route. The heading read, *An account from my childhood*.

'I thought you said this was a manuscript. I expected it to be written by hand in the ancient way,' I said.

'The original is,' said Nella, 'but this is my translation from the Greek.'

I read:

I, being Aeneas, son of Philippos, and drawing near to the end of my days, wish to set down a true account of certain events during my childhood by which the gods ensured that I should follow the same path as my father while my sister became a wanderer and followed her own fate.

I would also like to set down that my sister Homa and I, though estranged from our youth, were reunited and reconciled before her recent death.

My history begins with the happy times tending the summer flocks with Homa. That is how I would always wish to remember my childhood, ignoring the biting winds of winter and the weariness and forgetting the fear and shame which came later.

Homa was four years my senior and very strong and agile. For all that, my father's flock often spread far and wide while she sat beneath a tree daydreaming.

'Homa,' I would say, 'please let us round up the strays. Father will be angry and whip us if any are lost.'

'You go if you wish,' she would reply, 'I'll follow later. After all, they have to spread out and find fresh grazing. They would starve otherwise and then father would whip us for letting them die of starvation.'

Eventually she would realise that she had tarried too long and then would follow long hours retrieving the stock: Homa striding out, suddenly full of energy with me trailing, despondent, small legs tiring.

It was inevitable that accidents would befall our sheep and there were beatings. Homa suffered most. She was the elder child and in charge of me as well as the herd. I must admit I was whipped but once and liked it little. Homa probably had more thrashings than she need for she had a defiant tongue which provoked our father and all our mother's pleadings could not save her.

The summer after our mother's death was very hot. The slightest movement caused cascades of perspiration. Naturally, the sensible thing when tending sheep was to sit under a tree. I made no objection.

Often we had provision for several days and nights and we slept under the stars. On one such occasion Homa told me that she had had a strange dream of a monster who roared thunderously and caused a rushing wind. In her dream the monster had swallowed all of our sheep.

The dream affected Homa for we set off early that morning to check on our flock. In fact, we spent the next few days checking. There was no point in rounding them up for this was the time of year when they could roam far and wide to find the best grazing. Despite this, Homa encouraged the furthest of them towards the area where the main body was dispersed. I never expected to exert so much energy in that fierce heat but I accepted it. If all our sheep were swallowed by a monster Homa could expect floggings for the rest of her days.

The dream came true a few days later. We saw a monster near the high peak of the island and I felt the blood drain from my face through fear. Rooted to the spot we watched. It made no awesome noise. It was entirely silent which, in some respects, was more frightening. Although we saw it from a distance we could perceive that it was huge, a giant with great girth and enormous height. It had a grey shiny pelt and the shape of a man. Its movements were slow and clumsy. When it turned its head in our direction we could see that it had a ghastly blank face with one huge dark eye in its centre.

My heart has never beaten so fast as the day I saw that ogre. At first my legs turned to jelly but soon they were recovered enough for me to spring up and run from that place as fast as I could. But it was not to be. Homa grasped the top of my skinny arm with her long bony fingers and pulled me into the parched bracken.

'Keep down, you fool,' she hissed, bruising my arm with the tightness of her grip. 'Don't let it see us.'

So we kept down. Homa told me to stay where I was and wriggled forward like a snake to watch the terrifying creature. I was then convinced that she was the bravest person in the world. She came back to me and said that the giant had disappeared from view behind some rocks. We retreated, keeping close to the ground, to the place where we had slept that night.

'Homa, let's go home and tell Father what we have seen,' I said. 'We cannot stay here.'

'You shall go home and tell Father what we have seen,' she whispered. 'I shall stay here and try to look after the sheep. Tell Father to come as soon as he can and to bring his bow and arrows. Otherwise surely this monster will eat the entire flock just as in my dream.'

I was happy enough to go home, to get far away from the giant, though I felt guilty at leaving Homa behind on her own. I was frightened also at the prospect of being alone.

'Come too,' I said. 'I shall be afraid travelling without you.'

But she would not come.

'Father will whip me for leaving the sheep,' she said. 'You go and tell him that we need his help.'

So I went alone, feeling safer and happier the nearer I got to home. If I had foreseen my reception I would not have been so glad. My father would not believe my tale. I pleaded with him, I begged him to come and bring his bow. I told him of Homa's dream and how later we had seen the real monster.

He shook me until my teeth rattled.

'What nonsense is this?' he roared. 'Has Homa sent you with this rigmarole because she has lost more sheep than ever? Get you back to the grazing and tell Homa that when she returns she will get the biggest thrashing of her life if any of our flock are gone.'

'But it's true, Father,' I cried. 'I saw it with my own eyes. A great tall monster.'

I stretched my arms up and out the more to explain its vastness. My father gripped my barely perceptible biceps where Homa had already bruised me, making me shriek.

'Tell me lies would you, boy? Well, I know what is the best thing to do with liars.'

That was when I experienced my first and only whipping. It was a turning point in my life. After that I always told people what they wanted to hear and that, I suspect, is why I became a successful and prosperous man. I rarely said what I thought, and seldom did as I said.

Success was in the future and seemed all unlikely then as I dragged my painful body back up the mountain to the summer grazing to deliver the awful news to Homa.

'We are between Scylla and Charybdis,' she groaned.

'Between what?' I asked.

'On the one hand is a horrendous ogre,' she replied, 'on the other Father's wrath and the strength of his arm.'

I shuddered.

'There's only one thing to do,' said Homa, staring wide-eyed into my tear-stained face. 'We must kill the monster and drag it back home. Then Father will believe us.'

I was appalled.

'Kill it? How can we kill it?'

'With our knives. Creep up on it when it sleeps. Even monsters must sleep.'

I doubted that and said so.

Our knives were small and not very sharp. Mainly we used them to cut bread, cheese and fruit; occasionally to free sheep from briars. Then we would sharpen them sufficiently to saw through the tough tendrils.

Now Homa honed her knife as never before, not only the blade edge but also the end into a sharp point.

'That would kill anybody,' she said, 'even Cyclops.'

'Even what?' said I.

'Cyclops. That's what I call the monster because he has one huge round eye.'

Quaking with fear I accompanied my sister back to the area

where we had first seen the giant and there we saw it again. It lumbered around building a stockade. This was made of shiny silver wood but it was not birch and it was not cedar and it was not like any other timber I have ever seen. This fence when built encircled a wide area and also enclosed the mouth of a cave which was the monster's lair.

Imagine our horror when a second giant came out of the cave and began to help the first.

'Two Cyclops,' gasped Homa.

Many of our flock were in the vicinity and the two monsters began rounding them up and driving them inside the paling as if it were shearing time. They were slow and lumbering but for all that they managed to pen a score or more sheep. Homa looked on horrified. I looked on terrified.

Then they began to pick out one or two from those that were captured and push them through the opening into the cave.

'What are they doing with our sheep?' asked Homa. 'We must find out.'

The bravest thing I ever did was to follow Homa, creeping, crawling to the palisade, breath held, my tiny knife grasped in my hand.

We could not see into the cave and so we learnt nothing, but we saw the creatures close to. I believed at first that they were blind, for their monstrous single eye seemed to reflect the land and sky and did not appear to focus on anything or have the means of focusing. That explains my carelessness. I tried silently to indicate to Homa that I believed that they could not see but as I gestured my knife slipped from my hand. It clattered against the fencing as it fell and the nearest monster whirled round and began to lurch towards us. Homa and I jumped up and raced away, leaping over rocks and thorn bushes with the speed of fear.

I slept little that night. I racked my brains to think how we might convince father of the Cyclops' existence without having to kill them. Homa would deem it impossible to kill two of them, I decided, and I was heartily glad. We would not have to put her desperate plan into operation.

But Homa insisted that she could still carry out her plan. She would kill both giants swiftly and silently while they slept. I could see the impossibility of her scheme. The first creature attacked would cry out and awaken the other and she would be caught and probably killed. It needed two, acting in unison, for the plan to succeed but I could not bring myself to volunteer my services. Homa, in any case, made it clear that she did not want me with her as I might drop my knife as before. She would kill the first she said, and if the other awoke she would put out its eye with a sharpened stave before it could grab her.

The stave was whittled and at nightfall Homa crept down to their stockade planning to work her way slowly and carefully to the cave under cover of darkness. Later she would need my help in dragging one of the carcases home to father, she told me.

So I remained on the hillside alone in the darkness and full of fear. The dawn should have brought relief but it merely added to my anxiety, for Homa had not returned from the giants' lair.

I watched the cave mouth all that long hot day and saw no sign of her. I became convinced that she was eaten by the Cyclops.

If I could have foreseen how petrified I would feel that second night alone in the dark I would have set off home before dusk. I sat wide-eyed in the pitch black imagining Cyclops creeping up on me and about to pounce.

At the first glimmer of dawn I began to move towards home, slowly at first, making sure that I made no noise, then faster and less quietly, and finally I ran headlong.

My father accompanied me back to that place, tight-lipped, disbelieving, expecting only that many of his sheep had either come to harm or were missing. His expectations were fulfilled. The giants were gone, their sheep pens had disappeared and there was no sign of Homa. I was convinced that she was devoured by the Cyclops but would not say as much to my father knowing that he would not believe me.

Homa reappeared a day or two later. The Cyclops had kept her captive but had not harmed her. They had cooked and consumed scores of sheep and then driven her away to the other side of the island. When she felt enough courage to return, every trace of them had disappeared.

My father was contemptuous of Homa's tale of monsters and

I, past the turning point, would no longer corroborate her story. She was reviled, beaten and flung across the hearth where she struck her head on a cooking pot. My father never spoke civilly to her again.

The loss of the sheep was a setback to the family fortunes but we seemed to recover well enough. Soon Homa and I were out guarding the flock again.

Homa never lost another sheep. She worked hard and she worked long. She had great physical fortitude. She began to suffer from headaches which sometimes affected her sight but still she would work on.

When my father died all his goods were bequeathed to me. I would like to record that I did not drive a half-blind woman from my house to fend for herself. Homa chose to go.

It took her longer to assimilate the lesson which I had learned so young but eventually she did. She began to tell people what they wanted to hear. My sister, as you know, became renowned as a story-teller and much in demand. She is now much more famous than me although I am the richest man for many miles around.

Now I weep with joy that my sister returned home before her death and we were reconciled. I shall always remember her as young, strong and agile as in the happy days when we tended the sheep on the summer pastures.

Nella was staring at me when I looked up. 'Now you see, don't you?' she said.

I was still trying to marshal my thoughts and, in my mind, fit in all the pieces of the jigsaw.

'I see the problem,' I said, 'if these are genuine.'

'They are, they are. Professor Beck and Doctor Roskopf would not be going to such trouble if they believed otherwise.'

'Yes, what exactly are they up to?' I asked. 'I thought these documents were copies, transcriptions.'

'Yes. The space ship journal is a direct copy but the other is my translation. There are not that many people who could do such an accurate translation. They would feel pretty safe if they could destroy that,' she said, pointing to the typescript which I held, 'and put paid to me.'

'Would they really murder to suppress the truth? If there were a lot of money involved I could understand it but most people are not bothered about the past.'

'There is money involved, grants, sponsorship, livelihoods but mainly it is academic reputation and the opinion of future generations.'

'You say you're going to Earth, but won't that be very dangerous if they really are so murderous?'

'It would, but I'm afraid I didn't tell you the truth. I'm running away from Earth. I will return but only when I can reproduce these documents on a massive scale together with my own commentary on their discovery. There will be too many to track down then and therefore little to be gained from liquidating me.'

'And where are you running to?'

'Wherever I can reach without them knowing and following. It has to be somewhere sophisticated enough to have facilities to produce copies of my finished work in large numbers.'

I was not convinced of the life-and-death nature of the situation but decided to err on the side of caution where possible deaths were concerned.

'I can offer you a place on my ship to Sandergate Theta,' I said, 'but I would have to check your papers.'

'You would be welcome to check them but I cannot risk my name appearing on a flight list or going through the normal embarkation procedures. I'm sure every flight is being searched.'

'That's why I would have to check your papers. Your name would not appear on any list and you would by-pass all the normal procedures. You would be my personal guest and share the privacy of my quarters unseen by any other passenger, if necessary.'

Her face lit up with a wonderful smile and she produced her papers for me to examine.

'The truth is,' I said, 'I would be unable to get you an ordinary flight for we are fully booked. With the rare mineral finds on Theta it's becoming a very popular place just lately. Everyone is rushing in hoping to make a fortune.'

One or two irritating habits apart, Nella was an excellent

travelling companion. She was cheerful and helpful and during my off-duty spells adapted her mood to mine. She would make conversation when I needed chatter and could keep silent without seeming oppressive when I needed peace. There was plenty of time for me to pick holes in her thesis and plenty of time for Nella to refute them.

I helped her to disembark discreetly at Sandergate Theta long after the other passengers had left. I have never seen her since.

Sometimes I wonder if it was just an elaborate plan to get a quick and free passage to Theta. Certainly many people were desperate to get there at that time though the boom is over now. Yet those documents would have been hard work to forge and seemed so genuine. I feel better in myself for recording the whole affair just in case there is something in it. Naturally, the episode has made me ponder the origins of the human race.

One should never open conversations in Space Station bars but just occasionally I do. When you have seen every video and played every computer game and all other entertainments have palled conversation can seem a blessing.

Certainly it can be an improvement on staring into space.

PAMELA ZOLINE

Instructions for Exiting This Building in Case of Fire

Pamela Zoline was born in Chicago in 1941. Her work has been exhibited and published widely. She describes herself as 'neither a writer who paints nor a painter who writes'. She now lives and works in England and in Telluride, Colorado, a small, beautiful, rather remote town high up in the Rocky Mountains. She is working with her husband, John Lifton, on designing a radical mountain community; on the Telluride Institute; and on a real-time, interactive Computer Opera, The Life and Death of Harry Houdini. *They have three children, Abigail, Saskia-Jos and Gabriel. A collection of Pamela Zoline's short stories will be published by The Women's Press in 1986.*

'I wrote "Instructions for Exiting This Building in Case of Fire" because it seemed like an obvious, necessary story. It was more that I wanted the story to exist, politically, than that I especially wanted to have to write it, and I remember feeling rather hard-worked and rumpled as I laboured over it.

'I'm interested in the strategy within the story which unsubtly requires the reader to make some of the same moves between detailed memory and a kind of twice-invented reality that a writer must make in constructing a fiction; the barb in the fish-hook.'

First and primarily the reader is asked to Radically Visualise a particular child. Employing extreme breathing, sensory looping and the usual bio-psyche techniques, please call up into vivid present tense a real boy or girl, one whom you know well, and preferably one with whom you enjoy a largely positive relationship.

(If given the partitioning of modern life you do not know any children, you will have to borrow one from literature or painting, or perhaps from the movies. One candidate, an archivist, recently utilised the younger Shirley Temple, and another fastened on the tiny blonde Infanta Margarita looking warily out from the Spanish court, at Velasquez the painter and past him into the middle distance.)

We have found it useful to provide some framework devices to assist visualisation. Initially, call up the brute dimensions of the child: mass, weight, reach, height. You will find that you can revive, through whole-body recall, the received pressure from those occasions when the child's body has rested against your own. The next array includes the colour and fragrance continuum. Fill in hair colour, eye hue, the pigmentation of the skin and particularly the shades of mouth, cheeks, the palms of the hands and the soles of the feet, and the skin beneath the fingernails. Please be as exact as possible. Numbered swatches and colour chips are enclosed. Try next to specify the smells relating to mouth, hair, skin and gaseous emissions. What textures do you associate with this child's skin and hair? Characterise the teeth. We have found that the reconstruction of auditory sensa are especially difficult for some. It facilitates to summon up the image of the child in action, bending, turning, pausing to speak—insert here a typical utterance, coming from lips of such and such a shape, with the head tilted how many degrees from the perpendicular, and the brow set with just these curves and arcs, the nose at such and such an angle, the gesture, the gaze, the tone of voice.

Now quickly, at a grosser matrix, fill out the time–space context around the individual: specifying surroundings, time of day, presence of others, colour inventory, humidity and pressure, noises, smells, emotional tonus. There is your child now, squarely placed in an amply detailed continuum (I am reminded of the exercises in 'particularisation' in the Creative Writing Syllabus at Chicago Tertiary College), and there we leave her (my resolutions for gender-neutral language break down—when *I* tell this story, I see a little girl).

She is sitting athwart her young brother whom she has tickled into hysterical submission, they are wrestling in our back garden, sending up gusts of yellow aspen leaves which litter the ground like coins of fairy money. She is wearing hand-me-down denim overalls and a red sweater on which the motif ducks and rabbits have gathered for a pre-Easter meeting though it is only October. And one's sense of her person is of a highly variegated surface so covered is she with her usual rents, tears, bruises, paint marks and other smudges and her fine brown hair escaping every which way from the double security of braids and barrettes. Her earnest and passionate researches into the nature of things leave her decorated with testamentary marks of contact, stones and worms in her pockets, twigs in her hair, blue and green daubs across her cheeks and chin. She has the aspect of a tribal citizen, very powerful and intact, with an extraordinarily direct and unabashed intelligence. In the broad sunlight it is warm, though there is an autumn chill in the plum-coloured shadows. Her eyebrows are drawn with a two-hair Chinese brush, her eyes are blue. Now her brother is bawling over some rough justice, and to soothe him she delivers a new rhyme, a choosing device which she has learned, she is shouting out, '*My Mother and your Mother were hanging out the clothes/My Mother gave your Mother a punch on the nose/What colour was the blood? Shut your eyes and think/Green! G-R-E-E-N spells green and out you go/With a jolly good clout upon your big nose!*' Successful solace, and they are both laughing uproariously and will not stop.

And now, patient reader, without at this point questioning the mechanism, let the Goddess Hariti act as *dea ex machina*. She who began as a child-devourer but was converted by the Buddah into a cosmic nurse-maid will whisk that altogether palpable child to Moscow, to Gorky Park. It is spring and the ice is continually melting and freezing, and what is this child, my child, my luminous girl doing in Moscow, on a park bench, wrapped in foreign winter gear and licking a chocolate ice cream?

It was as the Middle East rended itself mortally, the crazed wolf in a trap biting his own flesh. And it was as the pendulous

Siamese twins of Africa and South America, now separated, seemed still continuous in their joint misery and suffering and accelerating frenzy. There were so many wonderful and urgent reasons for dissent, and only the one overwhelming reason for accord which was both absurd and too vast, so that most of the *homo sapiens* population, up on our hind feet, sundered from biology, found it invisible. The little wars flickered and acted as beacons to the larger interests; the global theatre was filled with acute excitement. The situation became daily more extreme. It was when the minute hand on the Domesday clock fluttered and hiccoughed in those rare seconds before midnight that we finally acted on this set of premises, to change history.

Angleinlet, Minnesota

Anyone viewing the video of Dakota Saltz and Michael Benjamin, the newly sunburned Saltz–Benjamins, making the beast with two backs in the 60s Nostalgia Room of the Hotel Sands Susie on election night would have concluded that her attention was only partly taken up with the bumpy union of their bodies. The camera, though expected, was tactfully secreted in an expensive lighting fixture which mimicked live candles. The décor featured hanging strands of beads and bells, souvenirs of Vietnam, political posters in four languages and voluminous folds of Paisley cloth. Spot-lit and bolted to the floor was a display case in which a bit of moonrock set in a lucite block was on show, and the theme was picked up by a 'one small step for man' photo mural.

'My mother was a hippy,' Dakota snorted, on top, lazing back and forth, she sneezed at a drift of smoke from the automatic, everlasting, self-igniting joss sticks. 'She believed that a creative and spiritually evolving life-style would save the planet.'

The television blatted out the terrible and expected results, the bright and dark forms of the victorious flickered across the lovers' substantial flesh: bad news, bad news. From all over the globe the media shepherds and shepherdesses rounded up and brought forward their unnatural flock, the members of the world's various governments to react and reflect upon the

American elections. Mesomorph, ectomorph or endomorph, bald or hirsute, rhetorical or confiding, pompous or humble, religious or secular, dressed in emblematic duds, they all bared their teeth at one another, and uttered patriotic formulae and threats.

Moaning, Dakota willed herself to focus on transactions between her body and her husband's. She called on some partially understood tantric discipline to transmute the corporeal into the spirit, to map the personal body onto the cosmic body, she meditated on a terrible form of the Goddess Kali seated in intercourse on the male Corpse-Siva, resting upon severed heads. The fanged and bloody Goddess is the same as the beautiful Mother and Lover. The images flickered and incremented, Michael's red mouth shaped an O, the pulses of orgasm married the opposites for a moment. Panting, grinning, tasting the sweet oxygen, the newsflash immobilised them as though it had been a jolt of ball lightning zapping through the room:

The young son of a top Russian general and the four-year-old daughter of a US Senate leader had both been kidnapped from their homes within the past twelve hours. BEGIN!

Dakota found herself standing in the middle of the room, holding some socks and underwear, starting to pack, standing still, tears flooding her vision. Michael side-stroked into view, looking preoccupied.

'*Kismet Hardy, or Kiss me, Hardy, pie in the face*', she babbled. '*Here we go!*'

The news bulletin is repeated on the screen. The relatives of the kidnapped girl are being interviewed, they seem hardly to be able to construe the reporters' questions, so deeply absorbed are they by the enormous event which has overtaken them. The father's brows leap and punctuate independent of his sentences. Dakota's mouth is a hot cave from crying.

'Crossing the Rubicon, I can't remember the Latin for the die is cast,' and she wept and roared for a few moments, into the labelled hotel pillows, and then she was calm again. She had her instructions with her, a microdot mole on the right shoulderblade. *Eat this note.*

The shaman reconstruction ritual was an eclectic and corrupt piecing together. About fifty women were bussed from St Paul, through the vast acres of sleeping suburbs, through the farmland, into the northern woods, and then deeper and deeper until they stopped at a place that looked to the untutored eye as leafy and indefinite as all the surrounding landscape. Dakota wondered afterwards whether the hot drinks passed around in polystyrene cups had been drugged. Certainly the colours in the nimbus around the fire began to vibrate brilliantly in distinct bands. They took off their clothes, undressing in the bus, joking and talking in the instant equity of bare flesh. Outside their breaths formed steamy clouds but the big fire heated them at least one side at a time. Silhouetted against the tall flames the organisers read out bits of potted prophecy from Hopi and Kiowa texts, from the Bible and the Koran, and also from Nostradamus and other dubious sources. Then all were encouraged to run around the fire circle springing and roaring, leaping, barking like a dog, sniffing, lowing like an ox, bellowing, crying, bleating like a lamb, grunting like a pig, whinnying, cooing, imitating the songs of birds, and so on. It is said that the descent of the spirits often takes place in this fashion.

And so, the preconditions having been satisfied, she was now an 'activated agent'. Outside the snow had begun again. Carrying messages too secret to entrust to technology, Dakota was on her way to Florida.

* * *

No one invented this, everyone did, all at once, like a miracle. No one is the leader, we all are, and it just happened that way. That's right. And if that all seems odd, unlikely, too much the paradigm of what used to be called new age organisation, then you will have to find out for yourself, if there's time, if it seems important. The stories we tell ourselves are whatever is necessary for going on. Personally, I've never really thought of myself as a group player.

In the crisis room in Kansas the red crisis lights are on, and the sirens blast at frequent but random intervals rendering all thought impossible for that period and leaving an auditory after-image suspended in time for a little, like the ghost flash bulb that hung over the head of the importunate school photographer. I am explaining this to you just as I find I am explaining it to myself, over and over, since I made the initial, irreversible commitment; since we began.

The very notion of approaching a family situation, and invading that family and violently removing a young child from that family, and taking that child away so fast and so far and promoting so many changes, that any future connection between child and family is uncertain: even *the idea* of that action is disgusting and abhorrent.

And so I come to you with unclean hands. And also, in the midst of so much distress and tragedy, I speak with the authority of my own, of our family's tragedy.

It was during the early months of the exercises, I had returned from Florida, we were aping normality and even the pretence was precious. Judith, our middle child, second daughter, first-grader, our blue-eyed indomitable, always joking darling, is late home from school. It's Halloween and we're going to carve the pumpkins and then go out trick-or-treating, so she wouldn't be late. The costumed figures of the smaller children stumble from doorstep to doorstep, the bigger children are readying themselves, and yelps and calls escape from the upper windows.

Where is she?

Checking the bus-stop, which is on our side of the street, a two-minute walk. Pacing up and down the street, making the phone calls to friends' houses to see if she has, please God, broken the rules and gone over to play without permission; walking around the empty school, the deserted playground, the town park full of children but not that one special bright face, green jacket, fast runner, good climber. Talking to her teacher, to the bus driver, the school head, to the police, the FBI, and for those few hours, until it grew dark, sustaining a hope that some reasonable logic was still operating and that she would be home for supper, our radiant girl! But the dusk gathered and the clouds grew bright, never have I dreaded more the sunset's gorgeous rose and cadmium sacrifice, so quick.

We had known, of course, that in order to remain covert, and also to maintain a basic justice, the members of the organisation would have to be part of the big computer's horrid lottery, along with everyone else. And now I think of Judith always, every hour, every time I look up at a peripheral flicker which isn't her. My dilettante's essays into non-attachment have been worthless, of no value whatsoever.

What could justify this offence to Person, Family and Natural Law? Only this. The extreme and growing likelihood that we are finally about to do it, blow ourselves to kingdom come, extinguish our species along with the multitudes of others that journey along with us, and perhaps the planet itself as a life-sustaining venue. That, coupled with the dreadful, finally unavoidable conclusion that sane, liberal, powerful, even very evolved persuasion cannot any longer save the day—simply because we've run out of time!

At the ultimatum meeting in the buried solar motel at the Kansas headquarters a fat Polish woman stuttered through the pandemonium to the heart of things.

'Suppose yourself in a burning building, full of confused adults and children, a trickle of blue smoke, the intoxicating scent of roasting hydrocarbons, soon it will turn into an inferno but the inhabitants seem not to notice. The only way, *the only way* to set off the alarm which will alert the crowd is to lower a child, yours or another's, out of a window and drop it to the ground to its probable destruction. *Would you do it? "Yes".*'

Key-West, Florida

The 'living diorama' Seminole village, which was said to be on the site of the *actual* Seminole village, was made up of two rows of structures that looked like giant, stripped-down four-poster beds minus the organdie. These Seminole dwellings were open on the sides and covered on top, some with a kind of rough thatch, others were roofed with sheets of galvanised metal. On the platform, families in antique dress were assembled, playing Canasta, cooking fry bread, singing to babies who were slung in hammock-like devices fixed to the corner uprights. In short, going about all their domestic business before the eyes of the

delighted tourists. These Indians were, on close inspection, a
savvy blend of warm humans and androids, the mix favoured by
the most successful modern theme parks.

Pearled, striped and blotched with sweat, Dakota followed
behind a group of heavily-swathed Jordanians, and was herself
followed by a cadre of handsomely equipped Japanese. She
limped along on her sore ankle, viewing this odd, highly
artificial and decadent interface between cultures, than which
there are no others. Peering into the faces of the native
Americans first to make the rough division between humans
and subs, then to enter behind the opaque gazes of even the
living Indians—'How can I find my "contact" if no one will look
back at me?' Just a trill of panic, had she spoken aloud? Their
eyes were obsidian. And so, not paying attention to what lay
immediately underfoot, and limping on her left, the ankle was
swollen and still swelling, progressively, a chronic sprain,
damn! and so she was next a victim of the instantiated national
characteristics of the tour packs who surrounded her. The
Jordanians, intrigued and amused by the quaintness of the
exotic infidel, dallied. They hung back to point and discuss,
they stopped to open picnic baskets and napkin sacks. They
planted themselves just so to clean the face of one of their
spotless children, they retraced their steps to catch another look
at some special sight; they gossiped, they lingered. The
Japanese, hung about with all manner of mid-tech recording
devices, pressed forward with determined enthusiasm. They
photographed, videoed, filmed, taped, they pushed. And so
Dakota is caught up between the aggressive Orientals and the
dilatory Arabs, the light dazzles her eyes and her leg is hurting
and she is getting too much sun and how would she ever connect
with her contact.

Thump! she is knocked flat into the pink dust, coughing, a
large pyramidal shape looming above her resolves itself into a
heavily draped Arab woman. Bending over the topsy turvy
'agent', she lifts gauzy purdah and speaks directly into Dakota's
large-lobed left ear.

'*Follow the squaw who overcomes the dragon-reptile*.' She
then shows the sign which marks her as indubitably part of the
exercises, the sisterhood, the Mothers of Invention dubbed by

some old lady who did or did not remember the 1960s. Spitting out dust, Dakota picks herself up and moves forward. 'Not a particularly glamorous bit of espionage.' Had she spoken aloud?

And there at the end of the street which is formed by the two rows of houses, a dusty widening, trampled clay pricked out with weeds, a primitive gas station with one pump, closed, and a café-type highway restaurant which had fallen away from its chipper franchise crispness and exhibited curl all along its perimeters. The multicultural crowd thronged and surged, according to their deep natures, towards a deep, flat-bottomed pit fortified by adobe walls. Dakota was bundled along, pushed forward on a wave, she could see at the bottom of the pit, crouched on the fissured red mud, the green, segmented, long-jawed, quizzical alligator, ticking its tail in display to impress the young Indian woman who crouched opposite. The woman looks both tough and oddly casual. Her blue-black hair is cut very short, her face, in concentration, contains but does not reveal. A fat Indian man in a Hawaiian shirt printed with orchids and parrots gives the signal for the 'gator wrestling to begin.

The woman enters within the attack range of the animal and, avoiding both the switching tail and snapping jaws, she flips the animal onto its back and manoeuvres to sit astride the beast, and then, most amazingly, she proceeds to rub its belly in a clockwise fashion. And thus did the reptile fall into an hypnotic sleep which continued until the young Seminole woman ceased in the stroking of its stomach's pale, shining skin. And then its eyes unbuckled and its body kinked and jerked and its tail began to pendulum again and the woman leaped off and out of reach and scrambled up from the pit to much applause and electronic whirr. It was only at the last that Dakota remembered she was to follow this woman, and she dodged through the crowd after her, into the café.

Having attracted the attention of her quarry by pouring bourbon on the rocks into her lap, the lap that is of Laverne BitterWing who, as a radical feminist 'gator-wrestling Seminole, had seen more politicking than Dakota had had hot dinners, Dakota apologised and bumbled out the password which was 'authenticity', and felt herself blushing head to toe as Laverne looked on with a kind of irritated tolerance. Drinking the replacements, seated in a red naugahide booth, Dakota gave Laverne the message, whispering about an exercise that involved Manila and Peru with Florida as the third critical point. She hissed the names of the children who had 'won' the lottery; she outlined the network for each child's retrieval. Laverne's perfume rose up into her nose, she was thirsty from the dust and the heat and the whispering, 'another scotch, or rather bourbon, that's what we're drinking.' And Laverne tells Dakota the scarey stories about the 'hot' submarines nosing in close to the Florida coast, playing games of chicken. Recently military chemistry has covered the beaches with stinking, phosphorescent fish. Obsidian.

* * *

Sometimes it seems to us that there are signs that the exercises are beginning to take effect. In the boardroom, the factories, the bedrooms, in the chambers where governments grind out their extraordinary decisions, everywhere human creatues act and move, there is now this enormous consideration. With the kidnapping and the 'specified' resettlement of all these many little children, increasingly, the *we* and the *they* have become irrevocably, irretrievably confused, all mixed. This mixing, this sense of shared consequences, is not of our making. The exchange of the innocents simply points out what is in fact already the case, that finally, at this extraordinary juncture of history, we are members one of another, not in some abstract rhetorical sense but at the most practical level of survival. 'The bottom line.' Who spoke?

We remind ourselves that some small initial success is not sufficient for us to do what we all long to do, to stop this terrible work. The danger of absolute conflagration is immense. We must not weaken. We must be resolute.

Yes, of course there are casualties. The child who fails to respond adequately to surgery, the anaesthetised child who aspirates vomit and suffocates, the families ruined beyond repair, the child who goes mad. Please refer here to your own illustrated file on the after-effects of nuclear war.

Lubec, Maine

Flying to Lubec, Maine, the Saltz-Benjamins, diminished with Judith missing, no longer fill the five-seat middle bank of the airline's economy class. Dakota finds herself between four-year-old Max who, naturally exuberant, has been numbed and practically muted since the kidnapping of his sister, and an extremely elderly man. This gnarled and transparent gentleman introduced himself in heavily accented English as the proven and established oldest man in the world, a claim he substantiated by drawing out of his wallet various laminated newspaper clippings which pictured him and explained that, as a political prisoner in the Soviet Union during the 1940s and 1950s, not a young man even then, he had undergone repeated hunger strikes which had provided just that periodic shock to the genetic material which was required, as science has since demonstrated, to extend the human life-span dramatically. The old man chattered on about his history, stories of doves and hawks and the species' ultimate games. He entertained Dakota with the recitation of a menu from a great diplomatic dinner in Geneva—oysters in truffle sauce, smoked swan, beef Wellington, eight vegetables, world-wide cheeses, six wines, black bread, baked Alaska, pumpkin pie, and a whole living peach tree wheeled in so that the guests, all now deceased save for her interlocutor, could pick the fruits with their own hands. Dakota yawned until her jaws creaked, she was desperately tired and, of course, it should be Judith sitting there.

Jenny, their eldest, turned pale and Max grabbed at his ears as the plane banked and made for Ape Island, the tear-drop-shaped artificial bauble of land which had become famous as an exclusive resort and tax refuge, it winked up at them out of the foaming, Guinness-coloured Atlantic.

Fragmentation of directions is necessary to confound our pursuers. Dakota walks, with family in tow, through the Theme Park of the Evolution of Culture, '*just pretend to be ordinary*', on the look-out for a sign. Displays, rides, exhibition halls, museum complex, *son et lumière*, the mother and father point out the items of interest to their children, see the walls, the cities, the gardens, the modes of transport, the sophisticated techniques of warfare, all the works of art and culture which make up the inspiring models of *homo sapiens* achievement. Jenny was paler still at the Rembrandt Arcade, and finally threw up just outside the Lincoln Compound, observed only by a group of robot darkies. *And on this hand is the special activated genuinely scientific demonstration and statistical display.* They walk under an arch lettered in Revival Nouveau vegetable cursive MONKEYS TYPEWRITERS SHAKE-SPEARE. A 'living exhibit' organised according to the premise contained in the 'archaic humorous saying' *Put enough monkeys with enough typewriters for enough time and they will produce the complete works of William Shakespeare.* (which see).

No doubt the recent cataclysmic events have interrupted the day-to-day running of organisations even so far from the epicentre as this bit of hypostasised pastorale. Notwithstanding the fascinating character of the display, the monkeys and apes disporting in a charming conjunction of nature and culture, there was on every hand the evidence of neglect and order distressed. Citizens goggled at the primates interacting with all manner of typewriters, word processors and computers. They applauded the drama of these hairy cousins reinventing culture in picturesque vignettes, 'the taming of fire', 'clothing our nakedness', 'invention of the fishing hook', 'the commencement of poetic diction', and so on. But, as father commented to mother, despite the lavishness of this rhetorical Darwinism, there were, to the observant eye, many signs of 'making do'. Since the cancellation of Malaysia the severe interruptions in supplies and personnel has resulted in a certain amount of barely adequate habitat and noticeable psychological dislocation among some of the animals.

They came upon a group of gorillas dressed in rough tags of Elizabethan costume, labouring away at the construction of a replica of the Globe Theatre. Max and Jenny press forward in a gang of children up to the barrier to watch the action. They have taken up with a charming, peach-skinned, French-speaking blonde child, smaller than Max, and Jenny struggles to lift her to the top of the barrier so that she can see. The apes swing gracefully about the building site, there is a sense of mock decorum about many of their movements. Dakota noticed that they seem to build and unbuild with almost equal assiduousness, and they frequently stopped in the midst of some effort to act out a line or two from one of the plays, or to quote a mangled couplet from a sonnet. Their language was vastly imperfect but it was language. They glimpsed Hamlet and Ophelia in conversation under a willow tree. Ophelia seems upset, and Hamlet grunts and plucks at her, then turns away. And then a massive young silverback male catches Dakota's attention. He is standing on a precarious canti-levered joist which swings, barely pinned, from the top of the north wall. He is mouthing a speech: '*Lie with her—We say lie on her, when they belie her—Lie with her! 'Zounds, that's fulsome! Handkerchief—confessions—handkerchief!'*—he gabbled. '*Pish! Noses, ears and lips. Is't possible—Confess?—Handkerchief?—O devil!*'

'Act IV, scene I', says a voice at her side. She jumps sideways, startled, it is the certified most ancient man. 'His name is called Otello, in the Italian manner.' Dakota watches *as though in slow motion* the gorilla Otello moves down through the construction and over the grass and the rocks to the barrier, and, at more frames per second, clambers over the moat and simply bounds to the top of the barrier. Voices cried out 'Otello, Otello!' And then, as Dakota realises that she has known that this would happen, with grotesque but inescapable logic, Otello reaches down and lifts the little blonde from Jenny's arms '*Daphne*!' An ear-splitting shriek from two throats, French, the armaments magnate and his spouse who are ravening bootlessly at the edge of the crowd. 'Daphne! Otello, Otello!' these two musical names curl out over the scene as the gorgeous Otello mounts the heaped elements of the theatre, the wailing baby in his arms. Perched on top we can all see that she is in grave danger as he dandles and dangles her and teases her with the unsecured space. There is nothing anyone can do without spooking the ape and endangering the child further.

'*Otello, Otello!*'

What are these words in her mouth? Dakota is calling to Otello, he listens, he replies. This woman who has always disliked and avoided heights is climbing the structure, scaling the walls, she has gained the top, she is facing the gorilla and flailing child. '*I'm terrified of heights.*' Had she spoken? '*Otello*' she said through dry lips, and he made a dignified nod and handed over the little girl who was rigid and purple with continued screaming. Dakota held her tightly and climbed, bit by bit, shakily, carefully down. As she touched the ground she heard the crowd sigh collectively, the parents were coming towards them. But Dakota felt with her hurt foot for the trigger to the trap door in the burned knoll. *How had she known it was there?* and it swung open to let them in, then snapped shut, decisively. The hammering continued against the massive door which fitted seamlessly into the bank, it held steady. Dakota exited, down and out. She injected the wretched child and watched her twitch into unconsciousness. As they transited, Dakota was apologising to the ashy, crumpled baby in her arms.

Cape Alava, Washington

We delivered Daphne to Cape Alava, Washington. She was to undergo further training, briefing and 'conditioning' which is a dump word for surgically and drug-induced consciousness alteration. Drop-off was a veterinary clinic in a shopping mall. Anaesthetic music accompanied their progress through the bland reflective corridors constructed at a giant's scale. Daphne held tightly to the collar of the bumptious Newfoundland puppy, her decoy. He terrorised hamsters and kittens in the waiting room, a distraction, until they went through to the examining room where the agents stood with sad, drawn, severe faces that Dakota recognised from the mirror. Then the child was screaming again, and trying to hold onto her, and the huge puppy was barking and leaping, and people were falling on the slippery blue linoleum, and Max yells out in a rusty voice, '*Daphne, Judith! Daphne!*'

* * *

Now, gentle reader, please call up into your mind's eye your selected child as already visualised. Go through the reification processing and mass out significant traits as indicated earlier.

(Refer to instructions.) Remember, having filled in the broad descriptive categories, it is often the subtle level of detail which strongly evokes an individual child's presence.

What is this child like in silhouette? The typical thrust of shoulders, the gait. What kind of temper does the child display? Describe the child's appetite, singing voice, mood spectrum. It is of utmost importance that you carry out this programme of recollection with maximum thoroughness, as recent evidence indicates that the psychic numbing of which we have heard so much cannot withstand this kind of focused attention to vital, loving detail.

How does the child look when asleep? What is the sound of your child crying? And now, place the child here, right here at this place in the text. PLACE CHILD HERE. It is *your* chosen child being viewed, stalked, snatched, taken.

As I write there are sounds of hideous wailing coming from the isolation ward above. And it is your child, your little Nan or Ted or Mary, your Miguel, Saleem, Makmuda, Ku, your Jonathan, Joseph, Mario, Zephyr, Chen, Boris, your Alice, your Sam who will be 'adjusted' to the fabric of another nation and culture.

And please let Judith play along with it, like a game, and not turn magnificently stubborn, our radiant girl!

And please let the big computer remember so that when we may find her, we can.

Some of the operatives have killed themselves.

Osborne County, Kansas

Good times, bad times. And now here we are, autumn on the Great Plains and the wind bowls down through the high grasses, juddering and wailing over Canada, all the way from the North Pole. In the grounds of the Best Western Motel which we have taken over as headquarters the gardens are being organised as a didactic and formal mechanism. To walk through its lanes and avenues, and to look upon its sculptures, ruins, topiaries and fountains is to move through the powerful arguments, logical, aesthetic, political and metaphysical embodied in the artefacts made by angry, grieving, grimly optimistic women.

Was Clio, the Muse of History, a mother? Did she grieve while the necessities of process destroyed her young? Now so many children have been shuffled and transported: Israeli children have been taken into all the Arab countries, and there are infant Jordanians, Syrians, Iranians, Libyans and so forth now living in Israel and in the West. As for the super-powers, Russian, American and Chinese children have been scattered over the planet like grains of rice; in Northern Ireland such is the nature of the horrid conflict that Catholic and Protestant babies have been exchanged and re-worked so that they are often living down the street from their biological parents. And so throughout the world, every barrier of nation, race, class and religion has been crossed and recrossed with our tender future citizens. And all over the globe, along with the massive grieving and anger, there is a kind of stirring of consciousness, a kind of glimpsed recognition of this pattern, the strategy and its point. Can humans, we sapient ones, come to take care of our offspring with the same concern and good sense shown by the other beasts? If a nuclear missile aimed at my 'enemy' is now, also, by definition, aimed at my children, will it stay my hand?

We strolled through the white garden, the red garden, the scented garden, the garden of physicks. We picnicked quietly by a vast turf maze. Max seems calmer, here in the open. He and Jenny are braiding weedy flowers together into a chain which they put around my neck. A bent figure bundled against the blustery wind approaches us, and as he unwraps several layers we recognise the 'oldest man'. We offer to share our lunch with him, and he sets to with gusto, launching with a full mouth into one of his rambling stories about past days and the adventures of his prime, about the cold wars and the hot wars and the chemical wars and the nuclear wars and the biological wars— As he talks we finish our meal and decide to wander together through the maze. The path winds round the reproductions of the Sphinx and Camel Rock, then through the water garden. Max is tired and I pick him up. Carrying one heavy, silent baby, longing for the lost one, we push on until we come to a life-size statue of Avalokitesvara, the Bodhisattva Mahasativa of compassion, eleven-headed, and there our ancient companion regales us with a tragi-comic tale of another elaborate conference on disarmament which had once again finished in histrionics. He told of a subsequent feast of fools in the Embassy and ended, '*I was at that feast and drank beer and wine, it ran down my moustache but did not go into my mouth.*'

Michael laughs *haha* at the ironic and habitual Russian ending to fairy tales and fables. Max is snoring softly. And here we are at the centre of the maze, a niche, a minor cave carved into the side of a hill, an invented hill in the flatness of Kansas. And in the cave there is a grotto, lined with seashells and fossils, and inside the grotto is a robot facing a bank of TVs which are showing the 24-hour news from all around the world, burning buildings and etc. Jenny says amazed, 'The robot is weeping.'

Mothers, forgive us.
Mothers, join us!

MARY GENTLE

A Sun in the Attic

Mary Gentle lives in Bournemouth. She is the author of A Hawk in Silver *(Gollancz, 1977) and* Golden Witchbreed *(Gollancz, 1983). She has had short stories published in* Asimov's SF Magazine, *of which 'The Harvest of Wolves' was included in Wollheim's* Best SF of 1984, *and 'The Crystal Sunlight, The Bright Air' in* Space of Her Own *ed. Shawna McCarthy (Robert Hale, 1984).*

Mary Gentle says of 'A Sun in the Attic', 'The process of writing is something best understood with hindsight. Looking back, a whole rag-bag of things came together for "A Sun in the Attic": Roslin and Arianne; the attractiveness of "alternative" technology, wind and solar and tidal power, coupled with the fascination that the Industrial Revolution has. And the (erroneous) conviction that there's nothing wrong with the eighteenth century that a good re-write wouldn't cure. "A Sun in the Attic" is my "hard" sf story: it isn't technological gadgets, but the scientific perception of the world that worries me. And no, I don't really agree with Arianne . . .'

The Archivist sits in a high room, among preserved (and precisely disabled) relics; sorting through notes, depositions, eye-witness accounts, and memoirs.

Outside the window, the city of Tekne is bright under southern polar light. The room is not guarded. There is not the necessity.

In the somewhat archaic and formal style proper to history scrolls, the Archivist writes: In the Year of Our Lady, Seventeen Hundred and Ninety-Six—

Then she pauses, laying down the gull's-quill pen, staring out of the window.

Beyond the quiet waters of the harbour, the slanted sails of the barbarian fleets have drawn perceptibly nearer.

The Archivist turns back to her material.

Tell it as it happened, she thought. Even if it is not in a single voice, nor that voice your own. Tell it while there is still time for such things . . .

An airship nosed slowly down towards the port's flat-roofed buildings. Beyond the harbour arm, the distant sea was white and choppy. Tekne's pale streets sprawled under the brilliant Pacific sun.

'It *may* be a false alarm.' Roslin Mathury leaned on the rim of the airship-car, protesting defensively. 'You know what Del's like, once he's in his workshops.'

'That's why you've brought us back from the farm estates a month before harvest, I suppose?'

Roslin busied herself with straightening the lace ruffles at her cuffs and collar. Without meeting Gilvaris Mathury's gaze, she said, 'Very well, I admit it, I'm anxious.'

The airship sank down over the Mathury roofs, the sun striking highlights from its dull silver bulk. The crew tossed mooring ropes, and house servants ran to secure them.

'I should have made him come to the country with us!' Roslin said.

'No one ever made Del do what he didn't want to,' Gilvaris observed. 'I should know. He's my brother.'

'He's my husband!'

'And mine, also.'

'When I married you, it wasn't to be told the obvious,' Roslin said, equally acidly; gaining some comfort from the familiarity of their bickering. 'Well, husband, shall we go down?'

The mooring gangway being secured, they disembarked onto the roof of the Mathury town house. The airship cast free, rising with slow deliberation. Its shadow fell across them as it went, and Roslin was momentarily chilled. She saw, as she looked past it, the crescent bulk of Daymoon, blotting out a vast arc in the western sky.

'*Se* Roslin, *Se* Gilvaris.' The house-keeper bowed. 'We're glad to have you back safely—'

Roslin cut the small elderly man off in mid-speech. 'Tell me, what's so bad that you couldn't put it in a message to us?'

'The *Se* Del Mathury worked while you were gone,' the shaven-headed servant said. 'He made some discovery, or thought that he did; he had us bring food to his workrooms, and never left. I think he slept there.'

Roslin nodded impatiently. 'And?'

'He saw visitors,' the housekeeper continued, 'admitting them privately; and received messages. Three weeks ago we brought his morning meal to the workrooms. He was gone, *Se* Roslin. We've seen and heard nothing from him since.'

Light sparkled from glass tubes and flasks and retorts, from coiled copper tubing and cogwheels. A half-assembled orrery gleamed.

Gilvaris turned, pacing the length of the workroom. Boards creaked under his tread. Sunlit dust drifted down from the glass dome-roof, and the swift shadows of seabirds darkened it with their passing. Their distant cries were mournful.

'He might have forgotten to leave word,' Roslin offered.

'Do you really think so?'

The caustic tone moved her to look closely at Gilvaris. Unlike his younger brother in almost everything: tall and dark where Del was fair, secretive where Del was open, slow where Del was erratically brilliant.

'No,' she said, 'I don't really think so. Where *is* he? Is he still in Tekne, even? He could be anywhere in Asaria!'

Gilvaris absently picked up a few bronze cogs and oddly-shaped smooth pieces of glass, shuffling them from hand to hand. 'I'll try Tekne Oldport. That's where he commonly gets his supplies. And I'll ask at the university. Also, it might be wise to discover who his visitors were.'

Roslin dug her hands deep into her greatcoat pockets, feeling the comforting solidness of her pistols. 'Damn, when I see him—'

'If he didn't go willingly? House Mathury has enemies.'

Her dark eyes widened. 'So we do . . .'

'Now wait. That's *not* what I meant. I know House Mathury

and House Rooke are rivals in trade, but—'

Roslin came over to him, took his hand. 'Trust me.'

'You shouldn't see Arianne.' Gilvaris put an emphasis on the first word.

'Should I not?'

'You don't have the temperament for it.'

'And you do, I suppose?'

Gilvaris raised an eyebrow. 'I have been told that I resemble my aunt closely.'

Roslin bit back a sharp answer. 'Don't quarrel. You go to the Oldport, I'll ask questions elsewhere. We can't waste time. I'll never forgive myself if Del gets hurt because we weren't here when he needed us.'

A summer wind blew cold through the streets. Roslin walked down to the wider avenues of new Tekne, under the tree-ferns that lined the pavements. Sun gilded the white façades of the city houses. Daymoon was westering, its umber-and-white face blotting out a third of the sky.

She stopped to let a roadcar pass; the engine hissing steam, pulling its fuel car of kelp and a dozen trailers.

House Mathury has enemies, she thought grimly, approaching the wide steps that led up to one of the larger houses. She passed under the archway and entered the courtyard beyond. Servants showed her into the house. As she expected (but was none the less impatient) they kept her waiting for some time.

'*Se* Roslin.'

She turned from pacing the hall. '*Se* Arianne.'

Arianne Rooke, being a generation older than her, still affected the intricately braided wig, the face-powder and high-heeled boots of that fashion. Her eyes were bright, lively in her lined face; and they gave nothing away.

'It is a pleasure, *Se* Roslin. You should visit us more often.'

Her smile never faltered as she ushered Roslin through into a high narrow room. The walls were lined with bookshelves. It smelled faintly musty: the unmistakable scent of parchment and old bindings.

'House Mathury has, after all, connections here.'

'Connections? Yes,' Roslin said bluntly, refusing her offer of wine and a chair, 'you could almost say I'm here on a family visit.'

'I don't quite understand.'

She looked the woman up and down. Arianne was small and dark and, despite her age, agile. Roslin didn't trust her. She was head of House Rooke; she was also Del and Gilvaris's mother's sister.

'Where's Del?' Roslin demanded.

'*Se* Roslin, I don't—'

'Don't take me for a fool,' she said. 'Our houses have fought for . . . but he's one of your own blood! What have you done to him?'

Arianne Rooke seated herself somewhat carefully in a wing-armed chair. Resting her elbows on it, she steepled her fingers and regarded Roslin benignly over the top of them.

'Now let me see what I can gather from this. Your husband Del Mathury is missing? Not your husband Gilvaris too, I trust? No. It would never do to lose two of them.'

Roslin said something unpardonably vulgar under her breath.

'And for some reason,' Arianne continued, 'you imagine that *I* am responsible? Come, there are far more probable reasons; you as a wife should understand this.'

Such delicate insinuations did nothing for Roslin's temper. 'I'm not as stupid as you think!'

'That would be difficult,' Arianne agreed.

'I ought to call you out,' Roslin said savagely, regretting that her pistols must be left with the servants.

'My dear, you're a notable duellist, and I have a regard for my own skin that only increases with age. So I fear I must decline.'

Roslin, aware of how much Rooke was enjoying herself, thought: Gil would have done this better.

'You're trying to tell me you don't know anything about what's happened to Del.'

'I can but try.' Arianne spread her hands deprecatingly. 'Would that I did. Would that I could help.'

That hypocrisy finished it.

'You listen to me, Arianne. I mean to find Del. And I will. And if you've had anything to do with this, I'll take my evidence before the Port Council, I'll bring House Rooke down about your ears, my friend. Or,' she finished, blustering, 'I may just kill you.'

'Isn't melodrama attractive?' Arianne Rooke observed. 'I'm sure you can find your own way out.'

She could not know that, when she had gone, Arianne Rooke chuckled a little. Then, sobering, took up pen and parchment to write an order for the immediate and secret meeting of the Port Tekne Council.

'Anything?' Gilvaris asked.

'No. She made me lose my temper, so naturally I didn't learn anything. Except that I shouldn't lose my temper. You have any better luck?'

'Not so far.' He sat back on one of the benches. They haunted the workrooms, he and Roslin. 'He could be held somewhere. Now we're back here, we may get a demand for money.'

Roslin looked round the darkening room. It was the short Asarian twilight: Daymoon had already set.

'Maybe . . . It doesn't look like there was a struggle here, does it?'

Gilvaris shook his head. 'It seems to me that there's equipment missing. I wouldn't know for sure—but it could be so.'

She knew he rarely admitted ignorance. Part of the reason for that was a life spent struggling in the effortless wake of a brilliant younger brother; if Del had not loved him so devotedly, Gilvaris's life might have been bitter.

Del, she thought. We're not whole without him.

'What I'm saying is, it's possible he packed and left. He's clever enough to do it without the servants knowing, if he thought it necessary.'

'You think he left us?' Roslin said, incredulous. 'Damn, you're as bad as Arianne Rooke.'

'I don't think he left *us*, specifically,' Gilvaris said, unruffled. 'I think he left. Those visitors he had: some were tradesmen, and some were from the harbour. But at least one was from the

Port Council. They're no friends of Mathury. I think Del's in hiding.'

Roslin considered it. 'Why?'

Gil shrugged. 'Haven't I always said, one day he'll discover something that'll get him into trouble?'

'It's amazing,' Roslin said, as they dismounted from the roadcar on the Oldport quay. 'I always saw Del as a loner, shut away in those rooms. He knows more people than I do.'

'He kept in touch with a lot of colleagues from the university,' Gilvaris said.

The wet morning was closing to a rain-splattered noon. They had seen and spoken with, so far, a maker of airship frames, a glassblower, a metalsmith, a windvane repairer, a clockmaker (this being a woman Roslin disliked instantly, knowing that she had been a frequent visitor to House Rooke before Roslin had), as well as printers of news-sheets, and at least four sellers and importers of old books. All knew Del professionally and personally. None knew where he was now.

'He was on to something. When he shuts himself up and works like that . . .' Roslin shook her head. Gilvaris linked his arm in hers as they walked.

'Metal and glassware. His most recent orders.'

'Meaning?' Roslin queried.

'I wish I knew.'

A harbour ship chugged past, and the smell of steam and hot metal came to Roslin through the damp air. Viscid water slapped at the quay steps. Out in the deeper anchorages, up-coast ships spread flexible canvas shells. Steamships wouldn't risk leaving Asaria's canals for the cold storm-ridden seas. Downcoast krill-ships were arriving from the southern icefields.

'If he was that desperate, he wouldn't take one of our ships,' Gilvaris forestalled her. 'I've made enquiries, there's one more chance. A barbarian ship.'

Roslin looked where it was moored by the quay, saw low sharp lines, great jutting triangular sails. And thought of Del: intense, impractical, obsessed.

'Would he go? Without a word to us?'

'He would, if he thought that staying would put us in danger.'

Roslin blinked. 'I—damn, I can't think like that!'

'There's plenty who can.'

After a moment Roslin put her free hand in her pocket, gripping the butt of the duelling pistol. They went forward to hail the barbarian ship.

'I have seen no one,' the barbarian insisted, in passable Asarian.

He was a tall man, taller even than Gilvaris, with pale yellow skin and bright, braided golden hair. His robes were silk, and from his belt were slung paired metal blades. Roslin recalled that rumour said barbarians fought with these long knives, like servants.

No one? she thought. He's lying.

'Perhaps I can speak to your captain. Will she see me?'

He said, 'I am captain here.'

'Oh.' Roslin sensed rather than saw Gil's amusement. Momentarily at a loss, she glanced round the bare cabin. Cushions surrounded low tables. The table from which the barbarian had risen was covered with parchments and thin ink-brushes. Seizing on this, she commented, 'Skilful work. What do you write?'

'Of my travels.'

Roslin studied the script. A scant number of repeated symbols were inscribed from right to left across the page, instead of from top to bottom.

Partly gaining time, partly curious, she asked, 'What do you say about us?'

He smiled. 'That the southern polar continent of our legends is no legend. That Asaria is a land in which women head the family; that women here take many husbands—where I come from, men take many wives. And that otherwise the strong oppress the weak, the rich oppress the poor; knaves and fools outnumber wise and honest men; and that the machines of peace are very apt to become the engines of war. In short, that Asaria differs very little from any other continent of the globe.'

'"Engines of war"?' Roslin queried.

'Why, ma'am, consider this: you have your cars not pulled by beasts of burden, what strong and tireless transport they might make for cannon! And your kite-gliders, they would let you know of the enemies' advance long before he sees you. You have ships that need not wait on wind or tide. You have ships of the air. Consider, there is not a city wall that could stand against you!'

Gilvaris Mathury, a little satirically, said, 'Ah, but you see, cities in Asaria have no walls.'

The barbarian inclined his head. 'Indeed, I have studied your Asarian philosophy: its alternative is to put walls around the mind.'

Roslin ignored that. 'In your history, sir, say also that in Asaria women love their husbands, and men love their brothers—'

'Man,' said Gilvaris, 'do you think *we'd* harm him?'

'Let us say,' the barbarian said carefully, 'that *if* there were such a man, and *if* he were due to arrive here, you would have but to wait until he came to the ship. But say also, that you may not be the only ones he is hiding from, and that—if you are seen waiting—you will not be the only ones to find him.'

Seabirds roosting under the eaves of the Oldport houses cried through the night. Roslin lay awake. Gil's arms round her were some comfort, but she missed the complementary warmth of Del.

Lovers: husbands: brothers. It was not in her nature, as it was not in Asarian custom, to compare. Two so different: Del with the obsessed disregard of the world that first attracted her, Gilvaris who had spoken of marriage with House Mathury (and only in that moment had it crystallised, to be without either of them was unendurable).

So she had spoken to her mother, head of house Mathury, and little help did she have from a woman whose three husbands had been acquired at different times from all over Asaria. Roslin, nevertheless, married the brothers. And a season later was, by virtue of the plague, left sole survivor and heir of Mathury, which served to bind them closer than the common.

Beside Gilvaris, aware of his quiet breathing, she knew he

did not sleep. They lay awake and silent until Daymoon rose.

'Are we right to be here?' Roslin sat on the edge of the bed, lacing up her linen shirt. She could see from their high window the steps of Oldport South Hill, the fishing boats at the quay. 'Can we trust a barbarian?'

'It's all we can do. Can *he* trust us, that's what he'll ask.' Gilvaris's voice was muffled as he pulled on his coat. Adjusting the mirror until the polished basalt oval gave back his reflection, he flicked the lace ruffles into place. 'It could take time to get a message . . . *Quiet!*'

For once he moved faster than Roslin. She barely caught the sound of footsteps on the stairs, and he was by the door, pistol raised. There was a sharp repeated knock.

Roslin grinned, relaxing. 'That's the landlord. Breakfast, I'd guess, and not Arianne Rooke's cut-throats.'

Without releasing the pistol, Gilvaris pulled the door open, surprising the visitor with his hand raised again to knock.

It was Del Mathury.

'It's no good yelling at me!' Del protested. 'I didn't want to be found. I wouldn't be here now, if the barbarian hadn't said it was the only way to stop you turning all Tekne upside-down.'

'What the—'

Roslin's temper cooled. She felt the sting of tears behind her eyes.

'What did you think we'd feel like?' she demanded. 'Damn, you might have been dead for all we knew!'

'You knew I'd be all right.' His open face clouded slightly. 'Didn't you? You didn't think I'd . . . it was a matter of staying out of sight until the ship sailed. I was going to send a message to you both then, so that you could join me on board.'

Roslin sighed, sat down on the chair-arm, and put her arm round him. Gilvaris positioned himself protectively behind Del.

It's like Del not to see the obvious. But you knew that when you married him, she reminded herself.

'Del, love, why would we want to go on a barbarian ship? And for that matter, go where?'

'Somewhere I can work without the Port Council bothering me.'

'You're the brilliant one,' Gil said. 'Tell us why we've got to leave, not Port Tekne, not the up-country farms, but all Asaria?'

'Don't be angry with me, Gil.'

'I'm not.'

Roslin had a sudden vision of them as children: the elder brother eternally trailed by, and eternally protective of, the younger. She wondered if either of them coveted the other's relationship with her as she coveted their brotherhood before they ever knew her.

'It was made very clear to me,' Del said, 'when I talked to people, that what I was doing wasn't liked. I don't know why. I don't expect it matters . . . Gil, Ros, I missed you when you weren't here. You'd better come and see what I've been working on.'

Del led them high up among the old deserted houses of the South Hill, below the derelict fort. Roslin was sweating long before they reached the ultimate flight of steps. She saw, across the five-mile span of Tekne, North Hill push out like a fist into the sea, and the kite-gliders and airships anchored on its crest. Inland from Tekne the country went down into flat haze, broken only by the vanes of wind- and watermills.

'We should have stayed on the estate,' Roslin grumbled. 'You and your machines—Gil's conspiracies—I don't like any of it.'

Del, who was perfectly familiar with that complaint, only grinned. He took them up to the top floors of a derelict mansion that jutted out over the streets below. The walls ran with damp, and clusters of blue and purple fungi grew on the stairs. A continuous thin sound broke the quiet: the sifting of old plaster and stone dust in decay. Roslin smelt musty ages there. The sound of the wind died, and with it the shrieks of birds.

At the very top of the house, in an attic with a shattered dome-roof, Del had set up his makeshift workshop. Half of it was in crates, ready to go aboard the barbarian ship; but Roslin could only concentrate on the massive structure of metal and glass that all but filled the room.

'Look at this.' Del picked up a brass cylinder. Roslin turned it over in her hands, then gave it to an equally puzzled Gilvaris. Del snatched it back impatiently, and manipulated some of the wheels jutting from it. 'No. Like this.'

Dubious, Roslin copied him, holding it to her eye. The metal was cold against her skin. Her lashes brushed the polished surface of the glass. She felt Del take her shoulders and turn her towards the window. She saw a white blur, felt swoopingly dizzy; then as her long sight adjusted she made out houses, streets, tree-ferns . . . And lowered it, and the side of North Hill sprang back five miles into the distance.

Roslin turned the tube in her hands. It was blocked at both ends by glass, one piece of which slid up and down a track inside the tube, adjusted by cogwheels.

Del took it away from her and rubbed her fingermarks off the glass.

'It's a pretty toy,' Gilvaris observed, making the same test, 'but as to people's concern, I confess I don't understand that.'

'The principle can be applied to other things. It's producing the lenses that's most difficult; they have to be ground.'

Roslin, gazing at the arrangement of tubes, prisms, lenses and mirrors that towered over their heads, began to make sense of it.

'Hellfire! I bet you can see as far as the barbarian lands,' she said.

'Further than that—' Del stopped. Gilvaris held up a hand for silence. 'What is it?'

Roslin listened. There was something you couldn't mistake about the tread of armed troops. She moved to look down the stairwell.

She said, 'It's Arianne Rooke.'

'One would suppose we were followed,' Gilvaris leaned over her shoulder.

Roslin saw the first shadow of confusion on Del's face.

'You led them to me,' he said.

'Looks like we did.' There was movement below in the shadowed stairwell. Deliberately she drew the pistol from her greatcoat pocket, cocked it, aimed and fired.

The report half deafened her. A great mass of plaster flaked off the far wall and spattered down the stairs. The scramble of running feet came to an abrupt halt. Roslin handed the pistol back to Gilvaris to reload. She leaned her elbows cautiously on the rail and called down: 'Come up, Arianne. But come up alone—or I'll blow your damned head off.'

Arianne Rooke gazed up at the spidering mass of tubes and mirrors and lenses. The late-morning sun struck highlights and reflections from them. Roslin watched her lined, plump face. Her heels clicked as she walked across the floorboards, circling the scope; and she at last came to rest standing with hands clasped on her silver-topped cane. Her braided wig was slightly askew; exertion had left runnels in the dark powder that creased her skin.

'I have thirty men downstairs,' she said without turning to look at anyone there. 'This must be destroyed, of course.'

'You—'

Roslin gripped Del's arm, and he subsided.

Arianne Rooke turned, regarding Gilvaris with some distaste. There was a distinct resemblance between aunt and this one of her nephews. Roslin wondered if that meant Gil would, when he reached that age, be like Arianne. It was an unpleasant thought. And then she wondered if they would—any of them—live to reach Arianne Rooke's age.

'You,' Arianne said, 'I thought you, at least, had some intelligence, Gilvaris.'

'This rivalry between Rooke and Mathury is becoming a little . . .' Gilvaris reflected, '. . .excessive, isn't it?'

The older woman inclined her head. 'Think that, if you will.'

'This won't give you any trade advantage,' Del said, bemused. 'Or is it that you can't bear Mathury to have something Rooke doesn't?'

Roslin caught Gil's eye, and saw him nod.

'Arianne,' she said, 'do you know a woman called Carlin Orme? She's one of my husband's colleagues. She has a printing press. You may know her better as editor of the Port Tekne news-sheet.'

Rooke frowned, but didn't respond.

'I spoke with Carlin Orme last night,' Roslin said. 'And with a number of other news-sheet editors. I thought, in fact, that it

would be a good idea if someone other than Arianne Rooke
followed us here. They'll be interested to see what my husband
Del has discovered. And to know that House Rooke is here
with thirty armed men.'

'My dear,' Arianne said, 'never tell me that was your idea?'

'Well, no. Gil's the subtle one. I'd settle for something more
straightforward. And permanent.'

The last chimes of noon died on the air.

'Call off your people,' Rooke said, 'and I'll do the same.
Quick, now.'

Roslin said, 'I ought to give them something, *Se* Arianne, if I
can't give them the treachery of House Rooke. Why shouldn't
Tekne know about this?'

The woman looked round at all three of the Mathury. Roslin
waited for the outcome of the gamble.

We have to win here, in Tekne, she thought, glancing fondly
at Del. Because that ship's a dream—there's nowhere to go.

'Oh, you children!' Arianne Rooke swore explosively. 'You
haven't the least idea of . . . Do you know that I can call on the
Port Council to silence you? Yes, and silence Carlin Orme and
her like too, if I need. *Se* Roslin, I don't want to have to do that.
Your husbands were Rooke before they were Mathury. But I
will if I have to!'

'Port Council?' Gilvaris demanded.

For answer, Arianne Rooke drew from under her coat what
even they must instantly recognise as being the Great Seal of
the Port Tekne Council.

We underestimated you, Roslin thought.

'What *is* all this?' she demanded.

'Delay Carlin Orme.' Rooke reached out with her cane to tilt
one of the great framed lenses. 'I'll tell you—no, I'll show you.
I'll show you without any of us having to leave this room.'

Arianne Rooke stepped back from the scope, which she had
most carefully adjusted. She handled it a sight too familiarly for
Roslin Mathury's peace of mind.

'I want you to look through this—*without* upsetting it.' She
arrested Roslin's hand. Her fingers were cool, almost chill.
'Each of you. And while you're doing that, I want you to listen

to me.'

'So talk.' Roslin, hands clasped behind her back, bent to the eyepiece—and forgot all about listening to Arianne Rooke.

It took a moment for her eyes to focus. One side of her field of vision was starred with the sun's glare, and there was the deep purple-blue of Asaria's summer sky. And . . .

She gazed through the scope at the surface of Daymoon.

All her life it had been familiar, the sister-world that dwarfed the sun in the sky. Now she saw lands, seas, icecaps. The webwork of dry rivers, the arid ochre land; and white cotton that specked the world under it with the minute moving shadows of clouds.

A bright metallic spark travelled across her vision, high over the deserts of Daymoon, a sharp, unnatural shape that fell into shadow as it entered the crescent's darkside. Roslin went cold. Another speck followed. Now she became adept at picking them out, their mechanically perfect flight (and thought, without reason, of Del's workshop and the half-repaired orrery).

'But—' she straightened, blinking. 'Then it's true, the legends are *true*. . .'

'No,' Rooke said. 'Not now. Now there is nothing there. In all the archives of the Port Council, we have no record of any life. Look at what you do *not* see: patterns, lines, edges. No fields. No canals. No cities.'

'But I saw . . .'

'What you see are machines. Del Mathury, you will most readily comprehend that.'

'I thought as much,' Del admitted, unsurprised.

'Tell me country tales, servants' tales,' Arianne invited Roslin. 'What is there on Daymoon?'

Roslin recalled shadows and firelight, and how tall the world is to a small child.

'Daymoon's a fine world. The people live in crystal houses, and their lanterns burn for ever. They build towers as tall as the sky, and fly faster than any airship ever made. Their carriages outrun the speed of the sun. Each woman there is richer than a *ser* of the Port Council, each man also. They cross the seas and span the land, and no disease touches them.'

Abandoning the child's ritual, still bemused, she said, 'So I was told, when very young. Servants believe it still, and think to go there when they die.'

'Which is well, since few of us can be *ser* here in Asaria,' Gilvaris commented acidly, straightening from the scope. 'Is that what you'd hide, that they've no paradise waiting? That Daymoon is a lie?'

'Daymoon is true. *Was* true,' Rooke corrected herself. 'And you see what is left. To put it most simply: I wish to keep us from that road, the road they followed to destruction. Del Mathury, worlds have been destroyed by those like you.'

Roslin stared blankly. Gilvaris, glancing at Del, thought, No, you're not the first. How many years has the Port Council studied, to be so knowledgeable? And how many years have they kept it secret?

'I have often thought, in all of *that*—' Arianne Rooke's gesture took in light-years, infinity, '—that there must be worlds enough besides us and Daymoon. A million repeated worlds, differing only in small details. No sister-world, perhaps, or no southern Pacific continent, no Asaria or perhaps a barbarian empire of the north, or . . . many things.'

Suddenly practical, she turned to Del. 'If you must work, then work *with* the Council.'

Del laughed. '"Must" work? If no one made anything new, we'd never change.'

'I should not be ashamed to stay as we are now.'

'No, I dare say *you* wouldn't.' Del was caustic.

Roslin said, 'We'd better work out something to tell Carlin Orme.'

There was some argument, Roslin hardly attended. She was watching Arianne Rooke, who stood there with one hand on her cane, and the other tucked into her waistcoat pocket, for all the world like a Fairday shyster.

'I'll talk to Orme,' Gilvaris announced, cutting off further discussion. 'Del, you'd better send word to the barbarian ship.'

Roslin quietly moved aside, to stand near Rooke.

'"Machines"?' she said.

'On Daymoon, they mock the dead race that made them. Is that what you'd have over Asaria?'

She heard unaccustomed seriousness in Rooke's voice.

'Do you think you can undiscover things?' Roslin asked. 'Silence every Del Mathury yet unborn? You're mad!'

'I'm not mad. But I do have visions.' Arianne Rooke laid a dark hand on the scope. 'I believe there is a choice at some point. Perhaps now: an age of reason. And then an age of passionate unreason, ending as you have seen . . . There are scars of war on Daymoon. No, I don't seek to take away the machines, so much as the desire to use them so poorly.'

Roslin said, 'I don't understand you.'

Del, as he went past them, said, 'Arianne Rooke, who gave you the right to play God?'

As close to pain as Roslin had ever seen her, the woman said, 'Nobody.'

Silent for a moment, Roslin watched through the attic doorway as her younger husband went to speak with one of Rooke's armed men.

'How long have you been watching us?'

'Some years. The rivalry between Rooke and Mathury hasn't made it any easier, I'll admit. And for that reason—that you're less likely to believe me—I've taken the rather extraordinary measure of summoning the Port Council to full session. They can confirm what I say.'

After a perfectly-timed pause, she added, 'We shall have to do something for young Mathury.'

'For House Mathury,' Roslin corrected, at last on sure ground. 'Shall we say, a seat on the Council? Gil would be good at that. You see, if Del's going to work with the Council, I think he needs someone there to look out for his interests.'

Arianne Rooke chuckled. 'You bargain well.'

'And you flatter a little, bribe a lot, and hold force as a last card.'

'Which is only to say, my dear, that I'm a politician.'

Roslin squinted up through the broken roof at the sky. An airship glided soundlessly overhead.

'I don't understand what's been happening here.' She met Rooke's gaze. 'I'm missing something. Some chance I ought to take, some question I ought to ask.'

Motionless, watchful, Arianne Rooke gave the conversation

more attention than an outsider might think it warranted, and thought to herself, Can this woman, who (let us be honest) is not altogether *bright*, can she come close to a Del Mathury's curiosity? Because if she can . . .

Rooke said, 'And shall I tell you more, *Se* Roslin?'

A silence fell. The sunlight sparked from brass, mirror, lens. And in the pause, it became apparent that Roslin Mathury could not summon so irresponsible a curiosity; did not desire, or see the need for it.

'No,' she said, smiling. 'Leave me to run the Mathury estates without your interference. That's all I want. Now do you think we should go and bring a little order out of this chaos?'

Rooke thought, I spoke with a barbarian once, what did he say? 'Putting a wall around the mind . . .'

The Archivist pauses.

That last sentence, true in its way, fails to suggest the whole truth. She carefully erases it.

Outside, bells ring gladly, and pennant ribbons uncoil on the breeze. She blinks away images three generations dead. Sees Tekne, now little changed. Fewer airships, fewer steamcars (but there are always servants to do the work). The only significant change is that there are barbarians in the streets.

But really, one shouldn't call them that. Not with the ser-Lords of all four continents here to celebrate the centennial of the Pax Asaria. And what better to encourage them in Asarian philosophy than a dramatic reading? she thinks, smiling at her own vanity.

Even if such turning points in history are largely guesswork . . .

In haste to join the carnival, the Archivist inscribes her final lines:

Arianne Rooke, alone and last to leave, adjusted one of the free lenses to catch the sunlight through the broken roof. She walked unhurriedly away. Where the sun focused, a thin wisp of smoke coiled acridly up from the wooden attic floor.

FRANCES GAPPER

Atlantis 2045: no love between planets

Frances Gapper was born in Stockport in 1957. She works on a horticultural magazine, and her publications include a children's novel, Jane and the Kenilwood Occurrences *(Faber, 1979).*

She says of her story, 'It took a long time to get written. I feel protective towards it, especially the first part. It is dedicated to Gill Hague, with love.'

It was June 2045, sometime after my sixteenth birthday. I was slowly sinking into deep lethargy. Family disapproval closed in around me, fog-like. I'd failed. No boyfriend—and that was a serious thing in 2045 for a healthy second-class sixteen-year-old. It brought shame; it meant moral visitors snooping, penalty points, the lot. *No one* in our family got penalty points. Not till me. My mother drifted round the house, white-faced, haggard, like a ghost, like a self-starving feminist from the early 90s.

June was the start of the social duties vacation. I should have been expanding my community knowledge, showing social awareness, helping on civic projects. . . Instead I was lying in the bath. All day, just lying there, passive, stubborn, absorbing energy quotas. ('Hot baths cost VITAL POWER,' said the posters. 'Self-indulgence—the country pays.' Two steaming taps, pouring away houses. Streets running down the plughole.) Voices—horrified, appalled—sounded faintly from the landing.

'For God's sake—' (my father). 'Look at the dial. I can *see* it going round. Get her out of there.'

'I am trying, darling. It's very difficult. . .' (my mother, who once got a certificate in Skills of Motherhood—Tactful Assertiveness her special subject—but in practice she was hopeless).

She hoovered pointedly outside the door; I sank lower, submerging my ears.

It was that June, my brother won the schools' literature competition. He wrote a poem against trees, proving how they drained civic resources. Ecology poems were in fashion; my brother's was quite influential. It was printed in the *National Bulletin*. Trees—all trees—were removed by order of central government, and replaced with oxygen hydrants.

Financially speaking, his social contribution points went some way towards cancelling out my penalty points. The general family atmosphere lightened, perceptible even through the bathroom door. I emerged cautiously. Meanwhile, my mother had been busy too, making sanction applications in my name. The process was complicated, but she was always good at forms; I was now a registered Social Invisible. For the next five years, until the case came up for reconsideration, my existence could be ignored—or at least fairly well discounted. This situation had its good side: social hours points for the family (for housing a non-wanted), also heating rebates. On the other hand, SI's quite often went insane. Or died. However.

My mother read the disgrace lists every morning, in the back pages of the newspaper; studied them with a ghastly, intent sort of fascination, all through breakfast. My father took the front pages. I sat in the middle, glowering, invisible, eating bits from their plates.

'You'll choke yourself,' said my mother coldly without looking up, to the air, to no one. Or, 'It's disgusting.' But she couldn't direct her words efficiently, they lacked force and purpose. 'You'll be in these, one day,' she said. 'Mark my words. Down in the disgrace lists. In the witch list, probably. For execution. She will,' addressing my father.

'Who will?'

'That girl. She who was—you know. . .'

My father's face went vague, as if he couldn't quite remember. He wasn't pretending: by that time, he'd stopped seeing me. 'Oh, her. Hmm. . .But she wasn't a witch, was she?'

'She would've been,' my mother said, darkly, 'given half the chance.'

My father put down his teacup, firmly. Conversation ended.

Witchcraft was a risky subject to introduce at meal times, bordering on the indelicate. His stomach was sensitive.

'What time is it dear, please?'

The art of writing was lost.
Lost by law, in the Great Silence.
What I do now, whatever I create, has no meaning.
Whatever I am.
Words hurt. Strain inside, in the mind. Pushing through a wall. Silence.
Speech hurts. Better not speak.
They've done something, I can tell. By their faces. Indifferent. Satisfied. What was it, what happened?

One morning, a letagram came. It came by direct air passage, across the city, fluttering, swerving. I loved letagrams, they flew so gracefully. Like birds, like I imagine birds might have flown, before the hygiene exterminations.

Of course, they were old-fashioned. Hardly anyone wrote, it was too dangerous. So easy to break the law, say something wrong. Thought messages were safer, via computer, using automatic censorship.

I used to letawatch with my brother when we were children. He grew out of it. Hours, days on end it seemed, watching. There's one, look. Oh, let it be ours. Please, let it come this way.

I raised the window, a tiny slit, two permitted centimetres. The letagram flew towards me, straight and beautiful, like a gift, especially for me; slipped inside, fell on the floor.

It would have found any gap, of course, waited outside if necessary. Still. I was living in dreams and hopes, possibilities; you get that way. Being invisible, anything might happen—or nothing.

Let it be mine, please, my future.

I stared at the letagram. It stared back at me, coldly. It was official, I could see by the stamp and the tracing devices.

My mother picked it up gingerly by one corner. The doorbell rang—remote control, from central post office—too late as usual.

Here is a window. Stand here, look through. Here is the world, the sky. Look. We have taken away nothing. It is all here, still here, always. You were dreaming. You had a bad dream.

But it was—different. The sky was a different colour . . .

The sky changes colour. It is often this colour. You were dreaming.

I stare out. The sky was orange, dead like this? The sky was never—the sky . . . I strain to remember. Holes in my head, empty, painful. My mind forms, tries to form, another colour, another word. I can feel something . . . in my hands. They've taken away, I think, parts of me. Parts of the world. Parts inside my head. I can tell by their faces, satisfied. No danger. Nobody left. But there was . . . somebody . . . something.

My mother said, 'Magda's coming back.' She dropped the letter. She was so shocked, she looked straight at me, trembling.

'Who's Magda?' I said, curiously.

'She's . . .' Just in time, my mother recollected herself. She turned away hastily.

'Who's Magda?' said my father.

'My—You remember. The one who was my sister. Who lived with us. The ghost.'

'Oh. I thought she was dead.'

'No. Changed. Ghosted. She's coming back. She's safe now, it says here, in this letter.'

There was a child. That's right. I didn't dream her, surely. In the quiet place, my sister's flat. Where I sat quiet, where I was kept, quiet, smiling. Place of approval, fragile safety. If you never moved. If you never spoke, if you never made a sound. But her—she was born wrong. Too much alive. Like an animal, something from another world. Exploring, grasping, crying out. She was too dangerous. They should have killed her.

I remembered my aunt. My beautiful aunt. My silvery aunt, the word-witch. She wrote: she was always writing, when nobody was looking, when nobody was there except me and my brother, and he was only a baby. Sitting bent over the table, writing, writing, her face all silvery, open and excited, beautiful. But still guarded; and at the first sound it would close over, she'd fold up the paper quickly, lock it away. And look at me, frightened, smiling. Finger on her lips. It was a game, our secret.

I remember coming home one day from school, and the whole flat was crowded with people. Grey people, police. The air full of flashing lights, electronic beams. My father talking, my mother crying and shaking.

'Witch! Witch! Blasphemer!'

My aunt was standing quite still. She seemed taller, but sort of empty, her face blank. The table was broken, bits of paper scattered.

'It's only what I think,' said my aunt. With her blank face.

'Blasphemy!' screamed my mother.

'It's only what I feel.'

Would she be changed? I supposed so. People did change in hospitals. And she'd be older. I thought she might be a bit different.

She was totally different. When she came in—I mean, when they brought her in—I felt sick. Her head was bald and sort of patchy, with places like wounds covered over. Her hands were the same, and so thin. They put her in a chair. And her feet. . .I thought, from now on, I'll be good. I'll never say anything, anything, or think anything, ever again.

'Magda, dear,' said my mother. 'How nice to see you. I'm Charla. You remember me, don't you? This is Dav. You remember him?'

She looked up, at me. 'Is that Jene?'

'No!' cried my mother, stepping quickly in front of me. 'She's an invisible. You remember what that means, don't you dear, invisible?'

'Are you Jene?'

'Yes, I am.'

She was mad, my aunt. It was generally agreed. Ghosted. You can see ghosts, but you don't take too much notice of them, or believe what they say.

First week, she said nothing. Just sat there, staring at her hands. Second week, suddenly, she said, '*Come the wind.*'

'What?' I said.

'*Come the water. Tear away her metal coverings.*'

'What? What d'you mean?'

I moved closer. We were alone, almost. There was a guard, of course, ticking quietly on the wall in one corner, recording every word. But it was only the small box type, no videograph. And it wasn't programmed for code, or poetry, or nonsense, or whatever this was. It would probably get cross-wired, or sparkled. I felt anxious.

She looked up at me, quickly, then down again.

'*Unmantle,*' she added. '*Grasp the hands of the enemy, to his own destruction.*'

'I think,' I said, tentatively, 'you'd better be careful. The guard's only basic, it might not assimilate. . .'

'*Dreams,*' she went on. '*World against world meeting. No love between planets.*'

The guard beeped twice, then fused. 'There,' I said. 'I told you. . .'

My voice died. I saw the smile pass across her face, quick as a shadow. I saw her eyes, narrowing.

'*Atlantis,*' she said.

'What?'

The door slid open. It was my mother back from culture classes. She looked briefly at my aunt, then through me; then saw the guard, now flashing silent emergency. She gasped.

'You can't come in,' said my aunt, with unexpected simplicity. 'It's against the law.'

'What law?' I said.

'The first law of the third constitution. "Two or more women shall not gather together in one place, without at least one fully operative guard, or alternatively, men in equal numbers".'

She was right. My mother fell back, panic-stricken. She looked awful. 'The police will be here soon,' I said. 'They should make up the numbers quick enough.'

'What's happening?' cried my mother. 'What's she doing? Stop her!' My aunt was standing now, in the centre of the room, fiddling with the main computer terminal. Her face was calm, concentrating. She was perfectly sane, obviously. I wondered who my mother was shouting at.

'She'll destroy everything!'

'On the contrary,' my aunt said, clearly. 'This is our last chance. If you still have eyes, use them. Look here. And look out of the window.'

The computer was partly dismantled. She was standing directly in front of it, quite still, her arms extended. Something flickered, between her hands. She moved them apart, outwards. Something was growing. A sort of picture.

I saw hills, low hills and grassland. A wide, empty territory, stretching out for many kilometres. No buildings, no people, nothing but grass, hills and sky. It gave me a strange feeling in my stomach. A torn feeling, between fear and longing.

'Look out of the window,' said my aunt, again.

Unwillingly, with a great effort, I forced my eyes away and looked. There was something in the sky, a darkness, spreading swiftly, sweeping towards us. Like a vast cloud, a great black wave, pouring down darkness.

'That is the end,' she said. 'There. The world is ending. If you want to live, break the laws and come with me. If not, you will perish. Choose.'

The other world, the new one, grew wider between her arms. Hills, grass. The sky such a lovely colour, pure and bright, alive.

I took a step forwards, then another step. It was difficult, more than you might think. Dying would have seemed more natural in a way. But I chose and went through. Into the new world. Created, programmed—whatever the word is—by one woman—with some help from a computer.

I looked back once, at my mother, before I went. But there was no way, not the slightest possibility, she would have come with us. And you can't take anyone by force.

LISA TUTTLE

From a Sinking Ship

*Lisa Tuttle was born in 1952. In 1974 she was given the John W.
Campbell Award for best new writer. She spent five years writing
for a daily newspaper in Austin, Texas, before becoming a
full-time freelance writer. Her publications include* Windhaven,
with George R.R. Martin (1981), Familiar Spirit *(1983), two
children's books,* Catwitch, *with artist Una Woodruff (1983) and*
Children's Literary Houses, *with Rosalind Ashe (1984), and
over forty SF, fantasy and horror stories. She is currently
working on* A Dictionary of Feminism.

*Of her story she says, 'I've wanted to write a story about
dolphins for at least ten years, since reading John Lilly's books
on his attempts to communicate with dolphins. Two ideas floated
in my mind, waiting to become a story or stories: 1. that dolphins
do have a language of their own, and are extremely intelligent
and capable of learning to speak a human language as well, but
that they might be wary of letting us know this, having
experienced the dangerous unpredictability—the violence and
cruelty as well as the kindness—of human nature. 2. that to an
outside, non-human observer, humanity might not be perceived
as the most interesting or valuable species on this planet.'*

Josie sang: a song of distance, of other stars and other seas, it
was a song of life and hope, but also of exile and loss.

The dolphins were leaving, bodies flashing silver through the
sea. Left behind, watching them go, Susannah felt more than
ever trapped by her human body, heavy and weighted to the
spot, dead and useless as a stone. Unlike a stone she could

think, yet thought in what might be a stone's one-note, monotonous chant: Gone. Gone. Gone.

Susannah woke with tears on her cheeks, chest tight with anguish. Josie and Elmer are in the pool, she thought. They haven't gone; I'll see them in the morning. But the image of the dolphins swimming away from her remained vivid, and it was no comfort to tell herself it was only a dream, for too often the truth—at least about the dolphins—had come to her first in a dream. Once, rather timidly, she had asked Stan if she was being silly to imagine that Josie and Elmer (really, she meant Josie, with whom she had an almost magical rapport, but she thought Stan might think it unscientific to favour one dolphin over the other) might be able to communicate with her during sleep.

'I don't think it's silly at all,' Stan had said. 'I think you understand the dolphins even better than you realise. You probably notice things—tiny, subliminal clues—which your conscious mind can't explain. While you sleep, your subconscious plays it back in the form of a dream, and you wake up knowing what you already knew on another level.'

Stan was Dr H. Stanley Mirabeau, recognised as the American expert on cetacean studies. He'd established the Center for Human–Cetacean Communication in Florida, and managed to keep it going for nearly ten years, despite increasing difficulties in getting funding for non-military projects. He spent more time than he liked away from the Center on fund-raising tours. He had hired Susannah six months earlier, choosing her over applicants who had better paper qualifications because of the empathy—obvious within minutes of her entering the salt-water pool—between her and the two dolphins.

For Susannah, meeting Josie and Elmer had been love at first sight. It had been like coming home after years of exile; finding her own people when she had nearly given up hope. She could ask no more of life than to be allowed to stay with them. Within a few days she knew that, of the two dolphins, Josie was the special one for her. Elmer, too, was intelligent, quick, receptive. . .but in Josie Susannah sensed a luminous quality of mind, a particularly generous spirit, something which transcended the boundaries and the incomprehensions inevitable between species. Perhaps it was love. With Josie, Susannah felt that any miracle was possible. She and Josie together would make it possible for cetaceans and humankind to speak to each other, would fulfill Stan's dream and end what he called the long loneliness of intelligent life.

Yet it was ironic, Susannah thought, that her job should be to teach the dolphins to articulate and understand English words when she herself would gladly have forgone all human speech and submerged herself in their underwater world. She longed to wake up transformed, to lose her cumbersome humanity. Since that was not possible, she did her job as best she could, glad that it enabled her to spend long hours splashing and swimming with Josie and Elmer, playing with them, stroking their abrasive yet tremendously sensitive skin, rewarding them with fish and praise whenever they articulated a new word, and herself mimicked, as well as she could, their own squeaks and squeals and clicks.

The other main aspect of research at the Center was a study of the dolphin's own language—if it *was* a language. Gordon Delafield was the young linguist currently attempting, with computer assistance, to crack the code of thousands of hours of dolphin sounds.

Gordon's previous work had been with signals from space. Were they noises or were they messages? He had never been able to break them down into any obviously meaningful pattern, but he had found similarities between them and the songs of the great whales—similarities which had seemed to him far too great to be coincidence, and which had led him to pursue the study of cetacean languages. He had come to believe that some extra-terrestrial intelligence far out in space was sending signals to communicate with Earth's intelligences, and that their first choice for contact had not been human. But were any of the cetaceans receiving these messages? Did they understand? Was it, on either side, truly a language, or was it something more like birdsong which marked out territory? Gordon was obsessed with finding the answer. He felt no connection with, no affection for, the dolphins who lived at the Center. He never swam with them as both Stan and Susannah did; he never played with them or attempted to communicate directly. He worked only at second and third-hand, through recordings and his computer. And yet it was possible, Susannah knew, that Gordon would be the one to achieve the first, undeniable, intellectual contact with another species.

She didn't mind. She had no desire for fame, no sense that she was working for all humanity when she taught Elmer to say 'ball' and she didn't need a linguistic breakthrough to know that Josie loved her. Despite the fact that she supposedly shared a language with Stan and Gordon, the two men felt more alien to her than Josie and Elmer ever had.

Now, thinking about her dream, Susannah wondered what it meant. What had the dolphins been trying to tell her? What did she know without knowing?

All week the dolphins had been restless, as if waiting for something to happen. Waiting for what? Did they *want* to leave, or did they know they would soon have to? Had something already happened which she should know about? Had funding been stopped? Was Stan in trouble?

Susannah was trembling. She sat up, reaching for the driest of the swimming suits hanging like a row of flags across the foot of her bed.

If only Stan were at the Center this week, he could tell her what it meant. She saw by the glowing digital clock that it was past three o'clock, and knew she couldn't justify phoning him at his hotel in New York. This wasn't an emergency, only a premonition. She might be wrong. The dolphins might be able to tell her.

Leaving her bedroom she was startled to see light, where there should have been darkness, in the main room. Her apprehension increased. Entering, she saw Gordon Delafield, his long, thin back hunched over the computer terminal, tiny headphones two bright orange dots against the sides of his shaven skull.

'Gordon,' she murmured, and touched his shoulder.

He jumped, then swore, then glared up at her. The whites of his eyes were red, the skin beneath them purple with fatigue. It disconcerted her that he didn't remove the headphones, and she spoke too loudly.

'What's wrong? Why are you still up?'

'I'm tracking the end.'

Her stomach lurched, she thought of dolphins swimming away. 'It's over?'

'Very soon now.'

'How soon? Why? What happened? Did Stan call? What did he say?'

'I haven't talked to Stan.'

'But. . .They can't just shut us down like that. What happened? There must be enough money to get us through to the end of the year, at least?'

'What's money got to do with . . . hey, I'm not talking about the end of the project, girl. I mean the capital E end.'

Now thoroughly confused, Susannah shook her head.

'War,' he said. 'The big one. The end of the world. This time we've gone too far. Look at this.'

At his invitation she moved closer and watched over his shoulder as his fingers dodged nimbly over the keys.

'I took the most sophisticated forecasting program on the market and then I played with it to make it even better, to make it more. . .cautious. Some of these programs give you a 90 per cent chance of nuclear war every time the Russian army moves across a border; every time one of our spy-planes gets shot down; every time some stupid threat is made. If they were right, we wouldn't have survived the Cuban crisis. But this program takes all those other crisis-points, and their outcomes, into consideration: if we didn't respond to *that* with a bomb, maybe we won't to *this*. I ran all the vital statistics about the Cuban crisis through this program and found there was, at top, a 75 per cent chance of a full-scale war. Well, hindsight is easy. And maybe this program is *too* cautious. You never hear the one that hits you, and that's what has me so scared. Just look at that,' he said, gesturing at the screen. 'The world situation today. . .It reckons on a 96 per cent chance. That's more than a probability, from *this* program. That might as well be a certainty.'

Susannah stared at the screen, but the lists and charts were so much static to her eyes, meaningless configurations of brightness against the green screen.

'I'm sorry to be so stupid,' she said. 'But 96 per cent chance of *what*?'

'War.'

No more enlightened, she shook her head.

Gordon reached with one long arm to disconnect the headphones from the radio, and now Susannah could hear what he had been listening to—the grave, measured tones of a reporter talking about casualties and shellings and tanks and a build-up of troops. She had to fight against her usual aversion to make herself listen and struggle to comprehend. But she lacked the background of understanding. She was deliberately ignorant of the world situation, preferring to live an internal, personal life. She couldn't break a life-time's habit in a moment, no matter how important it was. Because Gordon was watching her and waiting, she tried to respond.

'Isn't that. . .I mean, isn't he talking about Central America?'

'Mexico,' said Gordon, 'actually. On our doorstep, you know.'

'But. . .you mean we're at war with Mexico?'

He laughed. 'God, you really are hopeless. You really *don't* know what's going on in the world, do you?'

'Would it make any difference if I did?'

'Oh, hell, no. Not to the world. The war will get us both; you pretending it isn't happening, and me trying to know more than anyone else does, before anyone else does. Ignorance won't save you, and the facts won't save me. What I'm trying to tell you—what I was trying to *show* you so you wouldn't think I'd just flipped out or made it up—is that we're on the brink of another world war. And this time it will be *the* war to end all wars. Nuclear catastrophe. We've come close before, but this time I don't think we'll escape. The old men want death, and not just for themselves. They want to take everybody with them. And they will.'

'But, I don't see how they can. Nobody wants war—'

'How do you know? Just because you and your precious dolphins don't. . .The innocents aren't saved. They'll die, too, your precious dolphins. And all the little fish in the sea.'

She stared at him in revulsion, shaking her head, refusing the images that came unasked and unwanted. A child of the nuclear age, she had been unable to avoid knowing, unable to avoid the nightmares of that final, filthy death. Gordon's words were cruel and mocking, but she saw the pain on his skinny, hairless face, and knew that he hated the idea as much as she did. Hated it, and had to believe it. He and his computer were telling her the truth, so far as they knew it.

'I'm going out,' she said. 'I've got to check the dolphins. I'll be in the pool if you need me.' She paused before turning away, and said more gently, 'Why don't you go to bed. You won't change anything by knowing.'

'But I have to know,' he said. 'That's my kink. . .like yours is pretending you're a dolphin, and what we humans do isn't really your concern. No point either of us trying to change now. We'll be dead soon enough.'

He turned back to his console, and Susannah went outside.

The night was ablaze, black sky impossibly alight with luminescent falling objects. It was a psychedelic, schizophrenic, Van Gogh image of a starry night. It was as if all the stars were falling, flaring up in a sudden glow of clear, cold fire before extinguishing themselves in the waiting sea. Susannah was transfixed. She stared without comprehension, deeply moved and strangely elated without understanding why.

Gradually, the magnificence faded, as each falling, blazing star was swallowed by the sea. Darkness returned like silence, and the tiny, distant, ordinary stars reappeared in their usual places.

Then Susannah became aware of dolphin song. Josie and Elmer were vocalising their excitement in an eerie music which made her skin prickle, and brought a lump of loneliness to her throat.

'Hey you guys, what is it? Josie? Elmer? What do you suppose all that meant?'

In response, Elmer's sleek head thrust up through the water just beneath Susannah, and he spoke, forcing the alien sounds through his blow-hole into the air so she could understand.

'Out,' he said, with a click. 'Elmer go out.'

While Susannah stared at him in astonishment, Josie's head bobbed up alongside, and she opened her huge jaws in the uncanny image of a human grin, and said, 'Josie out. Let out.'

Susannah rubbed her bare arms, feeling the gooseflesh. The dolphins did occasionally speak of their own volition. They often greeted Susannah by name, or they might try to coax her into playing with them—but both of those could be learned responses, like a dog sitting up to beg, and did not prove genuine language ability, Stan had told her. But this—there could be no doubt about this.

'Why? What do you mean?' she stammered.

Josie said, 'Sea.' Or was it 'see'? It might have been either, and it was not a word she'd heard Josie use before. It was not a word she had tried to teach them.

Still rubbing her arms, Susannah looked around at the clear, dark sky scattered with the pinpricks of distant stars. Everything looked normal again. That brief glory might have been a dream; it might never have happened. But she knew that it had, and it had meant something to the dolphins, something she did not understand.

'What was it? Can you tell me?'

Elmer whistled and made a rapid, chattering noise before slipping beneath the water and swimming to the far end of the pool. There he surfaced by the sea-gate and leaped into the air again and again.

'Josie? What is it?'

The female dolphin, too, was restless and excited, but she remained directly in front of Susannah, staring at her and nodding her head. 'Out,' Josie said again. 'Out.'

'Why? The lights? Something to do with the lights?' Susannah pointed at the sky and made an arcing motion with her hand. In response, Josie shot straight out of the water, signalling *yes* with her whole body.

'But what?'

There must be some way to understand, even if Josie could not put it into words. And, quick as the thought, Susannah dived into the pool.

The water was like a second skin. She stretched out her arms and Josie came willingly into her embrace. As always, the sheer physical presence of the dolphin soothed her. She pressed her face against Josie's sleek side and wished for more than physical comfort. She wished for understanding.

She could hear Elmer calling to his mate. After all these months working with the dolphins, their whistles and clicks were still incomprehensible, but she sensed the urgency behind these sounds. She felt it in the tension, the barely restrained excitement in Josie's movements. She was—both the dolphins were—expecting something to happen, something which frightened them a little, and yet which they welcomed.

She realised then that it was not only Elmer who called to Josie from the sea-gate. There were other voices, merging into one, other dolphins nearby, calling to their captive friends from the open sea.

The wild dolphins had come before, although not for many months. They had been a regular presence at the beginning of the project, swimming outside the wall and calling to Elmer and Josie and receiving responses. Eventually—so Susannah presumed—the wild dolphins must have been satisfied that Elmer and Josie did not find their captivity too difficult to bear, and they had gone away. What did it mean that they had now returned? What did they know? Had the lights in the sky signalled an end to the alliance with humans? Did the lights have something to do with the war?

Despite the blood-warmth of the water, Susannah was suddenly very cold. Josie pulled away, and Susannah made no effort to restrain her. Staring in the direction of the sea-gate, the chorus of the dolphins ringing in her ears, Susannah wondered if the war Gordon had warned her of had already started. Was it possible those beautiful, brilliant fires in the sky had been a weapon?

She pulled herself out of the pool and ran inside, where she found Gordon exactly as she had left him.

'Gordon, what's happened? Has the war started?'

He looked up in weary surprise. 'Not in the last fifteen minutes. But I thought you didn't want to know?'

'I want. . .we must let the dolphins go.'

His lips stretched in a bitter smile. 'That won't save them. What do you think this war *is*? They can't get away from it, any more than we can. It doesn't matter how far out to sea they are. Nowhere is safe. It not just where the bombs drop that matters, you know. It's what will happen afterwards—the effects on the climate and the temperature and the atmosphere. There could be enough of a change so that all life in the sea would die. Your dolphins can't outswim death.'

'*They* want to go,' Susannah said sharply. 'They've asked me to let them out. This isn't my idea. There are wild dolphins just outside the gate, calling to them. They're all excited.'

'Excited.'

'Yes. Not frightened—' but she cut herself off, no longer certain that was true, realising she didn't really know what the dolphins were feeling, since she could not share it. 'But I think we have to let them go because they want to. You know Stan's idea that they shouldn't be treated as experiments, but as our colleagues, working *with* us. If we keep them here against their will, and they die. . .'

Gordon shrugged. 'Fine, fine. Whatever you say. If I'm wrong—well, we both get fired for irresponsibility, so what? If I'm right, this won't save your precious dolphins, but at least they can die among their own kind, free.'

He moved to key in the command to the computer to unlock the sea-gate when she stopped him.

'Not right away. I want—just give me three minutes.'

He looked at her sharply. 'You can't go with them, Susannah. That's not for you.'

She turned away from his gaze. 'Just let me say goodbye to them in my own way. Three minutes, okay?' She didn't stay to hear his response.

He had seen it—she meant to go with them—and she wasn't going to give him a chance to try to argue her out of her decision. Yes, it was irrational, probably impossible, but why should she let that stop her? If the end of the world was at hand, the usual considerations did not hold. She would rather drown among the dolphins, or die of hunger or exposure or exhaustion, than linger alone on land for the rest of her miserable life. She would be a dolphin before she died. She would die with them. As Gordon had said, among their own kind, free.

Josie heard her coming—Susannah never had been able to surprise the dolphins—and sped across the pool saying, 'Out. Out. Out.'

'Yes, we're going out – we're going out together!' Susannah said, and slipped into the pool. But this time Josie would not wait for her, but swam back towards the sea-gate, her impatience churning the water.

'Josie, hey, Josie, I told Gordon to open the sea-gate. In just a minute we'll be out—but wait for me; I'm coming, too.'

She realised she was babbling—even if Josie heard her voice over the noise of the other dolphins she wouldn't understand—and saved her breath for swimming, determined to reach the sea-gate before it opened. She would not be left behind.

The small lights on top of the gate began to flash green. Susannah slipped her arms around Josie loosely, so she would not feel restrained, and the dolphin butted gently, affectionately against her, just as the gate opened.

Elmer shot forward, too eager to wait, or perhaps fearful that the gate would close again. Susannah felt Josie's yearning, but also the affection implicit in the way she made no attempt to escape Susannah's embrace. Josie said Susannah's name, and then her own. Susannah had never taught the dolphins to say goodbye.

'It's all right,' Susannah said. 'You aren't leaving me. I'm going with you.' She pushed herself away from Josie, forward through the water, towards the gate and out into the open sea.

Josie was with her immediately, circling and nudging her back.

Frightened and exhilarated by being out in the ocean in the middle of the night, Susannah laughed aloud.

'Don't worry, Josie, I know what I'm doing. You lived with humans for awhile—now I want to return the hospitality.' She kept swimming, evading Josie's efforts to turn her back. The awareness that she was a strong swimmer gave her the confidence to continue, as did her sense of the dolphins all around her.

Despite the darkness, she caught glimpses of sleek bullet-shaped heads bobbing up from the waves, and she felt them passing her, circling her, as they 'read' her shape without touching, and tried to understand her presence. She knew from their whistles and clicks that they were puzzling over this human who chose to travel among them. Although she had lost track of

Elmer in the darkness, among all the others, Josie stayed close, guarding her. Susannah felt Josie's concern like a hand on her shoulder. It warmed and encouraged her. She felt happy, as near to belonging as she ever had, anywhere.

And then they were gone. All of them, even Josie. She was utterly alone. Panic gripped her so that she could no longer swim. She was all alone in the vast, dark, dangerous ocean. She sank, swallowed water and surfaced, choking and splashing. Old instincts asserted themselves and she was afloat again, treading water. She knew she would not drown, but her sense of direction, usually so reliable, had vanished. After a moment, though, she located the lights of the Center, and her internal balance settled. She had only to swim away from the shore and the dolphins would find her again. She did not believe that Josie had deserted her. She had simply tried to frighten her into turning back, and the shock treatment might have worked if Susannah had felt she had anything worth going back for. But she didn't, she would rather die, but she knew that Josie would not let her.

When Josie returned she was alone. At least, if there were any other cetaceans around they were keeping out of Susannah's limited sensory range. She felt an apprehensive sadness in Josie's manner which worried her, but mainly she was simply grateful for the dolphin's presence. Josie let Susannah lean on her, bearing her weight and giving her an occasional rest from swimming, but she kept the pace very slow rather than pulling Susannah along, so that the option of swimming back to shore remained open.

Susannah was very tired. She knew she could go on swimming for a long time, but mentally and emotionally she was exhausted. In her weary state, in the vastness of the ocean and the darkness of the night, she was no longer certain of the difference between waking and sleeping, between life and dream. Where were the dolphins going? Could she really go with them, or was she dreaming still?

Bobbing gently in the waves, supporting herself against Josie to keep her head out of the water, Susannah rubbed her face against Josie's, feeling her skin, hearing the motions of her blow-hole as she breathed. She could almost hear the dolphin thinking. They shared, if not the same body, at least the same dream. To spend the night in the water should have seemed alien and wrong, but Susannah knew she would be safe: she trusted Josie to watch over her and protect her from harm. Cetaceans always helped each other: they nursed their sick, providing company and psychological as well as physical aid. Sometimes they would risk their own lives, even die, rather than abandon a friend.

But where were Josie's friends? Susannah felt a faint, internal chill of apprehension. She had imagined that the other dolphins would stay with Josie as Josie stayed with her, but it hadn't happened like that. Where had they all gone? Had she forced Josie to choose between life with the dolphins and a lonely death with her? What did the dolphins know that she didn't, that Josie couldn't tell her?

Josie sang.

It was a dream-song more than dolphin speech, utterly strange and yet somehow familiar. And as she listened, Susannah began to understand what it meant. Rocking in the dark water, Josie's strong, solid body anchoring her to life, the music filling her mind, perhaps she dreamed. Perhaps Josie made her dream.

She was aware now of other presences, other intelligences. Not merely in the dark sea around her, but much, much farther away. She could neither see nor hear them, and yet she knew they were there, she *felt* them, a non-tactile yet definite sensation which she understood was a commonplace for dolphins. These others, these distant beings, she sensed, were different from the cetaceans she knew, yet not unimaginably so. They lived in other oceans, beneath another sun, and they offered a safe new home to their friends threatened by catastrophe and destruction. They sent a message of welcome, and the means of escape. They were waiting. There would not be much more time now.

Josie sang a song of farewell to Elmer and all her sisters and brothers, wishing them a safe journey and happiness in their new lives. She would have their memories to sing to herself, to keep herself company before her inevitable death. She knew the dangers, but she chose to stay behind, to look after her lonely, helpless friend.

Susannah wanted to cry, for Josie's love, and for her own selfishness. But tears were an indulgence and a waste of time. Maybe it wasn't too late to give Josie a chance to live.

Pushing away from Josie's beloved, familiar bulk, back through the water towards the distant shore, was like forcing herself back into a nightmare, but she did it. She felt Josie swimming beside her, but could not spare the breath or the energy to try to send her away.

Josie was still singing. Was Susannah still dreaming? If so, it was a dream they shared. All around them the sea turned from ink to molten gold as the lights emerged from the depths, bright bubbles rising to the sky and beyond, each vessel bearing a dolphin or a whale, carrying them to a new home far away.

Where the dream ended and waking commenced, Susannah did not know, but eventually she found herself on the shore. Josie's song was silence now, and Susannah stared at the black and empty sea, waiting all alone for the end.

PEARLIE McNEILL

The Awakening

Pearlie McNeill is an Australian writer now living in the UK. She says, 'I began taking my work seriously and thinking of myself as a writer from the late 70s. Since that time I have gained experience as a distributor, bookseller, publisher, editor and writing tutor. My first validation as a writer came following the radio broadcast of a play I had written about one woman's experience of madness. I live in London with my partner, her small daughter, whom I co-parent, and my younger, teenaged son.'

She says of 'The Awakening', 'I have been writing this story on and off for nine years. Accordingly, the first half of the story has always remained much the same and I have at last felt that it has evolved itself to a state that I experience satisfaction with. However, the second half of the story has had many variants and these are usually linked with my own emotional state at the time. I realise that I could probably go on writing the story ad nauseam, that I may never be truly happy with the plotting and resolution, and it may be that this reflects my ongoing pessimism versus optimism about the state of the society we live in.'

Lucy could see it from her kitchen window. A huge spawning mass. Engorged with contamination and encrusted here and there with weeping scabs of rotting matter. From time to time another dying tree would succumb; the trunk submerging slowly with a faint gurgling sound, leaving what remained of the foliage heavily draped with clusters of bubbles, thick with yeasty foam. It looked like some grotesque imitation of a well-decorated Christmas tree.

Once, it had been a river. The Hawkesbury river. What had it looked like way back then? Had someone looked from this very window, all those years ago, to see sailing boats scudding happily across its surface? Had there ever been blue water, healthy fish and screeching birds wheeling overhead?

Fortunately, the house had been built high to overlook the sweeping depths of a valley. It was a sturdily constructed dwelling wedged into the mountainside like new dentures in a tired old mouth. It had been built a long time ago by an elderly couple who had fond memories of the river.

Lucy felt very lucky to have bought the house so cheaply. There had been expenses of course. The necessary structural alterations, in compliance with the Property Decontamination Regulations, had been rather costly. Still, it had been worth it.

She moved away from the window. Near the doorway to the loungeroom she stopped. The pollution barometer was clicking loudly. Lucy watched as the morning's reading registered on the dial. Ten and rising. Resetting the meter at once, Lucy hastened to check if she had left anything on the kitchen table or workbench. Finding nothing, she closed both doors leading out of the kitchen, clamped the door-locks in place and turned on the geothermal, setting the dial on ten.

Next, she checked the bathroom. Towels in the solardome, all personal items in the airlock cube. Nothing left on the floor. Taps turned to vapour pressure position. Both doors clamp-locked. As Lucy turned on the switch a slow throbbing sound, barely audible, started up. She could never quite decide if the bathroom geothermal hummed or gurgled.

The two bedrooms didn't take long. As she checked the last switch, the alarm on the communication console sounded. With a quick look at her digital, noting to herself that she had just finished in time, Lucy turned off the alarm release, pressed the all-clear button, and immediately the heavily-bearded face of Communicator Tony came on the screen.

'Morning Lucy,' he grinned.

'Hullo Tony,' Lucy smiled back at him, her face warm with welcome.

Communicator Tony could be seen fiddling with some buttons and dials on a panel beside him. Turning his attention back to Lucy his eyes widened slightly. 'Looks like you might need a new ratchet clench for the bathroom geothermal, Lucy. All your other signals are reading OK. I'll notify Maintenance to put you on the list for today. What Task Procedure are you on?'

'I'm still on Craft, Tony, so I'll be here all day.'

'Righto. I'm switching you over to Identification Hook Up. Have a nice day!'

Before Lucy could reply he was gone. The screen picture blurred for a second or two, then wavy lines narrowing quickly into three sharp straight lines came into focus. Lucy pressed the Registration key on her console typeface, waited until the flashing yellow light signalled on the screen, and then proceeded to tap out the appropriate information for her Identification Hook Up.

FILE NO: LUCY/ARTIST/SINGLE PAR/FEMCHILD/HORNSBY/
6904328643.
ADDRESS: WHELAN PASS/EAST CORNER/VIA HORNSBY/N.S.W.
CODE: BLUE. AREA: FOUR.

Lucy checked for mistakes and then tapped the Record button. The information faded off the screen to be replaced by another smiling face, that of Resource Department Head, Steve.

'How are you this morning Lucy?' he greeted her.

'Fine Steve. And you?'

'Good. Very good. Ready for the News?'

Lucy nodded, wondering to herself as she did so what would happen if one day she said she wasn't. Probably Steve would act as though he hadn't heard.

The first report appeared. Lucy set her tuner pace to slow. The words began to roll up from the botton of the screen. She flipped her console seat adjustor onto PART RECLINE and made herself comfortable as she began to read.

HORNSBY CITY. NEWS REPORT
MONDAY APRIL 12TH.
1.
TWO TEENAGERS FOUND DEAD.
Citizen Security Officer Mark discovered the bodies of two

young men early this morning in scrubland north of the city. Teeth marks found on the bodies are thought to be those of a large reptile, possibly that of the deadly hump-backed lizard. Parents of the boys reported their absence when they failed to register their whereabouts after Senior Class yesterday afternoon.
CITIZENS ARE REQUESTED TO REPLAY THIS RE-PORT TO ALL YOUNG PEOPLE AGED BETWEEN TWELVE AND TWENTY YEARS. STOP. STOP.

Lucy's face tightened as she finished reading the report. No time to think about it now, item no. 2 was already moving up the screen.

2.
POLLUTION STRATEGY.
SPECIAL REPORT.
The Citizen Self-Help Strategy Department reports this morning that there have been some real success stories as a result of the Retraining Programme implemented by the Department late last year. Of the 2000 citizens selected for the programme, 1420 persons will now be eligible for Return to Home Environment application, following graduation from the programme later this week. It has been deemed necessary that the remaining 580 persons take further training until such time as their security can be assured. A listing of the graduates is available through Resource Department facilities.

3.
BREEDING DUTY ROSTER.
Parents are requested to register their daughter's name and mother's file-number before the end of the month, if it is desired that their daughter be considered for the next breeding roster. Applicants must be aged between fifteen and eighteen years. In the case of eighteen-year-olds, birth dates up to the 30th April this year are eligible. Parents must understand that their applicant daughter will undergo an extensive examination of physical, emotional and mental well-being, as well as counselling re suitability for such an

important community task. Applicants will need to have
completed three classes of Advanced Gymnastics, have at
least two credits in Gynaecological Study, and four credits in
Child Care. Applicants will also be required to present a
paper for evaluation to the Selection Board. Subject matter
will be 'WHAT AN HONOUR TO BE CHOSEN AS A
BREEDER'. Successful applicants will be informed of the
Selection Board's decision following the July sitting.

Lucy stared at the screen. Her spine straightened sharply in an
involuntary gesture and she reached forward to grasp the
console with both hands. She tried to keep her attention on the
screen but the words didn't mean anything at all. I must keep
control she thought. Lucy pushed herself back into her seat
taking slow deep breaths as she did so.

4.
CITY OF HORNSBY SHOPPING RESOURCE REPORT.
Pollution reading in the city at 5 a.m. Eleven and steady.
Citizens are requested to take note that previous information
given last Friday has had to be reconsidered due to a heavy
fall-out of contamination over the week-end. Areas 1, 3, and
4 are workable for limited periods only. Citizens are
requested to use their breathing apparatus backpack for all
occasions outside the home environment. Areas 2, 5 and 6
are not permitted any outside activity whatsoever. Shopping
facilities will not be available in the city today but information for tomorrow's shopping are as follows:
Code/Red. Area No. Three. Use of shopping facilities all day
except for the area north of the town square which is still
awaiting Decontamination Clearance. Code/Black. Areas 1
and 4. Use of shopping facilities permitted tomorrow
morning only. Identification Hook Up to be completed by
1.30 p.m.
WE CARE ABOUT YOU CITIZENS! PLEASE ASSIST
US TO DO SO BY GIVING US YOUR CO-OPERATION!
Have a good day citizens.

Lucy flipped the off switch, hastily checked the loungeroom and
from a nearby bookshelf she took a small protector unit, placed

it in position over her nose and mouth and left the house, clamp-locking the glass double doors behind her.

She ran down the track, her sturdy boots hitting the earth with a fast-falling thud thud thud. Near her craftroom she stopped and scrambled onto an overhanging ledge of rock. The gritty solidity of sandstone gave her a feeling of comfort.

She had to think this thing out. It was no use pushing her feelings away any longer. It wasn't just the uncomfortable thoughts that bothered her. The fact that she had even allowed them to exist at all was her greatest concern. Lucy had never questioned the policies and decisions of Administration before. She had always worked at being a good citizen. Her work was respected. She had many friends. Her life was full. Since Eric's death her life had revolved around Nancy and her work. Lucy had proved that she could do both equally well. There'd been no man in her life since Eric, and sometimes she felt guilty when she thought about that. What would it have been like if Eric were still alive? Could they have continued as happy as they'd been? Had Eric's death provided her, unwittingly, with the very independence she needed so much? That part of her life was over and she carried no regrets. Well, not these days anyway.

What would Eric have thought of his daughter? His photograph still stood in a small, gilt frame on Nancy's desk, though she seldom asked questions about him anymore.

Lucy suspected that Eric would have felt as unhappy about this whole business as she did. If only she could feel proud. Certainly, that was the way she was supposed to feel, but somehow her feelings refused to fall in line with the situation. She didn't want her daughter to be a Breeder and that was that! Lucy slapped her hand against her mouth as this new thought took shape. What had happened to her? How could she dare have such a thought?

Five years ago she'd not had a worry in the world. Five years ago. It was about then that Doctor Walter fellow had come up with his idea for Project Breeding Duty Roster. He called it his brainchild. The joke had evaded Lucy. There had only been four Breeder groups to date. Four groups of thirty young women in five years. He'd even been awarded the Human Life Protection Award! Lucy shook her head back and forth once or twice trying to make some sense out of the situation. How could Administration let such a project get started?

Each Breeder was expected to share her child with a designated number of people. Lucy had heard that in some cases more than a hundred citizens had been involved. Imagine, one hundred people attempting to share in the life of one small baby? And, if the whole thing was such a successful project, why didn't it appear more often on News reports? The only time anyone ever got to hear anything at all was when new Breeder applications were called for.

It wasn't that she objected to shared child involvement. Heaven knows, she could have done with a little of that herself when Nancy was younger—would have welcomed it in fact. But surely, there was a difference in the way it was arranged? Was it painful for those Breeders to have Administration dictate who was to be involved and how? Lucy shuddered at the thought. And what about all that deprivation experienced by those young women who failed selection? So many of them yearning to be Breeders, preparing for it for such a long time and then. . .

Nancy was obviously set on the idea. She had talked of nothing else for months. Lucy knew she could not hope to share her doubts with her daughter. After all, Nancy had been taught the values she now upheld and Lucy had contributed to the teaching of those values. What could she say? 'Now look here, love, I feel differently about some things now. . .maybe I've been wrong in what I've taught you all these years'. No. That was definitely not the answer.

Lucy wished that there was someone she could talk to, but the risk was too great. She knew what would happen if she did. Someday, somehow, that information would find its way into her file and once that first doubt had been formally registered, her credibility would remain in question for the rest of her days.

Of course there was one straightforward option open to her. She could report to the Breeding Duty Roster Committee her concern as to her daughter's maturity for the task, and much weight would be given to her viewpoint. She would even win for herself approval as a responsible citizen, but it was also very likely that Nancy would learn of her mother's intervention, and that would only undermine the ongoing trust between them. Besides, Lucy had no real wish to do such a thing.

Then too, how could she really know what was the best thing for her daughter? Maybe Nancy would benefit from the experience?

Probably she would meet all the necessary requirements for Breeder status and would prove that she could cope with the situation admirably

Were her fears for Nancy, or for herself and the way she might feel in Nancy's position? And if Nancy was not chosen as a Breeder, what then?

But, maybe, just maybe, Nancy's ability to cope with that rejection would be greater than Lucy could give her credit for. There was so *much* about this whole business that worried her. She must be strong for Nancy's sake. She would have to go on as she had been doing. There *was* no other choice. She could watch and wait.

Besides, maybe Nancy would change her mind.

She shook her head as she unlocked the craftroom door. Who did she think she was kidding?

Once inside her workroom Lucy looked around. She checked the pollution readout. Eight and falling. Slipping the protection unit off her face, she walked across to the middle of the room and lifted off the cloth cover from the sculpture she was working on. Pale sunlight, trapped between the wooden beams of the skylight, dropped a geometric patterned glow onto one side of the marble. Lucy traced the upward sweep of jawline with searching fingers. There was something about this work that baffled her. It had to do with the shape of the eyes. It was as though she were still searching for something; but what was it? Was it a certain expression? And yet, the more she looked at that face, the more she felt it was making a statement she had not intended. Surely not? No. It was those eyes. They held you. . .they were. . .well, sort of. . .defiant.

That was it! Lucy suddenly stepped back from the work-bench, hands rigid against her body, her mouth half open in surprise. Why the whole piece is full of defiance; that uptilted mouth, the resolute chin.

What a fool I am, she thought, it's been there all along and

I've been so preoccupied, I've not been able to see what it was I was trying to say!

Lucy couldn't decide if she felt relief or shock. She couldn't continue with the work, that was obvious. She'd have to disfigure or destroy it. As it was a commission and she was well ahead of schedule, it would not present too many problems. For one thing her costs were down. Why, just the other day the Director had congratulated her on her low expenditure for materials. She'd have to choose something other than the human form. That would be the safest thing to do. Lucy checked her digital. She'd have to make a decision and quick. This was important and she knew it. She couldn't afford to be sentimental. Too much was at stake. Lucy stepped towards the sculpture. Deliberately not looking at the face, she placed an arm either side of the base, braced her feet on the floor and heaved.

The crunching sound of marble hitting sandstone lasted only a second. Lucy dropped to her knees and pulled the marble slab upright. Then, she sat back on her heels and surveyed the damage. The fall had done what she hoped it would. The facial features held no threat now except for the left eye and one side of the jawline. She reached for a chisel. Satisfied finally, she stood up. Then suddenly, Lucy clung to the workbench and sobbed.

* * *

It was the last week in June. Nancy's application for the Breeding Roster had not, as yet, been rejected. But already the numbers had dropped from around 1000 applicants to less than 400.

The physical fitness exams had come first. Nancy had experienced no problems here at all. Her talent on the bar had even drawn comment from two of the examiners. Lucy had watched her daughter's performance with mounting anguish. Nancy's lithe form had seemed to fly from bar to bar and yet, thought Lucy grimly, this wonderful ability might prove to be a major factor in my daughter's unhappiness.

Nancy had sat for the Gynaecological Study exams in May.

The results were due to be announced any day. In the meantime, Nancy had been assigned to work in one of the local Child Protection Units. These places offered short-term residency accommodation to the sons and daughters of citizens no longer considered suitable for the task of parenting. Children were assigned to these units until more acceptable arrangements could be made on their behalf.

Lucy had taken to watching her daughter intently. Was the strain beginning to show she wondered, or was Nancy just tired? The stories Nancy told about the children in her care did little to ease Lucy's burden of anxiety.

How much else was there to question in the Administration's handling of citizens' affairs, she asked herself over and over again, and each time she was able to find another area of doubt and then more questions. Although she couldn't understand it fully Lucy sensed that she had started along a path of thinking from which she could not turn back.

* * *

Nancy's son was born the following summer. Informed of the birth by a member of the Breeding Roster Committee, Lucy was advised that her presence at the Birthing Bay would not be welcome until four days had passed. As the committee member pointed out to Lucy, the health and care of mother and infant was the most important consideration of all.

Lucy arrived early in the morning of the fifth day at the Birthing Bay. The reception attendant helped her unstrap her breathing apparatus backpack, gave her a ticket for it and then pressed a button on his intercom panel. Lucy was instructed to wait. She looked up when she heard footsteps nearby. The three young men appointed as Nancy's Breeder Germinators smiled at her warmly as they approached. The tallest one, Alan, pointed down the corridor and Lucy fell in step behind him. The other two men remained in the foyer chatting with the reception attendant.

Alan led the way up three flights of stairs before opening the door into a brightly painted room where Nancy lay in bed, her right arm encircling her newborn son.

Nancy smiled at her mother and stretched out her free arm in a welcoming gesture. There was something in that smile that gave Lucy a sudden surge of hope. Both women dropped their glances quickly. Alan stepped forward, picked up Nancy's child and indicating a chair to Lucy, came and placed the baby in her lap. Lucy looked down at the sleeping face of her grandson. The fingers of one hand lay curled tightly against his cheek. His thick black hair lay like a wreath above his forehead. As Lucy sat and watched the sleeping infant she could feel a new determination take root in her. This baby needed a future, not just an existence. Until that very moment Lucy had not admitted, even to herself, that she'd been waiting. Her plan might just work. For Nancy and her child's sake, she had to give it a try.

But it was to be another six months before Lucy could take matters any further. Her first problem was Nancy. Not that she was the problem exactly, it was more a question of how and when she could find the time to talk to Nancy about what she had in mind. And Lucy had to ask herself many times if it was fair to raise the matter with her daughter. Should she think of endangering three lives based on what she thought she saw in Nancy's smile that morning in the Birthing Bay?

As it was, Nancy's obligations as a Breeder had proved very taxing. There was not just the care and comfort of a baby son to take into account. As each of the three Breeder Germinators had come from big families, Nancy was, of course, expected to comply with their family responsibilities. In attempting to fulfill these expectations, Nancy had little time left over for any of the usual sort of mother–daughter chats they'd both been used to.

Yet, as it turned out, it was Nancy herself who seized an opportunity to spend time with Lucy. Darryl had come down with a cold. Using her child's health as a reasonable motive, Nancy had sought permission to stay with her mother for a few days, explaining that Lucy's assistance with the care of mother and child would be invaluable. Noting the circumstances and the strained appearance of the young Breeder, the Breeding Roster Committee had granted the necessary permission.

In the next few days, during Darryl's frequent naps, mother and daughter discovered that a similar trend in their thinking and approach to Administration had developed. Once and for all, Lucy dispelled whatever illusions she had left about the society in which she lived. Finally, she told Nancy how she'd overheard scraps of conversation about a small community of people said to be living in a distant valley. She didn't know how easy it would be to get there, nor how they would be received, but she felt they must make the effort, not just for themselves, but for Darryl.

Nancy thought they had to take the chance and made suggestions as to what food and equipment they might take. Size and weight would be important as there'd be Darryl and the backpacks to carry before they could even consider anything else.

They agreed that the best time to make their escape would be in the spring when the pollution levels were usually lower. That meant waiting another three months. Lucy agreed with her daughter that it would be best not to see each other in the intervening period, in case their behaviour aroused suspicion.

They used the time together to think of every difficulty they might encounter. Lucy undertook responsibility for setting the date for their escape. She was to contact Nancy through one of the Germinators and arrange a visit. Nancy was to understand that the night before the date mentioned, would be when the escape was to take place. In turn, Nancy was to confirm with her mother about the visit and if Lucy didn't hear back she'd know that Nancy was unable to get away as planned.

* * *

It was a crisp, clear night in spring. Lucy crept down to her craftroom, unlocked the door and stepped inside. She unclasped the backpack belt around her stomach and eased the buckle a little looser for greater comfort. From under a table she took a cane basket filled with several small packages of food. Lucy checked her digital with a torch that she then placed in the basket. Nancy should be here soon she thought. Outside again, she waited for her eyes to become adjusted to the darkness before finding a suitable spot to wait.

A few minutes later she heard soft footsteps coming slowly down the track.

'This way,' Lucy whispered.

Nancy came alongside her mother and handed her a few parcels whilst she eased Darryl into a more comfortable position in his carry-sling.

'We'd best be off,' whispered Lucy and led the way down the steep track that wound down deep into the valley.

It was hard going at first. Nancy found the steep descent difficult. But, as the track levelled out they made better time. It was almost daylight when Lucy suggested they stop and rest.

They stopped beside a dead eucalyptus tree.

'Is anyone likely to get suspicious about your absence?' Lucy asked.

'No. I don't think so. I told Peter I was going to Alan's mother's place and I told Alan I was going to visit Darren's sister. It will take them a while to figure things out.'

'Good. We'd better not speak unless we have to. There could be patrols nearby.'

When the sun came up both women were fast asleep. Darryl, held tight against his mother's breast, drank and slept his way through the morning.

It was almost two weeks before a border patrol party found them. Lucy was shot straight through the neck as she threw herself forward in an effort to protect Nancy and the baby.

It all happened so fast Nancy had no time to do anything. She fell to her knees beside her mother in time to hear the older woman's last words.

'We had to try, Nancy,' Lucy croaked, blood pouring from a gaping hole in her neck. 'We had to try.'

'Shh, Mother, shh.' Nancy couldn't believe her mother was about to die. She reached inside her jacket for a cloth to stop Lucy's bleeding. Fortunately, she didn't see the patrolman raise his rifle and take aim. The shot blasted part of Nancy's head off and she fell across Lucy's body almost suffocating her son as he landed between two warm bodies.

Darryl was freed unharmed, and taken to the nearest Child Protection Unit.

Next morning the events surrounding the death of both women were reported by Administration in the following manner.

HORNSBY CITY. NEWS REPORT. OCTOBER 23RD.
Citizen Security Officers Wayne and Mark found the bodies
of two women this morning in bushland close to the river
once known as the Hawkesbury. Injuries found on the body
are consistent with teeth impressions taken from a hump-
backed lizard. Evidence of a hump-backed lizard in this
district has been found and earlier casualties have been
recorded.
CITIZENS ARE WARNED NOT TO LEAVE THE
SAFETY PERIMETERS AS NO GUARANTEES OF
SAFETY CAN BE MADE.
One of the women, Lucy, was an artist and it is thought that
she and her daughter Nancy were looking for twigs and leaves
to be used in a Nature montage planned for Lucy's
forthcoming exhibition. Nancy was one of the successful
Breeding Roster applicants from last year's group and her
son Darryl is now in care.

The news rolled on.

NAOMI MITCHISON

Words

Naomi Mitchison is the author of some seventy books. In the early 1930s she was much involved in work on family planning and was one of the original committee of the North Kensington Birth Control Clinic. She had seven children, of whom five survived, and now has five great-grandchildren. She has been in socialist politics 'for a very long time', and is closely connected with Botswana where she is a full member of the Bakgatla. She now finds herself 'somewhat out of sympathy with mainstream feminism. I have never been treated in any sense as an inferior by my male friends or relatives, but do prefer them to do car repairs and work out VAT. . .' Her classic science fiction novel, Memoirs of a Spacewoman, *has been reprinted by The Women's Press (1985).*

She says about 'Words', 'I have always hung around on the edge of science, but could never have made a good scientist because my imagination has always been too wild. Scientists need imagination, but not as something overwhelming as it must be for a writer. I have been particularly interested in recent work on brain physiology, both at Cambridge and across in California, and in the problems of perception. This led me, so to speak, to doodle on the edge of the pages of Nature.'

I remember her so well. She was rather small, but one was only aware of that if one measured her in one's mind against the filing cabinets, and who wants to do that? I noticed that she did not wear glasses but had a large square magnifying glass on the table beside her—why? I never found out. She seemed no particular age, just herself, and she treated me, though after all I was only a visitor from Arts, as though I could understand. It was an ordinary enough room, partly lab, partly library, with the kind of books and journals one expects, a different lot from those in Arts. No pictures, nothing that was just for decoration, but some interesting photographs, and on the big table beside her, among some moderately tidy papers, a bowl of roses, all, I noticed, different.

She knew I wanted to write something about her work for our magazine and, like most scientists faced with this kind of confrontation, felt sadly certain that I would get it wrong. In fact I found it quite hard to follow during our interview. But at least I did listen carefully, and tried to take it in.

'It's the difference between the perceived world and the— perhaps—real world,' she said, sitting there, the university's Dr Toni, straight in her chair but not tense.

'You won't remember,' she went on, smiling a little, 'the days when all films were black and white, but I'm sure you've seen plenty of black-and-white flashbacks and documentaries. We colour them in our minds, somewhere between vision and perception. In fact we did it better with those old ones. We knew so well that grass was green and lips were pink, that it didn't disturb us that the colour wasn't there. I don't think we do that as easily now that we are so used to colour films.'

I murmured something, but she frowned a little and went on: 'Also of course we make a mental stereoscopic image. They talk about making that the next great improvement; but it hasn't really worked out so far.'

No, I thought, our imaginations are better at turning the ordinary world into something genuinely pleasurable than those special spectacles!

'But the other perceptions?' I asked. 'Hearing?'

She nodded 'We fill in more or less, the bird-song or the whisper if, for instance, the sound is turned off. But not perhaps the full orchestra, or even the pop singer at full blast. Just as well, perhaps. But the hearing channel is different from the seeing channel. That is to say, anatomically, in the brain. You know that?'

'Of course,' I said, 'and there's the nose as well as the ears.

Though the clever boys say we'll be treated to the smellies soon.'

She laughed. 'No doubt accompanied by the tasties. I think I might settle for the smell of new bread, or perhaps the first moment of opening a bottle of Burgundy, a good vintage naturally, I'm sure they could do it if we were willing to pay for it. A small technical matter! But they won't find it as easy as they think.' She smiled to herself.

'Touch?' I asked.

'We're going down the scale,' she said. Then slowly, 'Touch is the last hope when we're wandering lost through the real world, if that's what it is. Lumps and liquids and mist.'

She shook her head in a kind of irritation, it seemed, at being human, tied to the senses. Tied to the old words of description.

I hinted that it might be partly a matter of areas, thinking of the visible layout in so many animals that depend on smell or hearing—those big noses and ears!—maybe reflected in larger arrays of cells in the actual brain. Something I'd heard about.

At first she said nothing, then: 'Let's go up the scale again, past vision, beyond the block in the brain which there appears to be. So what do we find then?' I was a little uneasy. 'Isn't that what the drug-users claim? To go through the gates of perception?'

'Oh, that lot!' she said. 'They haven't got it right. Not even Huxley, who at least had a scientific approach—or should have had with that family.'

She sounded quite cross.

'I've tried most of their things and they always allow in the most atrocious side-effects, which do nothing but obscure the kind of perception which is—well, beginning to be possible.'

'You tried them? Yourself?'

'Yes. I had to, just in case they told me something. But no—no. The drug thing is really more of a barrier than a way through, and if it does begin to get through there's no control. You've got to have that, you know. Got to shut your eyes if you try to look at the sun. Got to stop your ears when the noise gets too loud.' She was silent for a moment, then said, 'Do you really want to understand about perception?'

'I can try anyway!' I said, or something like it. I was really excited. And then she began to explain, making me follow, flashing out the figures on the screen she had unrolled from the wall. Well, we all ought to know by now that the brain is an immense set of synapses, of cell pathways along which the perceptions run, triggered off through the channels we know. And the channels we don't know. No, that is too clumsy a way of picturing this unbelievable delicacy of cell life, which has itself to be assumed from a complex of other assumptions, since it is hidden from actual measurement by life itself.

'Oh dear,' she said, half to herself, 'if only I had the words!'

All the time I kept trying to keep pace with Dr Toni, trying not to allow myself, Arts fashion, to make quick, inaccurate pictures out of what she was saying and demonstrating, letting my attention slip. In the middle of it John came in. We all knew him, a kind of university father-figure, and with him one of the junior technicians a girl with striped hair gradually reverting to its original colour. There was a conversation largely in figures, and a piece of apparatus with dials on it and a kind of thin wire cage, or so it looked. He fitted it onto something on the far side of the room, showing it to Dr Toni. I only picked up the conversation when John said, 'No, Dr Toni, you shouldn't do that. Not the whole way. No, we want you back.' Then, 'Look. Try this adjustment, but not full strength.'

He was clearly worried. I wondered about it, but I was trying to puzzle out the whole thing in my mind.

What it came to was that in the 80s and 90s of the last century, it had been worked out by several groups of researchers, including Dr Toni herself, where the so many cell groupings and synapses lay in the human brain. This was what appeared to be responsible for the various perceptions of the world as we know it: the mapping of a universe within the unimaginable confines of cells, whose existence in the living subject could only be postulated, communicating in ways which are not yet understood. At least not understandable to me. But perhaps—yes, perhaps she did understand. What she and John had been discussing was how to define the cell groups; how to alert them without damaging them.

So I began to realise the possibility of some interference with living brain cells, some adjustments of the synapses, which would come back as a new kind of perception. For it seemed clear that the cells which received and made sense of the incoming signals and the cells which made this into a recognisable perception were not exactly the same. Oh that beehive we all keep in our heads! So somehow a new perception of the known world would appear, something immeasurably different from the delicacies of colour vision or of musical appreciation, so different from mere hearing. Something totally unexpected. Different.

'Better?' I asked very softly, tentatively, watching her face.

'Yes,' she said, and seemed to wait for—well, for something to happen, to be capable of being put into words. Then, 'But remember, switching the synapses with drugs means putting on violent pressures which are bound to be damaging. All the side-effects come in. This makes it impossible to be clear about the experience and is therefore scientifically useless. However we have discussed other ways. In fact, we have even tried certain possibilities.'

I was still floundering, trying, not very successfully, to understand what she was explaining to me. But at the same time—because after all, I am from Arts, I kept on turning a critical eye, looking for a straight analysis. I kept wondering what sort of woman she really was, under the lab coat.

'You have tried—your new way?'

'Yes,' she said, 'with some success.'

'You really had a different perception? Another world?'

'That? Yes. Undoubtedly. I can only say that I look forward more than I can express to repeating the experiment. But it certainly was—well, let us say, exhausting.'

'You are able to write it down? To describe it?' I could hardly wait while she seemed to be trying to answer.

'I'm sorry,' she said, 'I could, but I find no adequate words. They are by now tied to our ordinary perceptions. They have solidified into little blocks. I must persuade someone who is good with words to try my method.'

'Me?' I said with a little gasp. 'I'm good at words!' And then I thought, how can I be so arrogant? She'll jump on me!

But she didn't. 'Perhaps,' she said, and looked at me. 'You see, there is a kind of scintillation of movement. If only I could explain! No, I can't, I can't. You would have to experience it, and I'm not quite ready to risk another person.'

'Risk?' I said.

'Yes, that is the present position—At least John thinks so, and so do I. It's a different risk from drugs, but all the same, yes, undoubtedly there is a certain risk. However, I see you're a sensible girl, so you can look at my notes. . .No, you'd better take them away.

Now she was putting two or three bundles—all of them, I was glad to see, neatly numbered—into a large folder.

I was itching to look at them, but she put her hand on the folder and continued: 'I don't want to look at them, not for a long time, anyhow not just now. See if they give you any idea of how some of my experiences which that bit of hardware has made possible, could go into words.' And she glanced with a kind of twitchy smile at the piece of apparatus which John had brought in.

I was longing to get my hands on them, but she turned her back and pulled out another big folder from the filing cabinet.

'See if you can make head or tail of this.' Then she added, 'And don't come back till you have!'

I knew she meant it, but equally I knew that I was going to come back, and that was that.

Well, I sat down to read the notes. It wasn't easy. Parts were typed out neatly by one of the competent secretaries, but much was in her own handwriting. This was fairly legible most of the time, but occasionally became very difficult and full of crossings out. She was always very suspicious of word processors, saying they deleted things on their own. The bad bits seemed to happen after an experiment, when she was attempting to describe it. Three times at least. Clearly, what she was trying for was meticulous accuracy shout what she had perceived. But no, it wouldn't go into words. If I could find the right words to make it clear, to have the experience shout itself out of the paper. Surely I should be able! I became deeply involved, could think of nothing else, all to the detriment of my own work, as I was firmly told. But I felt that I had been chosen to help her—casually it seemed, but definitely chosen, by Dr Toni who was someone deeply respected and admired, sometimes envied, never spoken of disparagingly. So, as she said, I had to make head and tail.

I worked harder than I had ever done for myself. I wouldn't go back until I had made a decent job of it. It began to be clear—and also dangerous. I sat at my word processor tidying it up, erasing the soft, smudgy words, trying out alternatives, some way of tightening up what I was trying to make clear. All that. I wanted to show her that I could handle those words! To show this woman of enormous courage and intelligence, but who wasn't so good at explaining in words what she was about. For instance I began to see that the word 'perception' was used far too widely; it had to be split up and classified. I could do that for her. There were other words. She could talk, she could handle figures with no trouble. She could deal expertly with a complicated piece of equipment, but she was somehow not passing on her own experience, as I knew I could.

I'd spoken to her on the phone two or three times (she didn't like the videophone so I couldn't see how she was looking) and told her how things were going. Now I made a definite appointment. I had the copies; I felt tremendously excited and important, carrying them. I felt like dancing. But on my way down the corridor John stopped me and beckoned me into his room.

'Look,' he said, 'you've got to help. She's carrying these experiments too far. Too far, do you see? It's not safe. She—she's going to kill herself!'

And I saw he was in grim earnest.

Then the young technician (her hair almost back to normal) came in, and caught me by the arm: 'She might want you to try it too. Don't, don't!'

I didn't know what to say. I said she'd sounded all right on the phone. John said, 'After its worn off. Look Miss—(he never could remember my name), you can't go on doing things inside the brain where everything's so close and get away with it. Please try and make her stop. Please do that! Look,' he went on, 'we've got the techniques now to put pulses through to the cells, but—but it's fairly new. We aren't sure. We may be causing damage. And Dr Toni's that stubborn!'

'Has she,' I asked, 'really got through? To a definite change of perception?'

'Seems like it,' he said. 'But it's doing her no good!'

The young technician said, 'She was wanting me to have a go. Said she knew I'd love it. And when I said no, well, it was—like she was mad! Scared me out of my skin!'

John had hold of my arm. 'And all the good work she's done. Never a slip. All those papers. And all the years I've worked with her—' He was terribly upset. 'Telling me to set up the cell exciter. It's—it's like drink,' he said, 'wanting it! Alone in her room, without me watching, though I told her—' He seemed close to tears.

I thought for a moment. 'But she said there'd be no side-effects, this way. Not like drugs.'

He nodded. 'I know she said that. But it's worse than side-effects. You see, Miss, maybe you don't know, but those cells are small. Really small. You can only measure them in microns. If that. When the first papers on these brain cell synapses came out in the 80s or 90s, there was no way of getting at them. They're deep down in the brain. Protected. Then we got the new brain probes, and worked away at it through the 90s. Very dodgy, that. You understand, don't you, Miss, that you can't work with dead cells?' I nodded. He went on, 'We got on to hearing first. That started with noise, then got clearer—musical sounds. Vision started with coloured clouds, then got to lines and figures, kind of architectural. You saw them with your eyes shut. But that led on to asking, were these the only sense synapses or were there others for some other sense that we had never experienced? Cells that had never been animated, so to speak. Dr Toni thought there was evidence for this and we worked on it, her and me, and it seemed there was something coming through. We got it mapped—or thought we had. A new look at reality. But not looking, not as we know it. I tried it too.' He shook his head.

'But you were all right?'

'We were careful, in those days. Had to be! Give the cells a good space of time to settle. Months. And now she's trying to do it every week. Soon it'll be every blessed day!'

I was puzzled. 'How?' I asked.

He answered slowly, 'I made the thing to fit her. Comfortable. Velvet round the head. Thought she'd like that. Hand switches and dials. And now she keeps on—and it's doing her no good!'

I couldn't think what to say, what to ask.

The girl technician said, 'She doesn't even write it all down—sometimes.'

John went on: 'You just can't go on pulling the synapses about without—without something—' He shook his head. 'I've worked on the probes over a long period—finding the pathways so as not to destroy what we are looking for. Tried it on dogs. Tried it on myself.'

I asked, 'Did you have—well, a change of perception?'

'It left me muzzy.' He shook his head. 'She wanted me to try again. I did—once more. But, I was a bit scared, as if I'd been somewhere else. Where I wasn't wanted. Oughtn't to be. See what I mean?'

'But, did you find a new—well, a new way of apprehending the real world?'

He frowned. 'In a way. I'd look at something ordinary and it was different, as if it was someone else looking. But—I can't find words for it. No, I wouldn't like to do it again, not something I can't find words for.'

Words, I thought. How does one explain sight to a blind person? Words. My thing. I told them I would have a long talk with her and try to stop her doing anything dangerous. I had the feeling that they might be fussing. But if they asked me to try—?

Well, I went to her room. I noticed that it was full of flowers, especially rather complex ones, and a few bits and pieces which I didn't recognise. Before it had always been a rather austere, working room. I showed her what I had written, asking if I had got anywhere near the real experience, if the words had expressed what had actually taken place. Sometimes she seemed pleased, but then, again, she frowned and shook her head. Finally she said, 'I think you must have the experience yourself before you write any more. Would you like to try? You see I've got everything here.'

Yes, that appeared to be it. Harmless looking, but. . .She ran her hand into her hair, white over the temples but still dark on the top, parted it with her fingers and there was a small bald patch.

'This is easy,' she said, 'my mini-tonsure! Look how it fits.' She settled the thing over her head with those velvet paddings that good John had put on it.'And so,' she said, 'if I depress this and touch the switch—'

'Yes,' I said. 'But, if I may say so, aren't you overdoing it, dear Dr Toni? You don't look quite yourself. Please take it off. Please! Yes, I might try it myself, but not now.'

I took the apparatus. It was quite light, a really beautiful bit of craftmanship, a kind of fantastic crown, and put it carefully to one side. She seemed to be watching me in a way that wasn't quite—well, not quite our old Dr Toni. But then she smiled and seemed to come back to herself. Her hair fell over the bald spot.

'Is it so very rewarding?' I asked.

'Yes,' she said. 'Definitely. But of course a little tiring. And John fusses. As if I couldn't look after myself! But it means I can observe the ordinary world, the one you see, my dear, and remember how much more interesting it really is. Giving me so much more.'

'That's why you have that orchid?' She nodded. 'And that intricate carving. Chinese, isn't it?'

'Yes,' she said. 'And one begins to wonder—' But she didn't say what, just shook her head. Then she was back again: 'It is becoming such a bore perceiving things in the old way. How we all did nothing else all those years! But all the time I am conscious of this lack of words! Now I shall just put on my magic hat for a few moments and try to describe to you what marvellous differences there are and you will be able to translate. Yes, I know you will!' She snatched up the apparatus. I tried to deflect her, tried to argue, for it seemed all wrong for someone I respected and admired so much, someone who had trusted me to find the words for her great discovery, her journey into this other perception. She settled the thing on her head, giving me a wink and a chuckle. I suppose in a sense she knew she was being silly, not behaving strictly as a scientist should. And then she was off.

A few deep breaths and then she said: 'Now it's happening.'

There was a single flower, one of the composites standing in a small thin vase close to the chair. I saw her looking at it and her face changing, so that I could almost imagine how exciting, how marvellous it appeared with the new perception. I was beginning to think that I really ought to try it myself.

And then, suddenly, a wave came over her cheeks, a paleness, a hardening, and then her eyes closed and I knew, I knew. I ran to the door and shouted for John. It was as if he had been waiting, for he came running and switched the thing off at once, took it away so that her head fell back a little. But there was nothing to be done to alter what had happened. Only her lips were still smiling as if, perhaps, she had at last found the word to describe it all.

ZOË FAIRBAIRNS

Relics

Zoë Fairbairns was born in 1948, and 'has done quite a lot of writing since then, some of which has been published: e.g. Benefits *(Virago),* Stand We At Last *(Virago and Pan) and* Here Today *(Methuen).' She is 'an ardent believer in feminism, except when feminists go too far, or not far enough.'*

The Managing Director of Universal Magazines has invited me to lunch in his office and forgotten to get me any. I did wonder, when I walked in at the agreed time and found him coming to the end of a box of foie gras sandwiches, but I didn't say anything and now I know: I am not to be fed because he wants to get cracking.

'What I have to say is in the strictest confidence.'

Greg Sargent loves secrets, so I nod solemnly.

'I'm going to make you an offer. If you accept, the news will be released by us at the appropriate time. If you refuse—and you are daft enough—you're not to tell anyone that I asked you.'

'Isn't that what they say when they offer someone an OBE?'

'Don't be such a damn fool. How would I know? It's about that magazine of yours, *Women's Action*.'

He always calls it that magazine of mine even though it's years since I left the collective. I thought it went a bit too far. Now it goes even farther, but I still read it. So does Greg. It fascinates him. He's had his own personal subscription from the beginning, separate from the office copy that Unimag always takes of any publication presuming to survive outside its imperial boundaries. It is an embarrassing fact that Greg owns one of the few complete, bound collections of back numbers in existence. He reads it meticulously—often more meticulously than I do—a fact with which he loves to taunt me. For instance, I once remarked that I'd quite enjoyed a particular film and he said,

'Well, you do surprise me. That magazine of yours said it was quite seriously flawed.'

And on another occasion he looked up from a feature article and enquired, 'How is political lesbianism different from the other kind?'

Today he says, 'It's going to fold. I assume from your expressionless expression that you know already.'

I must watch my mouth. *Women's Action* goes much too far but I love it. I do not propose to admit to this powerful man that I too have heard rumours, the most alarming of which is that the magazine owes several thousand pounds to the Inland Revenue and cannot pay.

Greg doesn't care whether I admit it or not.

'We're going to buy it,' he says. 'Clear all the debts and relaunch.'

'They've agreed to sell to *you*?'

'I haven't asked them yet.'

'Don't get too excited, then. Things would have to get a lot worse before the collective would let it trot out as a stable-mate of *Unicorn* and *Women's Nest*.'

'If you wanted to run features criticising *Women's Nest* or *Unicorn*, you could,' he says. 'Do them good.'

'Doing them good wasn't quite. . .what do you mean, *you*?'

'I want you to be editor.'

'Now listen, Greg.'

'No, you listen. That little magazine's got potential and it's not just me who thinks so. My ad manager's waiting for me to fire the gun. He's got this scheme. For the first six months anyone who takes a full-price page in two of our other women's magazines will get the same ad half-price in *Today's Women's Action*. I've broken a few pencils on that title I can tell you, but today's woman's going to buy it. This'll age you and your friends on the *collective*: today's school-leaver was four—*four*— when you started. Today's woman isn't fighting men, she knows she's got them right here.'

He presses his thumb down hard on his desk-top in illustration.

'These advertisements, Greg—'

'You think today's woman can't laugh and turn the page if there's a silly ad? Well, she can. Not that she won't thank the advertisers in passing for keeping the price down for her and her less fortunate sisters who are on the dole. She *cares*. So don't go all prim with me about make-up. You think I wouldn't like to put make up on some mornings? You'll have as many editorial pages as you've got now and I'll be relying on you to preserve the unique character of the magazine. Keep us straight. Tell me where to get off if necessary. If you don't, I'll fire you. I'm as much of a feminist as the next man, but I'm a businessman and I don't make donations to good causes, I make investments, and the fact that we're having this conversation should prove to you that you can stop fighting because you've won. Stop laughing.'

'Greg. Do me a favour. Phone up *Women's Action* now and ask to speak to the editor. You'll soon hear what they think about hierarchies.'

'Their line is dead,' he says. 'Non-payment I expect. Run without an editor, can they? Can they run without a telephone too?'

'I'm not going to listen to this any more, it's irresponsible. Those women'll put out a welcome mat for the bailiffs rather than agree to what you're proposing.'

'Welcome them into their homes, will they?'

'What do you mean?'

'That so-called collective of yours isn't a proper limited company, is it? So it'll come down to individuals.'

'It'll be blood out of a stone.' Will it, though? Salaries on the magazine have always been tiny, but some of the collective have other jobs. They may have savings, houses, cars. They'll be cleaned out to pay taxes to the government and still there'll be no magazine.

'Greg, the magazine isn't mine to sell or refuse to sell. Make them your offer and see what they say. If and when you're the owner, ask me again if I want to be editor.'

'No,' he says. 'You misunderstand. We're not making any offer *unless* you'll be editor. Come on, you can't freelance on the fringes for ever. You must be nearly forty. I am. Come in from the cold and bring your magazine with you. Hey, didn't I invite you for lunch?'

* * *

I've never been to the camp at the base before. I've meant to but I've always been too busy.

Today is the day of the dragon festival. Dragon, according to the handouts, means to see clearly. In what language, I wonder, but that is a petty thought. If dragon festival day is the day for seeing clearly, perhaps I will see what I must do.

The women are going to make an eight-mile dragon and wind her round the base. She will then be sent on a world tour to embrace other bases. How do you make an eight-mile dragon?

'Please take your bits of dragon to Green Gate and start sewing them together!'

Bits of dragon! Sewing! I stare in horror at the woman with the megaphone. I never learned to sew, despite having had a skilled and irascible teacher in Sister St Laur. I remember the art room on Thursday afternoons. I used to fidget and pick at a grubby sampler, listening to Sister St Laur's bible stories which were far more interesting. I looked up one day and discovered I was the only girl still working on a sampler. Everyone else in my class was making a dress! I couldn't understand it. Was it one of those things that happened to other girls in the school holidays, like starting their periods or having holes made in their ears? It seemed better to get on with my sampler and say nothing. But now here I am surrounded by women with beautiful home-made tapestries, quilts, shawls and tablecloths, and I have nothing.

Somebody gives me a lime-green leaflet.

'Whatever your contribution, welcome! We cannot all go over the fence! We cannot all leave our homes! Whether you have been here two hours or two years, you are one of us!'

I have been here twenty minutes, but the perimeter fence is eight miles long, so if I walked round it I will be one of them by the time I get back to the beginning.

Under the high noon sun the ground is baked and cracked and tinder dry in places, hazardously slushy in others. Where the mud is worst, a causeway has been improvised: planks, poles, wire-netting, carpet. It must be crossed with care, one person at a time clinging to the fence for balance, and here and there little groups of women gather, smiling with shy friendliness, waiting for each other.

We are shadowed by soldiers inside the wire. They keep up a commentary over their walkie-talkie radios, in their odd, staccato language.

'Six females proceeding in a westerly direction. Over.'

I yearn for such language, in which everything is simple. Shall I stop a group and say, 'Listen, I've been made this offer, what do you think I should do?' But Greg has made my silence a condition of his keeping the offer open.

'One female proceeding in an easterly direction. Over.'

Beyond the wire and its gibbering sentries the base is flat and empty, the only movement the heat shimmering. In the far distance an aircraft takes off, swallowed up in the sky before its brief roar is even audible. There are foxgloves tangled up in the barbed wire and like Winnie the Pooh I make up a little hum as I walk and this is what I hum:

> Tangled up in the barbed wire,
> Tangled up in the foxgloves,
> Tangled up in the barbed wire,
> Tangled up in the foxgloves.

Which becomes:

> Tangled up in the firewood,
> Tangled up in the shit pits,
> Tangled up in the Green Gate,
> Tangled up in the Blue Gate.

'Appears to be making up a poem. Over.'

> Tangled up in the car park,

Tangled up in the death's head,
Tangled up in the fig tree
Tangled up in the chessboard.

It isn't a chessboard, it's Sister St Laur, decorating the fence.
She paddles deftly on her knees through piles of brightly-
coloured rags, her black and white rosary beads clicking a
rhythm like mine. She has made a lushly magnificent image of a
fig tree: burst figs hang like open green and black mouths with
white gums and seedy red teeth. I rush at her, shouting:
  'Why can't I sew?'
  'Because I can't either.'
  'How can you say that when you've made this?'
  'Appear to be having an argument about a fig tree. Over.'
  'This,' scoffs Sister St Laur, 'is not sewing.' She demons-
trates. All she is doing is to weave the rags through the mesh of
the fence, tucking the loose ends into the inside.
  'Appear to be, er—'
  'Oh do be quiet,' says Sister St Laur to the soldier. 'I am
trying to teach this child her bible.'
  She lets me weave brown rags into the earth around the tree's
roots. I hate this sort of work and time refuses to pass. The sun
hangs obstinately overhead still signifying noon, but the
women's leaflet said that I must serve two hours before I count
as one of them. I am tired of brown rags, but Sister St Laur will
not allow me to work on the tree itself until I am more skilled
and can recite verbatim from the relevant gospel. I can only
paraphrase.
  'Didn't Jesus want figs and there weren't any? So he put a
curse on the tree.'
  'Exactly. Disgraceful. *He found nothing on it but leaves for
the time of figs was not yet.* Didn't stop him, though, did it? If
the tree had sprouted figs out of season he wouldn't have liked
that either, which just goes to show—'
  The sky is split by the scream of a siren. The soldier jabbers
into his radio and the radio jabbers back. The earth is shaking.
Hordes of women rush past bearing bits of dragon, screaming,
'The convoys are going out! Stop them! Stop them!' Deathly-
white slipstreams criss-cross the vociferous skies, the fig tree is

putting out dead arms to cut itself down. The arms are the arms of soldiers in thick protective clothing. They have bolt-cutters in their hands. They clip and wrench until the tree hangs only by a hinge in the wire, and no barrier remains between us the women and them the soldiers. The air is rigid with wings, the rags of the tree are dead in the mud. Sister St Laur is doing a little dance of rage. The soldiers are coming to get us.

'Into the shelters,' they shout. 'Get into the shelters!'

'You're letting *us* into the shelters?'

'We'll need you for after,' say the soldiers. 'Why d'you think we've kept you handy?'

I won't enter their shelter. I won't walk willingly to my own death. But I'm not being asked to, I'm being offered a chance to survive. My feet teeter at the top of a staircase of a thousand steps. I have never been afraid of heights, but depths I cannot stand. This can't be it. This can't be death. I had hoped there would be a resignation, a quiet closing-down when it finally came. But my senses, my faculties are putting on fireworks: *See what we can do. Don't close us down. Don't, don't!* The soldier has me in an arm-lock and all I can feel is the sweetness of contact, contact with warm flesh that has living blood running through it. My eyes glorify in the flaming light; the rumbles and roars are music; my brain can still think. Why didn't we realise? We knew there were shelters. We knew there were plans for rebuilding the world afterwards. We knew that soldiers and politicians, senior police officers and town clerks were to be preserved. How did it escape our attention that such groups were unlikely to contain women of childbearing age and consequently other arrangements would have to be made?

Will we be together, those of us who are brought down into their shelter? Will we be able to plan? The underground room is cold and full of confusion. I can't see who else is here. It's not one of these bureaucrats' shelters we've heard about, with desks and telephones and wall-charts. There's nothing like that. But there's food for a long siege: rows and rows of deep-freeze cabinets.

'Get in,' my captor says, lifting a lid. 'It won't be no worse than falling asleep in the snow. Nice and cosy you'll be, better than up there.'

He puts me into a deep-freeze cabinet. There is one last gleam of rainbow light through the whiskers of ice before the lid comes down and all is darkness. My ears are lined with frost and when I hear more thumps I cannot tell whether they are the sounds of other lids closing, or the bunker collapsing on top of me, or people being shot. The soldier has lied, it isn't nice and cosy at all; I'm freezing.

* * *

'I knew it, I knew it, I knew there would be some left somewhere!'

Somebody has lifted my lid. I can't see who it is through all the ice, but the voice sounds male and I am uneasy. I have no illusions as to what I have been preserved for. Whether it is the fear associated with this thought that causes the frost in my eyes to melt I cannot say, but I am able to make him out: a short creature of scholarly bearing with a file of notes under his arm, a clipboard in his hands and an expression of intense intellectual excitement on his face. Apart from an overlarge head he looks physiologically normal, but I can't see clearly.

To my irritation, he offers me a visiting-card. What am I supposed to do with it? My arms are still pinned to my sides and the print is too small to read. Does he suppose that it is normal for women to be coated with ice? The heat of my anger clears sufficient space for me to move my lips and shout,

'Defrost! Defrost!'

'Good gracious, silly of me, I really am most frightfully sorry, it's the excitement—'

I feel a switch go, and soon I stand dripping before him. He places his card on the edge of the cabinet and steps back. I pick it up. It says:

> MR CONSTABLE
> DEPARTMENT OF RELICS

'Your name?' he asks.

'I think it's . . . it used to be . . . it's no good . . .'

'No-Good?' he repeats, referring to his file.

'I mean, I can't remember.'

'Don't worry, I have a collection of women's names and very pretty some of them are too, like you if I may say so.'

He beams and blushes and bows as he says this, as if he has been practising. Pretty! I look down at myself and feel my face. I am certainly well preserved.

'Mr Constable, how old am I?'

His blush deepens. 'This is hardly the time or the place . . . before I even know your name . . .'

'Have you got a towel?'

Again he misunderstands and consults his list, muttering:

'"A–Towel". I don't have that, but I have "Scrubber".'

'That was never a name, Mr Constable, it was a job. I should like to get dry.'

'Then come up into the sunshine!'

He points towards the staircase. Light is filtering down, but I am starting to remember something that makes me anxious.

'Is that really sunlight?'

'Oh yes.'

'It's not a nuclear winter, then?'

'On the contrary,' beams Mr Constable. 'Please. After you.'

His distant courtesy intensifies my loneliness. I ask if we might not look in the other cabinets first.

'All in good time. I want to show you where you will be kept.

'What are those?' He points at my face.

'Tears, Mr Constable.'

'I have heard of those.'

'Mr Constable. I'm sorry, but—it's been such a long time since I've seen anybody and such terrible things have happened. Would it be possible for you to *greet* me in some way before you do your research?' I offer my hand for a handshake; I long to hold a human hand, but he steps back, at once shocked and reassuring.

'I understand your anxiety,' he says. 'But nobody is going to touch you.'

We are walking together through clear, brilliant air. I keep my eyes down in order not to have to take in too many horrors at once: but the turf under my feet is perfectly green with not so much as a puddle or a patch of mud, and the only sound is bird-song. I allow myself to glance about. There is no sign of weapons, soldiers, aircraft, destruction or danger of any kind, but of course I cannot yet see clearly. He has brought me to an arrangement of benders and tents, neat but uninhabited.

'This is where you will live,' he says.

'How?'

'Precisely as you please. Mine is a ministry for preservation, not control, and we rely on you to recreate your historic way of life from which we in the human race may learn to live as you lived, in peace. I think you will find that my research has enabled me to anticipate most of your wants, though not without opposition from my committees. "Where *are* these creatures for whom you want public funds to reconstruct the Peace Camp, Mr Constable?" I have been asked down the years. But I have soldiered on—I beg your pardon, *struggled* on—sure in my heart that one day I would find you. Let me show you round. This is where the fence comes closest to the Viewing Platforms so it might be best to begin your decorations here. Let me have a list of the materials you will require, wool, photographs, and so forth. That part of the fence over there is for you to cut down. Well, it would be a pity to cut down what you have decorated, wouldn't it? Whenever you cut it down it will be restored within 24 hours so you will be able to cut it down again. This is probably the point at which the fence is easiest for you to climb—after you—and this is where you may dance.'

'Are there missiles under there?'

'Goodness no. They are on the moon, out of harm's way.'

The birds are still singing but I can't see them. Now Mr Constable is singing too.

'Tangled up in the fox-gloves, tangled up in the barbed wire, tangled up in the . . .'

'What's that?'

'I thought you would recognise it. Isn't it one of your songs?'

'It began to be. It was never finished.'

'We have them all in the archive. You can't kill the spi-i-rit, she is like a. . .' He catches my glare and stops. 'I am doing my best,' he says huffily. 'You must forgive me if I make the occasional gaffe. And now. . .now that you understand the situation, shall we go and melt your friends?'

Sister St Laur is a head and a half taller than Mr Constable. As she brushes herself down she showers him with sharp icicles.

'I say!' he protests.

'Piss off,' says Sister Laur.

'You'll have to be polite to him,' I remonstrate in a whisper. 'What choice do we have?'

'We have all the choices in the world. As I was saying before I was interrupted, fig trees are always in the wrong, so it doesn't matter what we do. Who is this little twerp?'

'I don't understand it, I don't understand it,' mutters Mr Constable to himself. 'The clothing suggests a nun, but . . .'

'Nun nothing. Let's play chess.'

She takes off her head-dress and a layer of her skirt. She arranges squares on a sheet of ice, then starts to make pieces and pawns. I advise Mr Constable to get on with defrosting the others. One by one they come out of their cabinets, weighed down and immobilised by their icy shrouds. But once Mr Constable has explained about the Department of Relics, the renewable fence, the Viewing Platforms and the missiles on the moon, no further action is required to melt them. They stand before him like a row of blowtorches.

'If you think we are going up there to be made an exhibition of!'

'Come and play chess,' calls Sister St Laur. 'The Queen is the most powerful piece on the board.'

'Ladies, ladies,' says Mr Constable tremulously. Behind his hand he whispers to me, 'Is that what I should call them?'

'What do you mean, *them*? I am one of them.'

'Oh no, you are not like them. They are not real peace women, are they? They must be the ones who only came for the day. Better than nothing, though, better than nothing. Ladies, women, girls, sisters. I must ask you now to follow me to the camp which has been prepared for you. You have my personal guarantee of safety and privacy, other than. . .'

'The purpose of the game,' explains Sister St Laur, 'is to checkmate, that is, trap the king. It is not difficult, the king can hardly move. Once the king has been disposed of, the game is over.'

'. . . other than on the occasional Open Day, which would be arranged with your full. . .'

'It used to be the rule that white moved first, giving black a built-in disadvantage, but there is no reason for us to stick to that rule, or any other.'

'All right!' shouts Mr Constable. 'Play chess! Stay down here! See if I care. You are not what I was looking for in any case! But be warned! I shall make a full report to my committees! Not everyone is as committed to your preservation as I. . .have been.'

Shaking his enormous head, more in sorrow than in anger, he climbs the stairs alone. Sister St Laur is setting out her pieces and the other women are improvising rules for a form of chess in which queens and pawns can only triumph and colour is irrelevant. I am tempted to join them but I am afraid for our safety. I pursue the sulky Mr Constable. At last he allows me to mollify him. He suggests that I come to the city. There will probably be sufficient interest in me, he says, to take the minds of his committees off the disappointment they will undoubtedly feel when they hear what the others are like.

High above the rows of sharp-edged boxes that constitute the city, gleams the Reliquary: round as a rollerball, white as the moon, it hovers on legs so thin as to be almost invisible. We enter through an automatic opening and are conveyed along a corridor. There is no need to walk, the floors move. Open escalators criss-cross and radiate in circular tiers: glass-walled lifts whisper up and down, bearing huge-headed staring replicas of Mr Constable.

'My committee,' he says, 'waiting to meet you.'

'Show me round first.'

'Very well. But we mustn't be long.'

'Please,' say the notices, 'go slowly to adjust your eyes to the light. Be as quiet as possible. Follow the arrows. Do not take pushchairs. Beware of pickpockets.'

I look quizzically at Mr Constable: Pushchairs? Babies then?

'Indeed. Embryos can be grown in any bodily cavity.' And he taps his head.

A tortoise eats leaves behind glass, watching me. It pokes out its pink tongue. Another flash of pink causes me to spin round to where a sting-ray is pressing its gorgeous rose-coloured belly against the inside of its tank. An elephant limps an endless circle, its foot tethered to a stake.

'By slightly restricting her liberty,' Mr Constable explains, 'we can give her much greater freedom, train her better and make her life more interesting in the long term. After the meeting I should like to show you my research archive. It may be that there is some help you can give me, identifying documents, and so forth. Some of them are very puzzling.'

I am starting to cry.

'What's the matter?' he asks tenderly.

'I'm so lonely.'

'What does that mean? How can I help?'

'Just take me away from here.'

It is night-time when we reach the point where the city ends and the wilderness begins. We walk in silence through the dead, treeless rubble, the warm moonlit dark. The moon is brighter than I remember it, as if it were on fire. I suggest that we stop in a cave. After my long ice age I feel needy and tender and sharply alive. I hold out my arms to Mr Constable.

'Oh no,' he says primly. 'It would be an act of conquest.'

'It doesn't have to be.'

'I knew I should have asked you to explain those documents to me!'

'We were never all the same, Mr Constable. You have to understand that, even if it does spoil your research.'

After a little coaxing he creeps into me like a cat. He is a joy to teach. He has never dreamed that such things are possible. Through the waves of our ecstasy I seem to see the moon explode, but I cannot see clearly when I am doing this.

I certainly thought it was *our* ecstasy. But when we yawn out naked into the morning with its odd patchy light, the moon vanished, the sun racing with clouds, he says:

'I cannot think what came over me.'

I avoid the obvious riposte. Flippancy would not be appreciated. He is metaphysically troubled, as one often is on the first occasion.

'We will look upon it as a relic,' he says at last and with some relief.

'But wasn't it good for you?'

'Penetration, invasion, war. . .'

'You want to start a war?'

'That is not what *I* feel but the others are not all like me.'

'I wasn't planning to do it with the others, Mr Constable.'

'I would like,' he admits, 'to snuggle against you and sleep for ever.'

'Well then! And listen. I have been calculating at what point in my menstrual cycle the world ended. I think I may have a child!'

He stares at my head, aghast. Smiling in gentle reproof, I direct his glance lower down. He refuses to look. He straightens his shoulders and pulls on his clothes. He throws my clothes at me, none too gently.

'We must return to the city,' he says. 'I have betrayed a trust.'

'But it was my idea!'

'The trust of my committee. They will be *furious*.'

He seems terrified. He appears to have thought of a remedy, and calms down. Speaking very slowly, he says:

'I have a suggestion to make. If you agree, I shall inform the committee. If you refuse—and I am sure you are too sensible—you're not to tell anyone that I asked you.'

'Isn't that what they used to say when they. . .Oh, never mind.'

'We will say that the recent event was proposed by me as participant-observation research. In furtherance of this research you will give birth in the Reliquary. Women are my subject as you know. But I don't do favours, I do research, and the fact that we're having this conversation should prove to you that you can stop fighting because you've won. *Stop laughing*.'

He tries to restrain me from running off but it is easy to

escape from the little twerp. Finding my way back to the place where the women are is more difficult. Forty days and forty moonless nights pass before I am home.

I chuckle to find the camp deserted, the fence undecorated, the silo undanced-upon. They must still be playing chess in the shelter. As I descend the steps, though, my optimism takes on an edge of unease.

The air is very cold. Bits of makeshift chess pieces litter the steps. There is no one about. The lids of the cabinets are down, the switches locked to FREEZE.

With effort I can raise the lids but I cannot throw the switches. The women have been violently flung back into cold storage. Their postures of struggle are frozen in blocks of ice.

For a long time I am immobilised by despair. Then it occurs to me that sooner or later, one way or another, my womb is going to bring forth warm water or warm blood or both. Either will serve to start the melting process.

The cold, cranial obstetrics of the relic collectors will not have allowed for this! We will have to wait of course, but not for too long.

Actually we hardly have to wait at all. To pass the time I start to talk to myself, recounting the various offers I have received. My words seem to arouse strong emotions inside the deep freeze cabinets, because with growls and roars and gushes of water the ice breaks and the women sit up as one and shout with incredulous laughter:

'He wanted you to do *what*?'

* * *

Thanks to Carol Sarler, Elsbeth Lindner, Jen Green, Robyn Rowland and Sarah Lefanu for help with this story; also to Sunderland Polytechnic for hosting me as Writer in Residence, 1983–1985.

PENNY CASDAGLI

Mab

Penny Casdagli was born in Greece, trained as a dancer and went to drama school. Since 1968, she has worked as an actress, and more recently as a director and playwright. Five of her plays have been for deaf children.

'I have no children—as yet—but have fantasies of bearing them. "Mab" is a result. I want to see every creative act as birth, and many different forms of caring as mothering. "Mab" is my second story for adults. At present, I am working on some more which take up issues touched on in "Mab", such as spirituality and feminism, disability and power, and what opportunities there are for the event of love.'

The yoga* teacher looked as if she had a dead canary stuck on her face. There was a large greenish lump the size of an egg on her cheek-bone, and bruises as yellow as egg yolk beneath her eye. She said she had walked into a lamp-post and all the women in the class, including Iska Battenbury, tried hard to believe her.

'Virabhadrasana Three, Warrior Pose,' said Lillian, the teacher.

'Oh no, not Virabhadrasana Three,' groaned the class. It too

*To give total period accuracy to this herstorical resumation of those events of late '82, the Authorisors' Elective have reployed words in their retrospective, not momentary resonance. Therefore 'yoga' is used here in its original pre-parthenogenic meaning of 'union', its etymological derivation being from the Sanskrit 'yuj', to yoke, and not in its present-day sense of yoga as preparatory or central to the study-praxis of parthenogenesis, or in its applied form of practical parthenogenesis.

was Iska's least favourite posture.

'Inhale. Jump the feet three or three and a half feet apart. Stretch the arms up, left foot in and right foot out. Tuck down buttock bones. Exhale. Turn the back leg into a beam of light. Vision is the first step.'

Iska Battenbury admired Lillian for what her father would call 'moral fibre', for teaching physical skills so energetically and precisely when she must be in pain herself. She forgave her the loose metaphor about the back leg. Iska was extremely fastidious herself both in her professional life and what there was of her personal life. The Cathcart Institute had not had a female head before. It was mainly due to the impressive influence of her academic publications outside the Institute on structures in therapy groups that when the post fell vacant, Iska's persuasive application for the job could not be rejected. She knew, however, that the Governors had disliked promoting an existing member of staff to such a high level and a woman to boot.

She had joined the yoga class six months ago and although she was older by years than most of the class could do Virabhadrasana Three with the rest of them. With the exception of Leonard, a Rastafarian who occasionally came, the class was all women. They had jagged hair, strong bodies, earrings with fists of silver, and T-shirts that said 'No to Male Violence', 'Women do it Better' and 'War is Menstrual Envy'. Intelligent young women. During the course, one of them, Ginnie, had become pregnant. Childless herself, Iska watched her grow with interest and relief that she was past lump-bearing. She had always disliked children and delegated child therapeutics, traditionally an area women therapists did well in, to others. Perhaps that explained her antipathy. She enjoyed being skilful and successful in the 'male' territory of power breakdowns.

'Relax. Good. The other side,' called out Lillian.

'Why is it called "Warrior Pose"?' asked someone in a brave attempt to delay doing it to the left.

'You're not going to like this,' said Lillian, looking at the women. 'It's called that because it is dedicated to Virabhadra.

The god Shiva got angry, tore out a lock of hair, and where it fell to the ground, Virabhadra, the Warrior, sprang up.'

'We could reclaim it,' suggested Ruba, one of the black women, 'and make it a female freedom fighter.'

'I thought it was called "Warrior Pose" because it was such a struggle to do,' said Ginnie, stroking her tummy, and everyone laughed.

Lillian walked round the room correcting. When she came to Iska she said, 'Lengthen the neck.'

Iska was in a tangle of limbs and hardly knew where her neck was. Lillian took a handful of hair from the top of Iska's head and tugged rather roughly.

'Extend into the hair.'

Iska groaned.

'Let pain be your guru,' said Lillian cheerfully and passed on.

After the class, as she sat trying to rub the dirt off her feet, a refinement no one else went in for, she overheard Ginnie and Ruba talking quietly with Lillian.

'Lillian, there's quite a lot coming up for all of us around yoga, like some of the women have been saying they feel quite emotional after the class. . .'

'Like our muscular armature is being displaced,' added Ruba.

'And we were thinking, could there be a space—'

'A time—'

'For us to debate it all as a group?'

Iska recognised the first buds of a power-struggle and collected up her tights and blanket.

'Yeah, I know what you mean,' said Lillian. 'Yoga can act as a catalyst for all sorts of things. I identify with what you are saying. When I first learnt yoga, I had to work through all these issues by myself.'

A classic, thought Iska. Isolated individualism equated with value; the confusion of effort with virtue. 'You can only reach me if you have spent as much effort to become as isolated as I am.' Sequential paying-out of knowledge ratifying the existing hierarchical power structures, particularly prevalent in theistic contexts. How is it the same patterns occur and recur? Because we are all the same.

'Goodbye,' she said, and the women stopped talking and smiled.

'Bye, Iska. See you next week.'

Outside, it was bitingly cold. Frost persisted at noon, whitening the grass, fretting the road with threads of ice, seemingly lifting detail out of object and freezing it into a bitter dimension. As Iska got into the car, the doors opened and the three women came out. Lillian got on her bicycle and Iska wound down the window.

'Can I give you a lift? It's so cold.'

'That's really nice,' Ginnie and Ruba climbed into the car and after a few false starts, they pulled away.

'When's the baby due?'

'In the new year, I can't wait to get back to my old shape. I feel huge today.'

She may well not be married, thought Iska, so she asked:

'Will the father be at the birth?'

Both the women laughed.

'There isn't one!' said Ginnie.

'Sorry?'

'Ginnie self-inseminated by donor,' added Ruba. 'there are three of us co-parenting. We'll all be present!'

Iska kept the car on the road.

'We were asking Lillian if we could discuss what yoga was bringing up for us.'

'Is that something you recognise?' said Ruba.

'Oh yes. It would be nice, but isn't the overall issue whether we're a class or a group?'

'Right,' they agreed, 'right. That's really crystallised what we've been feeling. Are we a class or a group?'

Iska dropped them where they wanted to be, at the Women's Centre, and drove back to the Institute, her thoughts full of the moral complexities of women literally taking birth into their own hands, how it would affect the power dynamics of early infancy, and whether it would not be an excellent idea if the Cathcart were to plan courses for just such eventualities. Her talent lay in spotting and adjusting to new ideas and phenomena; it was her capacity for flexible and therefore saltatory thought that gave her the edge over her colleagues. Years as a therapist had made her virtually unshockable. It had washed off judgemental morality—as distinct from her analytical observations—as surely as yoga lengthens ligaments. Any residual crystals of disapproval or censure had dissolved in obligatory and vigorously sought-for loneliness. Or so she hoped. She must go into this more profoundly with her Supervision Group. But these women were at the grassroots, and despite all the differences, she felt close to them. As she neared the Cathcart, she found herself illogically repeating nonsense words:

'All we need to be complete is grass growing beneath our feet.'

She parked the car in the space reserved for her. What could it mean—'All we need. . .', where had she picked that up from? As she opened the car door, chill air blasted in. Iska sneezed. It *was* cold. She blew her nose and saw blood on the tissue. A nose bleed. Her nose was bleeding! It must be the change of temperature, the car had been cosy. The bleeding was light. She made nothing more of it.

No one could do the next class. Lillian demonstrated knot after new knot of asana while they watched. When they were resting in Corpse pose she gave a talk on yoga from the viewpoint of 'a feminist and a Buddhist'—a harder position to take, thought Iska, than any they had tried and failed that morning. Lillian said yoga was a way of breaking through to the ultimate and of taking evolution into their own hands. They were more likely to believe that she'd walked into a lamp-post last week. She also recommended honey for healing bruises.

Ruba came up to Iska as they changed.

'Well. That's settled it.'

'What?'

'We're a class.'

'Yes,' said Iska and smiled.

'It's not what I want.' Ruba laced up her boots.

'Do you want a lift?'

'No, it's okay. We're on our bikes today.'

Iska went to wash. She took off her tights and froze. It was impossible. Blood, like a heavy period. But at fifty-six. . ! What could explain it, spotting, injury, a cut, hot flushes, break-through bleeding?

'None of those applies to me,' she said out loud. She had to get back to the Cathcart and give a lecture on the acausal relationship of greed and gratitude. There was no time to go home. She dressed, dirty feet and all, and returned to the hall.

'Er—could anyone. . .could anyone give me a tampon?'

She was sure they would laugh at her embarrassment, but they didn't.

'Don't look at me,' Ginnie grinned, patting the unborn child.

Lillian looked in her bag.

'Thought so. I've got one.'

Iska felt the need to explain the exceptional situation. 'I'm sorry, it's just. . .'

'Don't worry,' said Lillian. 'Pay me back next week.'

Iska didn't go to yoga the next week, nor the next, nor the next. In thirty days she had three periods. They were regular in that they happened regularly every ten days. She kept it to herself because it was ridiculous but she couldn't turn the tides away.

Eventually, in the last week of the yoga term, she went to the doctor. The practice served a vast urban catchment area so there was no continuity, a different doctor every visit. Today, he was plumpish, a keen young man with sleepy eyes.

'I've had three periods in thirty days. Old blood followed by new. I went through the change of life seven years ago.'

'I see. General health all right? No problems?'

'No.'

'Eating and sleeping normally?'

She nodded.

'No pain anywhere?'

'No.'

'I see. The most likely explanation is. . .Could there be any chance that you are pregnant?'

'I'm fifty-six years old, doctor.'

'I take your point,' he said, hastily consulting her records.

'Too old even from an extreme case of palaeoprimogenesis,' she added.

'But when in fact did you last have sex?'

'I take it you mean partner sex?'

'Yes, indeed.'

'October '72,' answered Iska without turning a hair.

The doctor tried to hide his surprise. 'And is this lack of a boyfriend. . .?'

'Over the years, I have fulfilled my own needs by masturbating.'

'Of course.' The young man looked increasingly uncomfortable.

'That's the only conceivable way I could be pregnant unless the change of life can reverse itself. Although it *is* coming up to Christmas!'

'What? Oh yes,' the doctor chuckled.

'So what's happening to me?'

The doctor took off his glasses, sighed on them and wiped them clean. 'I'll take a swab, but quite frankly I haven't the foggiest. Misplaced stigmata?'

Iska drove home. She cut the Cathcart, and the teachers' training group she was to lead. Being teachers, they hated being taught and tried to renege on their class tasks by taking refuge in group identity. They then behaved divisively, demanding exclusive communication with Iska, parodying what she had said the week before, and throwing up absurd notions of hierarchy and power abuse. Very childish. The conflict simply was, were they a class or a group? Both, obviously. Suddenly, she thought of the yoga class and had a pang of longing for the young women. There was a patch of blue in the Christmas sky just large enough to make a Dutchman a pair of trousers. And tomorrow. . .but there could be no yoga now until the new year. Term had finished.

As soon as she got into the flat, she kicked off her shoes and dragged the armchair to the side of the room. She rolled back the rug and wound the flex of the television into a coil and tucked it out of harm's way. She drew the curtains and undressed. The central space of the room was clear. She stood in it, spreading her toes, pulling the inner ankle up and rooting into the ground.

'All we need to be complete is grass growing beneath our

feet.'

The words haunted her but did not irritate or bewilder. They were just there, part of a process. Inhale. Arms wide. Jump the feet apart. She was stiff. Her body felt like a cage and when, as she moved, bones clicked, it was as if birds flew out of her joints. She heard Lillian's voice but Iska Battenbury was gone. She was only that which does yoga, that which has moved furniture. There was nothing else. That is, she was defined solely by activity. And everything was the same, part of the process. There was no barrier between that which was herself and the environment, nameless meditation. Her arms stretched up. Intuition is experience brought into the present. Once there, it has always been there. Because it is customary to place experience in the past, insight or intuition, the ability to see round corners appears to be a perception out of time; or at least, an apprehension of the future. Virabhadrasana Three. Her back leg was shot through with light. The impulse ripped through her body. Her limbs formed a neon hieroglyph. That was it! Bodies were filaments made incandescent by messages of light. Each yoga pose was a letter in this evolutionary language. Lillian was right! She came to standing and saw the eyes of her father staring at her from the photograph over the mantelpiece. She went to her desk and got scissors and tape. She cut a square of paper from yesterday's *Times* and stuck it over the frame.

'I'm not talking to you,' she cried. 'People are taller in the morning, sleeping lessens gravitational pull!' She hurled the picture against the wall and heard the glass break in its paper shroud.

She sat at the desk and wrote:

'I don't want to put my hand on anyone's knee until I have understood the place and consequence of sex.'

She stared in horror at what she had written, so firmly, so fluently. She held the pencil in her right hand. But she was left-handed. Who or what was writing this? And with what hand? She thought of the neon hieroglyphs. That was the answer. The right side of her body had been brought to life. Sinister and dexter. Perfect balance. Yoga. 'All we need to be complete. . .'

She had a splitting headache and rubbed her eyes. When she opened them, blood spilt across the desk. The walls were daubed with it, the television a tank full of blood. Blood had eased its way into the pile of the carpet, washed the curtains, and soaked like syrup into the cushion of the armchair. Moggy, the lucky black china cat, bled by the phone. The pain in her head was organising into excruciating, regular rhythms with parent spasms occurring every few minutes. Iska became aware of a harsh noise. She glanced round the reddening room until she realised it was her sobbing. She steadied her vision. Vision is the first step and she took down from the shelf a volume of Hildegard Kalkhoff's *Exposition of Image*. Index: blood. Yes, there it was: 'Blood—rites, initiations of'. She turned to the page and read the black and crimson text.

'There are initiations of blood. These rites reflect the mythic and genetic fact that dreams and memories are stored as latent sub-material in the structures of the blood.'

'Thank you,' she whispered as she closed the book. Her head quaked and instinctively she put her hands up to protect herself from the pain. On the very crown of her head there was a lump. She staggered to the bed and got in. Please, no more lumps, no more lamp-posts, no more dead canaries. No more blood.

'All colours will agree in the dark' (Francis Bacon).

Note the masculine use of the imperative 'will'. She switched off the light and did what children often do in the face of danger or acute distress. She fell into a sound sleep.

In her dream, Iska stood in a field green and four-square. Along one side, she saw the women from the yoga class and in the middle, on a pillow of earth, there was a scarecrow. His coat was patched with scraps of paper, each with a strange letter or sign drawn on it in different colours. Lillian stepped into sight and snapped a branch from a sapling overhanging a ditch, and tucking it under her arm, she charged full tilt at the scarecrow like a jousting knight on a transparent horse. Iska watched Lillian trying to tear a letter from his coat but the scarecrow melted into life. He looked like Leonard, the occasional man in the yoga class. He turned from her, drawing his arms in close as if they were angel's wings. He was the colour of open mouths in the darkness, or a flight of pigeons over a city at dusk. He was a nest of grey flame, soft, flickering, insubstantial. Woman after woman challenged him but none could grasp braided shadow, a man made of dust and feathers. Over a corner of the field, seven stars came out before their time. Iska decided to risk her luck and managed to rip a letter from his coat whilst he looked at the new sky. She ran away as fast as she could, her heart pounding. She scrambled over a gate and down a shallow incline into a small wood. The letter was red, a spiral daubed in blood, a birthmark. She knew that with the logic of dreams, lucid dreaming. She heard a twig crack behind her, something moved. Someone, something was there: an invisible companion. Both of them saw a path worn black in the grass and followed it to a clearing. She looked down and saw blades of new grass pushing upwards between her toes. The ground was liquid and the grass with a sudden shift became opaque, the skin of the water, glass. Fish with low green eyes twisted and fed and Iska threw them the paper with its sign. The invisible companion—it could have been a dog—dived in after it and retrieved it and lay on the gently lapping ground waiting for approval. She discerned it only by what it displaced in the environment, the shape flattened in the grass. Iska touched it. Her hands told her it was made of jelly and membrane, had a head and a body hardly more than a tail. It was an embryo, and unseen at that.

The next morning the pain of the previous night seemed like a nightmare—nightstallion, should she say, thinking of the fastidious attitudes to language taken by the women in the yoga class. She stretched and rubbed her eyes. The lashes of her left eye were sticky with sleep. She rolled out of bed and bathed her face in warm water. Better. Gone. Then she noticed something afloat in her water almost transparent, except for a reddish hue. She scooped it out with her hands on to a towel and went to the study. The displaced furniture made her pause until she remembered she had moved it herself. She found her reading glasses and switched on the light. Immediately, the jelly clouded, and the warmth of the lamp made it contract and pulse. Bewildered, Iska looked round the room wondering what to do. She pushed the armchair into its place and caught sight of herself in the mirror. Her forehead was split by a silvery mark running right into her left eye. She peered closer. It was sticky, like a snail's trail. Had that thing. . .She remembered the lump. She bent her head and saw the lump had gone and in its place the hair had parted like a clearing in a wood. She touched the spot. Both skin and skull were soft and resisted the pressure of her finger no more than the fontanelle of a newborn baby. She must put honey on it to heal it. Honey in the rock. . .

Whatever it was on the towel was still pulsing, almost—she caught her breath—as if it were incubating. Even as she watched, gorgeous colours, prismatic and various, shot through the membranous sac. Activity within intensified, and without, the surface was put under considerable stress. She heard a sequence of sound, like disordered bird-song, and at that exact moment the room filled with the mingled fragrance of rose and lemon. The skin tore, the waters broke, wetting the towel, and in the beam of light stood a perfect hatched human female of exquisite beauty no taller than a toe. When she saw Iska, she lifted up her arms and laughed.

Iska Battenbury cancelled all her plans for Christmas. She was too involved in her own experience of parthenogenesis to participate in someone else's. She looked after her daughter who grew three-eighths of an inch, and read. She read all she could lay her hands on. She read about rabbits, Zeus, the Virgin Mary and her cousin Elizabeth; from psychology, physics, biology, mythology and poetry to Tom Thumb and the homunculi of the Gnostics. She put honey on her head which was healing nicely and wore a woolly hat. She wrote a letter to the Cathcart saying that due to family matters she would miss the first week of term. She needed time to think—something she would not have dreamed of before, but things undreamed of had happened to her. Above all, she delighted in Mab. She found the name in Shakespeare and often muttered the lines to herself while she watched her daughter at play:

> 'Oh then I see Queen Mab has been with you.
> She is the fairies' midwife and she comes
> In shape no bigger than an agate-stone. . .'

It was the happiest Christmas she could remember.

The yoga class wondered why Iska kept her woolly hat on all through the morning. They did not know that under it she had made a nest for Mab to keep her safe even when they did the hardest postures. She couldn't leave her at home. Ginnie wasn't in class. She must have had her baby. Lillian seemed very relaxed, changed somehow. She asked them to sit on the ground in dandasana.

'Would anyone like to say anything?' said Lillian.

Ah, the class had democratised in her absence into a group. That must account for the lovely atmosphere. Good.

'Yes, I'd like to say something,' Ruba spoke. 'I'd like to say that it feels really good to have Iska back.'

'We thought we'd lost you,' added Lillian.

Iska blushed. The woolly hat prickled.

After class, Ruba and Lillian invited Iska to go to the Women's Centre where they were going to meet Ginnie for lunch. They went in Iska's car. Ginnie's daughter was called Quincy. She had been a difficult birth and Ginnie still looked exhausted. Iska was introduced to Liza, another of the co-parents. When Iska saw Quincy at the breast she felt a stab of pain that her own daughter was so different.

One of the women asked her. 'Did you have a good Christmas?'

'Winter Solstice,' corrected another.

'What? Oh yes.'

'What did you do?' asked Ginnie.

'Oh, I. . .I. . .' something broke inside her. 'It's so. . .I. . .' She could not speak. Her eyes filled with tears. Carefully, she took off her hat and laid it on the table. Her voice had an authority when she finally said,

'I—I very much want you to meet my daughter, Mab.'

An hour later the group were still making plans. Lillian was so excited she had abandoned her macrobiotic diet and was tucking into a plate of baked beans. She had left the Buddhist boyfriend who beat her up just after Christmas, on Boxing Day, in fact. Liza worked in a school for deaf children and confirmed

Iska's suspicions that Mab had little or no residual hearing. It was a blessing as no entity so tiny could have borne the volume of everyday city noise. Indeed, it was possible that she had been deafened in the first few hours of her life.

Liza tried her with some simple sign language and Mab danced for joy.

'I shall teach Mab signing. That will be my present. If there's a problem reading back because her fingers are so minute, I shall use a magnifying glass, even get Mab to go behind the glass when she needs to communicate.'

'She's growing all the time,' put in Iska, looking anxious.

'Fine. Of course, you'll have to learn too,' said Liza.

'And I can look after her when you're at work. I'll be with Quincy anyway,' Ginnie added.

'But. . .'

'Why have we established support systems if we're not going to use them?'

'Don't worry,' said Liza. 'We'll help you care for her, and there'll be times when we need help with Quincy. And your car will be really useful, you know.'

'I'd like to teach Mab yoga,' said Lillian. 'After all, she's a yoga child.'

'But I feel I'm building up a debt of gratitude I can never repay. I don't know what to say.'

Ruba leaned over and grasped her hand. 'You will. You'll know.'

The Cathcart year climaxed in the Hildegard Kalkhoff Memorial Lecture. July sun streamed in at the windows of the packed hall, with the yoga women occupying the front row. There was one empty seat next to Ruba. An expectant hush fell as Iska Battenbury took the stand.

'Good afternoon and welcome to the Cathcart Institute, where it is my great honour to be giving the annual lecture in memory of a very great woman, our psychological mother, so to speak.'

There was a polite chuckle and a ripple of applause. Lillian arrived flustered and sat in the empty seat. She leaned across to Liza and whispered something. Iska looked at them from the platform while Liza signed: 'Yes, pregnant. Definitely.'

Iska beamed at Lillian. 'Where?' she signed.

'Tell you later,' signed Lillian. And Iska straightened her papers.

'My talk is entitled "Metaphorical Birth", and I would like to think that if Hildegard herself were here today she would take a benign interest in these proceedings. She was an innovator who gave birth to some extraordinarily original ideas whose consequences may be even more far-reaching than any of us have yet realised. I shall be giving the talk in English and British Sign Language for the benefit of my daughter and any other deaf person present.'

There was a stirring among her staff and colleagues who had no idea Miss Battenbury was a mother.

'There exist today two facts whose implications both psychically and physically are so highly charged with significance that even restating them may appear banal. These two facts exert a mutually polarising energy as do any play of opposites: birth and death, weight and feather, water and land—throwing up between them the antithetical landscape which we too often inhabit, in which we are too often lost. These facts are that all the trees in Hiroshima are exactly the same height and that conception may be a spontaneous creative act involving one individual or many but not necessarily two. I'll explain.'

Transparent, unwritable language streamed from Iska's hands. They fluttered, entwined, they moved in the wind, became lovers, finger-spelt the name of the Japanese town, made concepts into pictures, irony into cartoons, and let windows into emotions.

'Mankind—and I use the word advisedly—' she broke off to smile at the front row, 'is capable of inflicting collective planetary death. By contrast, if every male human dropped dead now,' Iska rapped the lectern with a dry knuckle, 'humanity could continue not only biologically as species but with those qualities we designate "human" quite secure. Some would say potentially enhanced. This is not speculation but hard fact. Incidentally, those trees in Hiroshima. They are of course the same height as they were planted at the same time. So what we are examining is the conflict between fission and fusion, between destruction and survival, that crude debate between bombs and sperm banks.'

There is no formal sign for 'sperm bank' in sign language so Iska had to mime it out. The yoga women laughed but elsewhere in the hall chairs scraped, buttons were twisted and throats cleared in the first fidgets of dissent.

'Mass contraception programmes have carried over the notion that relationships between man and women are somehow sterile. The connection between sex and its function of genesis has been ruptured and sex as pleasure and means to ownership substituted. A parallel compensation for this one-sided attitude has been the stimulation of the latently-held belief in parthenogenesis, a really cheering concept, especially for "women-identified women". The union or yoga of women in one-gender relationships is felt by those involved to be a profoundly creative act and resultant in metaphorical, if not actual, birth.'

Some of the psychotherapists in the audience were getting to their feet to protest.

'Please, ladies and gentlemen, do be patient. I shall speak for no longer than absolutely necessary, as I intend to pre-empt discursive argument by the force of example. But first, I should like to reiterate some simple facts of life: those relating to the method of birth. There is birth by egg, by water, by womb, and some would add by miracle. Then there are the means of conception. These are as various as the science that has transformed them, and we are forced to challenge and expand our definitions of birth until birth becomes vision upon vision of wholeness which gives a new meaning to the word "culture".

'If a hydra, one of the simplest forms of life, is cut into two, there are two. Spontaneous generation. Cut off a lizard's tail and it will go and grow another. Generation. Fruit trees and earth worms are hermaphroditic. Dandelions self-propagate. There may even be regenesis. Not strictly speaking examples of birth unless we define "birth" as an event and struggle towards wholeness, however partial. In humans, reproduction is complex. Heterosexual conception demands the female be penetrated by the male. But to that we must add artificial insemination and test-tube babies, cloning and genetic engineering. There is also self-insemination, a woman inserting donated sperm into herself, and sperm inserted by another woman—or even man—in a non-medical context would constitute an example of what I have called "shared insemination". Here we are talking about teaspoons and syringes as reproductive organs. These new forms of genesis raise moral and philosophical questions which we must confront. If there is no father, is there a father-rite? We must look into the eyes of our fathers, before we are able to extricate ourselves from their influence which is now biologically highly suspect.'

Iska could barely be heard above the furore in the hall.

'And now we come,' she continued speaking loudly into the microphone, 'to perhaps the most contentious form of birth—that of parthenogenesis—so-called "virgin birth"—in which an exterior impregnating agent is absent. Rabbits and people are parthenogenic. An act between members of the same gender producing an offspring will be rejected as scientifically inadmissible, and yet I name it as "partner parthenogenesis. . ."'

Ruba and Lillian smiled at each other.

'There are reports here of two black women in Port Elizabeth, South Africa, who after a sea bathe gave birth to a love child. And another. . .'

It was virtually impossible to hear her. Those leaving stayed by the doors to shout. The meeting was in disarray.

'. . .of an Asian woman who lived with other women in a village near Rimtek in Northern India and gave birth to a girl child out of her thigh. It seems there may be mythological retribution at work, a reversal of the monstrous usurping of the mother-rite by such inflated patriarchs as Zeus and. . .'

A surge of noise drowned her voice.

'. . . and then there is self-parthenogenesis, or miracle birth, the root fact of Christianity. Miracle is no exceptional event, though it has been made so by religious organisations who, by wrapping it in swaddlings of mystery, seek to rob us of our power. Miracle is a random act in which evolution leaps beyond itself; it is that movement in which the fine line of metaphor crosses into fact, "as if" becomes "that which is". It is conceivable that we are on the threshold of a matriarchical parthenogenetic dawn in which we shall create and nurture and in which the children within us can be born. A baby. Perhaps a book. Whatever. And we shall be kind to those with insight. And at this point, I would like to introduce my daughter, Mab, who as I explained is profoundly deaf. She could not have been born without the strengthening influence of the women of Beginners Yoga, Star-Crossed Institute of Further Education, whose interest and warmth was a primary factor in her conception and incubation. I shall read back her signs with some interpretation as Mab signs in a particular way and invokes different meanings of the same sign by the way in which she juxtaposes them, putting such pressure on language that at moments it becomes three dimensional.'

She laid her flowery hat on the lectern and sat Mab gently on its crown. Mab stretched for she had grown. When Iska held up a magnifying glass, the hall fell silent. Mab started to sign.

'My daughter says: "*name mab deaf hearing gone mum*—"'

'Mab is pointing to me and making the sign for "birth" which is two hands moving down either side of the abdomen, but she is making the sign on the head for Mab is my brain-child.'

The audience surged towards the platform, not believing their eyes, not believing Mab to be more than a turning plastic dancer on a music box. The yoga women stood—even Lillian—and faced them, forming an impenetrable barrier.

"'*you touch sky tall*
me—"'

'Here Mab is miming something very small pushing through something very hard,

"*—blade of grass*
when mum asked speak meeting
shocked trembling red shame
can't believe it
too small deaf

mum: *please*
me: *impossible. . .*"'

'This is an untranslatable deaf idiom meaning "devalued" or "useless".

"*see on table flowers*
think: got it hide hide long day

peep mum walking looking looking
shouts mab
laughing me like game
mum looking suddenly happens phone
sister. . ."

'Mab is referring to our friends in the front row,
"me lipread mum:
mab gone crying crying
me out flowers mum nothing see
shouting me mum not hear
finally mum see happy
say sorry trouble will speak meeting
people laugh size nervous
won't hear my little shout no good
mum, sisters: don't worry people ok
what say
don't know thinking thinking
what true important must say"

'Here Mab is miming scales with her hands. This is the sign for "doubt", "weight", "balance", "equality", concepts very similar in sign language.

"means same you tall same me small
you old equality same me
you poor me poor"'

The yoga women laughed and Mab smiled at them.

"'equality means love same you love me same
so all all same
all union decide best precious union"

'Mab sometimes signs "union" or "yoga" as linked fingers, which is also the sign of communication or relationship; but more frequently she uses her own sign, a composite of "women" and "together", because for Mab, that is what the world is. Hers is a world without fathers. She can see men just as she can see the difference between herself and the hearing world but she does not understand what men are for, although it has been explained to her. In Mab's eyes, men have no conceivable relevance and are an unfailing source of puzzlement to her.

"want me want all women together

> *freedom birth choice change*
> *agree?"'*

'Yes,' said a woman Iska recognised from the teachers' group. She was startled to see her face was wet with tears. Iska looked around. Only women were left in the hall now, although two or three men stood at a respectful distance near the doors, watching carefully.

'Agree,' said the woman next to her.

'Mab is deaf. She can't hear you.' The women looked at Iska blankly. 'This is the sign for "yes". Nod your fist.'

They did so.

'What's the sign for freedom?' asked someone at the back.

'Both hands out from the heart. Freedom. Freedom.' Iska showed them the sign, and those for 'birth' and 'choice' and 'change'. 'Put them together. That's it. Look, follow Mab.'

And one by one, woman by woman, everyone joined in, some clumsily, some gracefully, some smiling and some as if in a dream. Mab led them in the chant and they shouted with their hands, all in complete quiet. You could hear the grass grow. Then Mab made a fist with her tiny hand and held it in the air and that in any language is the sign for power.

RACCOONA SHELDON

Morality Meat

Alice Sheldon, also known as James Tiptree, Jr. and Raccoona Sheldon, was born in 1915 and spent her early years trekking across Africa and Indo-China with her parents. During the second world war she became a major in the US Air Force, and the first US woman photo-intelligence officer. She began publishing science fiction in the 1970s, under the name of James Tiptree, Jr, a pseudonym she chose from a jar of marmalade on a supermarket shelf. She won several Hugo and Nebula awards for her short stories and novellas. In 1977 it was discovered that Tiptree, acclaimed as an 'ineluctably masculine' writer, was in fact Alice B. Sheldon, a retired experimental psychologist. She has also written under the name Raccoona when she 'felt the need to say some things impossible to a male persona', producing 'a few overtly feminist tales' like 'The Screwfly Solution' which won a Nebula in 1977.

She says that 'Morality Meat' arose out of 'a very emotional outrage against the current savage proposals to force women to carry to term and give birth to, at risk of life, any fertilised ovarian cell, with no concern for the need for, or fate of, the human being thus coercively produced. Such initiatives may be seen as covert forays against women for their personal sexuality, carried so far as to punish them for being raped. It is also an unfavourable comment on the present moral tone of the US, where the greed of the rich has found an ally in government, and threatens to devour all.'

Cold, drizzle. Dark coming on.

Trucker Hagen is barrelling up the interstate in his eighteen-wheeler, trying to make time. He's bound for Bohemia Club North, and after Carlisle the road will degenerate to double-lane blacktop and twist up through the mountains. The north end of the interstate has only been finished this year; Hagen hopes they got as far as Carlisle.

Darker. He switches on his lights. A mile or so behind him another pair of lights comes on. That green Celica Supra is still hanging on his ass. But a glare on the road takes his mind off it: the drizzle is freezing in the dips. Yeah, and his brakes aren't all that good. He eases down a few clicks.

The lights behind him brighten briefly, then fade back again. Pacing him, all right. Hijackers, maybe, waiting to move in?. . .But the same thing had happened on other runs up here, he remembers. And nothing had come of it, nothing at all. Probably just part of the general Bohemia Club weirdness.

It has a funny atmosphere, that place, he muses. All men, most of them old. Not fags, no way. But not a woman there. Not one. And the old men are dressed all alike, some kind of shorts and badges too—almost like a bunch of senile Boy Scouts. Not Scouts, though—the place stinks of money. Very big money, if Hagen is any judge. Has its own airport, he glimpsed several private jets. And some of the cars by the main lodge made his eyes pop. The kind of money that's so big it hides, Hagen thinks. Hides out on uncharted islands, or like here in the mountains behind God knows how much private club property. The unmarked gate, with its gatehouse and dog patrol, is ten kilometres out from the lodge. Rich old boys pretending to be kids again, camping out in a fake wilderness. Pathetic.

But they want their city luxuries—oh, yes. The Bohemia fridge modules that fill most of the trailer behind him are full of steaks, chops, roasts—*meat*, for God's sake. At forty bucks a pound. Since the droughts and grain diseases finished off most of the US's meat production, Hagen hasn't tasted anything resembling beef in five years. Vegburgers. Soya everything— and that one rotten little so-called steak he and Milly had for their anniversary; fifty whole dollars. Even poultry got wiped out by that epidemic, and decent fish is hard to find. Hagen hates fish. But those old boys have their beef regularly.

Hagen spends a minute purely loathing them. But then he

remembers that the supply boss he delivers to is okay. If he's still there, chances are he'll bed Hagen down for the night in the help's compound. And maybe he'll even get a piece of real bacon with breakfast. That'd be a nice start for the rest of his deliveries up here in ski-lodge country.

Just then he hits the slick. A bad slick, very bad, running out on a curved bridge. Damn, real ice on that bridge. The clear air has momentarily fooled him. And now he sees the roadbed is graded wrong, it cants outward to a right-hand exit just beyond the bridge. Oh, Jesus. He gears down, down, braking all he dares.

The big rig is halfway round the curve when he feels the cab wheels start to follow that outward grade. Jesus, Jesus—can he possibly go with it and make the turn into the interchange road? Too sharp, no way. He's fighting to get her off that slide, to get back on the high inside of the curve. Too late—too late; the tonnage behind him is tracking the cab, with that sickening greasy feel of ice. And a big concrete divider is coming up dead ahead.

Panicking, he wrenches the wheel too hard, brakes screaming—and feels nightmares coming true.

The rig is going to jack knife over him.

There comes a forever minute of ghastliness—slow toppling, crashing, grinding—an impossible tilt. The wheel is in his gut, his forehead is wedged on the icy windshield. And then the beast behind him takes control of the cab, flinging it back and over and sideways, banging Hagen into blackness in a thunder of clanging and monstrous rips—

—They are down.

And Hagen is still alive.

From somewhere below he hears the crackle start. Fire! He gets one leg braced and heaves up at the cab door with all his might. Brokenness is all down his other side and arm. The door gives. In a pain beyond pain he crawls up and out onto the cab side, trying to see ground. The trailer has ridden partly up over the cab, split open, and from the broken fridge module a rack of cold slippery things are hanging around his head confusing everything. He bats at them, trying to see.

Light is coming from somewhere now—that following car, he thinks dimly. It's slowing. They have to see him. And the fire noises are getting louder—he has to get down out of there, *has to*.

As he pushes though the cold things, he gets a look at them in the stranger's headlights, and despite his agony he twists back for another look. He thinks he has gone crazy—but then he sees they have little curly ends. Tails—pig-tails. Frozen piglet carcases, is all. He goes sliding, scrambling down the cab side, lunging for the big front wheel. He hits it, steadies himself, sees a clear path to the ground and falls down it, crumpling as he hits. The broken oil-pan has sluiced all over his head, but he can move.

Through the oil he makes out the green Supra, stopped in the ring of fire-light. Two men are getting out. Hagen crawls toward them, hitching his broken side along the ground. Why don't the men help pull him away? Don't they know that rig behind him is about to blow to kingdom come, don't they know they're in danger too? He writhes, crawls, trying and trying to call to them for help. They'll help him, when they understand; they have to.

* * *

Earlier that same day, in the city far behind, a young girl carrying a baby struggled through the crowds to the L9 bus-stop, on the unfamiliar uptown side. She's sixteen years old and her name is Maylene; a small, *zaftig*, very dark black girl who moves tiredly. It has been a hard day at the K-Mart complaints terminal, a long trip home to fix up the baby and get her here.

The bus as usual is very late. Maylene watches two L9s go by without stopping.

By the curb is a clutter of streetpeople's box homes. The authorities don't bother bringing the fire-engines around here much. Maylene feels sorry for the streetpeople, but she's afraid of them too. She hates to see them burned out. The last time there'd been an old woman back in one of the shelters who couldn't get out.

The wind is icy cold. Maylene moves further back, into the shelter of the Drug Fair entrance. A gilt light falls on her from a display for PainGone. The light puts gold tints around her soft hair, and on the head of her pale-skinned infant, whose thin baby hair she has painstakingly corn-rowed and tied with a yellow ribbon.

The Drug Fair assistant manager, coming out to disperse the waiters, catches a look at her, and looks again. Something in the light on her narrow shoulders, the hollows under her cheek-bones that came from trying to feed two on wages that barely sustain one, maybe the very large brown eyes that seem to be seeing a crazy hope invisible to the others, jogs his memory. His Christmas window display has to be finished tonight.

At that moment an L9 arrives. It's crowded, but the driver stops. Maylene squeezes aboard, last as usual. She has the right notes in her cold hand. The baby, small as it is, weighs her down; she braces both legs, leaning against a seat-corner. She'll have to watch carefully, she tells herself she's never been this way before. Into white territory. Is that good? Maylene can't tell, but closes her eyes an instant in a silent prayer for guidance. And luck. Then she has a feeling she shouldn't petition the greatness of a male God for a trivial thing like her luck. Maybe His mother will understand better, she thinks, and changes her prayer.

The woman whose seat she's leaning on suddenly jumps up and ducks away through the aisle. A black lady sitting by the window reaches for Maylene's arm and gently pulls her down into the empty seat before the man beside them can take it. The seat feels warm. Involuntarily Maylene sighs, smiles with the comfort.

'How old's she?' The lady is smiling at Maylene's baby, who opens her own huge eyes and smiles her unearthly smile.

'Two months.' Maylene hopes the lady won't go on. As if catching the thought—or perhaps just too tired—the lady sits back up and rides to her stop with no more than a 'Good luck, dear.'

Now they were coming into an odd part of the city—one of the clean-looking little industrial parks with low office buildings, that sprang up after the bulldozers knocked down people's homes. What they called slum-clearance. Maylene unfolded the paper clenched in her hand and peered out. 7005. . .7100. . .the next block would be it, 7205.

Yes, there's the sign, gold on white like an expensive candy-box. The Centre is on the ground floor of one of the little office buildings, with a big carpark at the side. It is about half full.

Just as Maylene gets out and starts towards the Centre's doors, there's a snarl of truck gears and a man's voice cursing. A huge truck comes backing out of the carpark and turns heedlessly across the walk. Maylene glances across the cars and sees his trouble: a big fat pipe runs from the second storey of 7205 to the small manufacturing plant next door, with a sign saying CAUTION, 13 FEET 7 INCHES. Steam, or something, Maylene thinks absently, all her mind on what lies ahead.

Holding her baby close against the wind, she scurries up the pathway. The double-doors say in gold script, 'Come in! Come in! Welcome! For Blessed are they that give Life.' And then, in the lower corner, 'RIGHT-TO-LIFE ADOPTION CENTRE NO. 7'.

Maylene stops, her baby held so tightly that it murmurs. She *can't* go in. But there's another woman coming behind her. This gives Maylene strength to pull open the door and hold it for the other, a grey-haired, drawn-faced, white woman lugging a large, angry-looking infant wearing an engineer's cap. Behind her Maylene sees other figures converging on the Centre. Most carry babies, but there's a childless couple—no, two. People looking to adopt babies? Maylene sighs and goes on in, wondering if one of those couples will take her baby away.

She's in a warm, bright room, facing a plastic-padded counter, behind which white-clad nurses are coming and going. But she has time only to notice that the walls are papered with pictures of little animals in dresses—mice, maybe—and that there's a row of empty high-chairs by the counter, before a nurse is beside her and the other mother.

'You've come in the wrong side, my dears.' The nurse—she's white, like everyone Maylene can see here—urges them back. 'Unless you'd like to adopt another pretty little baby?'

No smiles from Maylene and the other. The child in the cap lets out a loud squall.

The door marked 'Baby Reception' is next to the one they'd come in. Inside is also warm and bright, with another padded counter. The walls are papered with foreign-looking flowers.

Several mothers are ahead of Maylene, talking about their babies to the nurses behind the counter. Each place at the counter has little side-walls for privacy, like in a bank. The nurses seem kindly and patient. But Maylene is wondering if her little one will be expected to eat sitting in one of those high-chairs. She had always eaten in Maylene's arms; Maylene could never have afforded a high-chair in any event. Will her baby be frightened, or cold?

Her baby—oh, how she dreads to give her up. She's the only thing Maylene has ever had all to herself; the love between them is like a living current. She doesn't dare even think about the days ahead, alone. . .

Whoever had given it to her she will never know. One of her brothers had found out where she lived, and suddenly he showed up at her room one night with bottles and what seemed at least a dozen wild young men; one or two of them looked white. He'd forced the drink down her, holding her neck and nose until she gagged it in. After that she recalled less and less, and finally nothing. . .but only came to in the morning alone and naked and sick, in a torn-up room.

She'd used no precautions, of course. She had no men friends and wanted none, and no one wanted her. She hadn't been quite a virgin; there'd been that terrible afternoon with her uncle when she was eight. And of course she knew what it meant when she started throwing up.

But quite soon she discovered that she very much wanted this baby. Even before she was born Maylene felt she knew her. The birth wasn't too bad, and after that their weeks together had given her all the joy she'd ever really known.

But then she started fainting at work, and the doctor at K-Mart laid down the law. She couldn't buy the baby's supplements and feed herself, too. And she might harm her child.

'People who adopt children take the very best care of them,' the doctor told her. 'They want them so much.'

So here she is, feeling like death.

Suddenly these thoughts are sent flying—a white girl waiting behind Maylene stamps past her up to the counter, dumps her baby on it, and bursts out loudly, 'To hell with this! You made me have him. Take him! He's yours.' She whirls and heads for the doors.

'Oh—but. Oh, Miss—Missus—you can't! You have to sign a release!' A nurse darts around the end of the counter to intercept the girl.

But the girl is big, and determined. 'Release?' she mimicks. 'Hell!' She slams out the doors.

An older nurse in the background is calling at an intercom: 'Doctor Gridley? Oh, Doctor Gridley!' From outside comes the racket of a car starting roughly. It accelerates away.

A tall man in doctor's whites comes out through a door in the back wall. 'Another dumper?'

'I'm afraid so, doctor. We were a little crowded here for a few minutes.'

'Well, just stick an 'X' on an orange label and I'll double-check it.' He sighs. 'Damn.'

Meanwhile the baby left on the counter hasn't made a sound. Now it begins to gurgle softly and turns its face toward Maylene. Something is wrong with it, she sees. Dreadfully wrong. It seems to have no upper lip, and there's what looks like part of another mouth, or face, merged into its cheek. And its legs and one arm are all short and twisted, too, and it's wearing a smeared bandage-thing instead of a little jacket. But it gurgles and slobbers happily enough while a nurse bundles a baby-blanket around it and lays it in a crib-cart. She ties a big orange label on the cart handle, and holds it up for the older nurse to mark.

'Doctor won't have to do much checking on this one,' the nurse smirks. The older woman, who seems to be the Head here, shakes her head crossly at the girl.

Maylene sees that all the newly-filled crib-carts have coloured labels tied on them. Some have big letters: 'CS', 'DF', 'S', 'BF'. Nurses are starting to wheel them into the back room.

The girl ahead of her turns away sharply, bumping Maylene.

Oh-h-h—it's her turn.

She slowly steps up to the counter, but her arms won't loosen. Unable to do anything at all, she stares mutely up into the face of the head nurse.

She looks down at Maylene's delicate little figure with its buttoned bodice, and understanding comes. 'I bet your baby is breast-fed.'

'Uh? Oh, yes,' whispers Maylene. 'What will. . .'

'Not to worry. We have two grand wet-nurses here.' The nurse turns to the back. 'Oh, Mrs Jackson! Are you free?'

'Coming!'

Mrs Jackson is a large, gloriously endowed, Indian-red, warmly-smiling lady. In no time Maylene finds herself releasing her precious armload into the other's friendly, capacious grasp. Mrs Jackson's bodice falls open and the little corn-rowed head burrows greedily into the source of all good things.

'I. . .I didn't have much milk. . .'

'Poor little creature,' Mrs Jackson croons impartially.

'We just slip a warm bottle to her one day when she's feeding, and she'll learn so fast you wouldn't believe it,' the head nurse tells Maylene. 'Now, dear, there's only this little paper to sign, right here. You take my pen.'

As Maylene goes out, numb, empty-armed, several pairs of hopeful parents are crowding in across the way. An idea comes to her: if she can just find a spot to wait out of the wind, maybe she'll see who takes her baby. She can see that bright yellow bow a long way away.

* * *

The six middle-aged people coming up the Centre pathway are clearly not prospective parents, although they turn to the Adoptions door. They are, in fact, the Right-to-Life Committee, or rather one of those few remnants of the Right-to-Life movement whose interest in other people's babies had persisted after their births had been legally enforced. Their visit is expected.

They come shivering into the bright room, hugging coats about them and exclaiming about the cold, to find six easy-chairs ranged invitingly along the lefthand wall. Head Nurse Tilley hurries out through the small crowd around the counter to welcome them. They can see the high-chairs, now occupied, and several white plastic baby-baskets on the counter, almost hidden by three sets of excited parents-to-be. Occasional glimpses of waving pink toes appear from the baskets; the future parents coo.

The Committee comprises four women and two men, who seem well acquainted with Nurse Tilley. When they're settled down, and a nurse's aide has offered hot coffee, cocoa or tea, Nurse Tilley produces her accounts file and presents it on a lapboard for the group's accountant, Mrs Pillbee, to examine. The other members turn beaming smiles on the infants and the adoptions in progress.

In the high-chairs are picture-pretty babies, all dressed in the Centre's white teddy-suits with different-coloured bows on their baby forelocks. Three are clearly white, one dark, and there's an enchanting brunette in a gorgeous cornflower-blue hair-bow who is so pale it's impossible to be sure of its race.

'Just to think,' says Mrs Dunthorne, the Committee's leader, 'if it hadn't been for our work, all these lovely, lovable little people would have been *murdered*. Murdered in the womb by unnatural mothers!' Her voice becomes choked, she dabs at her eyes with a scrap of lace. 'A Constitutional Amendment,' she says reverently. 'To think that the terrible crime of abortion is forbidden for ever now! Oh, we owe so much to you, Mr Seymour. No one could have fought harder against those cold, heartless, people.'

She sneezes, and gets up to take a closer look at the babies in the baskets. A moment later she's joined by the lady who was sitting on Mr Seymour's other side.

'If *only* he'd have it cleaned,' Mrs Dunthorne whispers to her friend. She is referring to Mr Seymour's trenchcoat, from which flows a powerful odour of formaldehyde. Her friend nods, also dabbing her nose. 'I expect he's not too well off.'

'But is he going to spend the winter in it? I mean, no one could be a nobler soul—Oh, you cunning wee thing,' Mrs Dunthorne says hastily as a nurse goes by.

Head Nurse Tilley is also glancing curiously at Mr Seymour.

She has long known him as the flaming figure of outrage who produced trimester foetuses in bottles at legislative hearings, and thrust them full at the TV cameras so the little faces and fingers showed, demanding to know who in the audience could kill or deliberately tear apart this 'beautiful little person?'

The TV had not, however, shown the last Alabama ratification hearing, when Mr Seymour had manipulated his bottles with so much emotion that one broke in his pocket, and he had bolted for the corridor crying, 'Get this *thing* off me!'

Mrs Dunthorne and others had surrounded him at once and no one ever mentioned the episode. But it is becoming clear that someone—perhaps their new male member, Mr George?—must tactfully raise the question of coat-cleaning.

Mr George, at the moment, is questioning Nurse Tilley. He seems to have more interest in figures and details than Mrs Pillbee. Nurse Tilley is all smiles; she has never been sure how far the Committee was clued into the Centre's total operations—the operations that made the Centre possible—so she played it safe. These people might still be under the illusion that the trickle of adoptions and voluntary contributions could do it all.

'That's right,' she says. 'All one hundred and thirty-four infants cleared for adoption have found parents since your last visit. Plus six in long-term hospital care. I'm happy to say we even found a home for one mild case of Down's syndrome. The mother had been told that hers would be a Down's baby, and when she found she couldn't obtain an abortion, she made several attempts to self-abort, and then refused to eat until her life was threatened so she had to be forcibly fed. But the child survived all this and came to us. The adoptive father is a child psychologist who believes Down's babies can be greatly helped.'

Murmurs of gratification.

'Oh, my,' Mrs Dunthorne exclaims, 'Mr Seymour, we simply *must* get more publicity for the work our Centres are doing! Wouldn't that help you, my dear?'

Nurse Tilley assents a trifle dubiously, as Mr George breaks in.

'Now tell me, Nurse. You show the adoption rate of babies

that are cleared. But I don't see your total intake, your holding of babies both cleared and uncleared.'

Nurse Tilley smiles harder. 'Oh, that figure can be reconstructed for any day, even any hour you choose.' She shuffles papers expertly. 'But frankly we haven't found it useful, because, among other things, times vary so wildly. It can happen that a baby comes in, gets checked, and goes out adopted in two hours, while another one with a case of the sniffles is held for two weeks. And if a baby is suspected of a communicable childhood disease, it can mean holding quarantine for a large group. You know how *some* mothers are about vaccinations. . .' Her tone is pointed and there are responsive sighs, as if she had held up a cue card saying 'Black Welfare Mothers'.

'And weekends—the labs are closed, you see, but people come anyway; even the time of day makes a difference—' She chats on automatically, trying to dispel the image behind her eyes that haunts her life—the vision of babies, babies, babies inexorably being born, unrelentingly flooding down over Centre Seven and the rest. Sometimes she felt she would drown in surplus babies, babies at first individual, tragic, then finally only figures. Figures which bore no relation to the hundred and thirty-four she had cited to the Committee. Numbers which her job depended on obscuring from the prying eyes of the Mr Georges.

'—and people holding responsible jobs tend to come in to adopt quite late in the day, even at night. We never close. So our population fluctuates.' Big smile. She hopes it will quiet Mr George. But he has one more question.

'Do I understand that you keep them all on these premises?'

'Oh, yes. We have plenty of room back there, and luckily we've been able to obtain some holding space upstairs too. Of course, we have a full paediatric staff, a cook, and two wet-nurses for infants that need weaning. Excuse me, is something wrong, Miss Fowler?'

While she was speaking, several couples have made their selections, checked in at the legal desk, and gone. But one couple is upset. The woman's voice is loud, touched with hysteria. 'But there *must be one*, Nurse. We called.'

The nurse at the counter explains. 'They had their hearts set on a fair-haired baby with blue eyes.'

'Everyone in our family,' the woman cried, '*everyone* has golden hair and blue eyes. Show them, Hugo!' Rather sheepishly, the man pulls off his fur cap, revealing a crest of ruddy gold. His eyes, like the woman's, are bright blue.

'I know this is a darling baby—' the woman gestures at a basket, 'but her eyes are hazel. It's no use, Hugo. Let's get out of here.'

'Oh wait, please,' says Nurse Tilley. 'I see we must let you in on our little secret. First, please, can I count on you to keep something *really* confidential?'

Puzzled, the couple nod.

'Very well. Miss Fowler, would you bring in the blue-ticket basket in the reserved—' her voice drops to a murmur. Miss Fowler nods and goes. While they wait, Nurse Tilley explains.

'You see, my dears, there's such an unthinking demand for blond, blue-eyed babies that if we displayed them normally, the others who may be lovelier and better in their own right wouldn't be looked at. And people would even quarrel over them—dreadful. So we reserve these few for people like you, with a special need. By the way, the baby I have in mind is a girl. Does that make a difference?'

'Oh, no! Oh—that's what we—'

Smiling, Nurse Tilley holds a finger to her lips and they fall silent.

In a moment Miss Fowler comes back in, carrying a white baby-basket. Nurse Tilley glances over and nods her head, Yes. The basket is placed before the waiting blond couple. Miss Fowler opens a dimity flap to display the infant. The Committee, staring frankly, see them both gasp a long breath, and then explode together in almost incoherent expressions of delight. Miss Dunthorne and Mrs Pillbee edge closer to look.

In the Centre's white blanket lies a peaches-and-cream baby; her forelock is true yellow gold, tied with a little green bow, and her large eyes look up with the deepest gentian-blue gaze the ladies have ever seen. In the gaze is a beguiling hint of curiosity, and she smiles with great sweetness.

'She's just been fed, she doesn't feel too active,' Nurse Tilley tells the enraptured future parents. The brilliant blue gaze hides as the baby's eyelids droop. She yawns like a kitten, then looks up again at the huge faces pressing lovingly toward her.

Nurse Tilley continues smiling automatically as the papers are filled out, the deliriously happy adopters dropping pens in their reluctance to free hands of their treasure. The nurse's work over the years has taught her much about infant development, and she has carefully observed this angelic-looking child. What she has been watching is a trace of—call it slowness. Perhaps it will wear off. But in her heart of hearts, Nurse Tilley has a prevision. That wonderful blue, blue, faintly questioning stare, that smile, will exert their magic through the first years. And motor development will probably be okay. But by the time she's about ten the smile will begin to lose its charm, and the little problems with reading and maths will begin to loom larger. With puberty, the reactions will begin to change from exasperation to tragedy. And then. . .Nurse Tilley's vision ends in the unchanging light of an institutional day-room, where a greying blonde woman will look up from the picture magazine with that same bright blank wondering smile. And the peaches-and-cream forehead will wrinkle as she wonders why the kind people who'd taught her to say 'Mummy' and 'Daddy' don't come around any more. . .

Nurse Tilley shakes herself. She could be wrong—she has to be wrong. And the couple had asked for a blue-eyed blonde. Which was what they had, no more, no less. From outside comes the quiet starting of a big, expensive car. Nurse Tilley has checked enough to know that money at least will be no problem here.

'Do you have many like that hidden away back there?' one of the ladies is asking.

'Oh, no—just when we get an unusual type someone might ask for. Oh! Oh, Mister George! We don't go back there, if you please.'

But the quiet Mr George has quietly vanished through the doors to the back room, with Nurse Tilley in hot pursuit.

She has him back in a moment.

'I should have explained. We do try to keep conditions as near sterile as possible. Of course they're not truly sterile, but for instance we wear different shoes from our counter ones. And feeding is just over. If one baby gets frightened of a stranger you could have the whole place yelling and losing their dinners. And the doctors are doing their rounds. If you'd care to watch, I should have opened this for you—'

She draws back a vertical blind to reveal a big plate-glass viewport in the back wall. Long lines of crib-carts can be seen, extending to the distance. 'Here are some paper shoe-covers, if you'd be so good.'

As the group gets shod and shuffles to the glass, Mr George says drily, 'That fellow in the red cap and bloody sheet doesn't look very sterile to me.'

'No, he doesn't. And I'm going back there right now to find out what's going on. If you'll excuse me—' She leaves the party clustered around the viewport.

Through it they can see Doctor Gridley and his two colleagues working down a line of cribs quite near. The babies' temperatures are being taken. Mrs Pillbee turns away, slightly pink around the nose. In the middle distance Nurse Tilley has intercepted the strange figure, a man in workman's clothes covered with a blood-stained sheet worn like a cape. He's holding one forearm with the other. Doctor Gridley goes over to speak to Nurse Tilley. He gestures to the man's feet, and the watching group sees the man is in his stockings. In a moment or two Nurse Tilley, smiling, comes back out to them.

'An emergency,' she explains. 'Really life or death. One of the workmen in the plant next door got his hand caught under a blade and nearly severed it. Bleeding terribly, of course. They made a tourniquet and took him to the back door here because they knew we had a doctor. He even had the sense to kick off his boots before he came in. Poor fellow. There's a good chance he'll keep the use of his fingers because the doctor got to it so quickly. But if he'd had to wait for an ambulance he might well have died from loss of blood. I can assure you, Mr George, that this sort of thing doesn't happen often! Well! Is there anything else you'd like to look over?'

'Lots of black kids over on the far side there,' remarks Mr George, still peering. 'I suppose you quarantine them?'

'Oh, my goodness, no. That's just pure chance tonight. See,

there're whites among them if you look.'

Eyes followed Mr George's gaze to the right side of the big room, where crib after crib holds a small black head; several of them wear coloured bows. The back wall of the room turns into an offset, where a medical station might be, and the group of crib-carts are lined up as if awaiting treatment.

A medico carrying a trayful of little syringes is at the line.

'What's he going to do?' asked Mrs Pillbee. 'Vaccinations?'

'No, I think not, that's usually done individually. I think that's the evening shot. Vitamins, and an infant tranquiliser. One of our worries is that a restless baby might start the whole roomful howling just before bedtime.' She glances at her watch. 'I think that's what's going on now—he's putting them to sleep.'

'What does DF mean?' another of the ladies asks. Nurse Tilley frowns.

'DF. . .DF. . .D'you know I can't remember! I know BF means 'Breast-Feed', and CS means 'Cleared for Show' and an orange tag means all data missing—the mother just dropped it and ran away. DF. . .must be something to do with vaccinations.'

'Are there really that many black families wanting to adopt a baby?' asks a lady who hasn't spoken before.

'Looks like it!' Nurse Tilley laughs. 'Of course, they may all give out suddenly. But we absolutely discourage cross-racial adoptions,' she adds soberly. 'It's not fair to the child. One thing about black adoption, you see much more of parents who already have two, three, even four kids adopting another, or even two. With whites it's your childless couples who adopt. Anything more? No?'

Coats and scarves are retrieved.

'Of course, you can always go over and watch the receiving side, but frankly, I'd advise against it. Here you've seen the happy endings of a few little stories, but at the input you get a steady diet of depressing scenes. Of course you might be interested in the unobtrusive methods we have for keeping new babies quarantined, and I'm very proud of the staff over there, they do a wonderfully sympathetic job at high speed. If one dawdles about sympathising *too* much, you know, people break down and lose their resolution to do the right thing. Takes quite a knack. I'm proud of those girls. But there doesn't seem much point in your depressing yourselves after you've seen how well most things turn out, does there?'

The Committee couldn't agree with her more.

* * *

Outside, the wind has grown even colder. Maylene can't find a sheltered spot where she can see the doorway well enough.

The plant next door is working on night shift, but when Maylene goes close to it her view is blocked by two big trucks. Finally a Burger King trailer pulls out, and Maylene stands by a warm vent from which she can keep watch on the Adoptions door. She's right under that pipe from the plant to the Centre, it should shed some heat.

But just as she's getting warm, a guard comes and shouts at her. She can't hear what he's saying because of a rumbling, scratching sound in the pipe overhead, more like a conveyor belt than steam. But his gestures are unmistakable—he wants her away from there. Maybe he thinks she's a streetwoman. But she has to go. And anyway, the vent and the rubbish smell bad. So she just keeps walking fast, to and fro in front of the Centre.

As she's about to freeze, a girl's voice calls softly, 'You watching the door?'

'Uh—yes.'

'Not there. Round here. They come out the side.' The girl ducks back into the carpark and Maylene follows to the shelter of an old van. From here she can clearly see the side door; it has a light over it. At that moment a couple come out with a baby in a plastic shell-basket. Maylene gets a good look at the baby's head. No bow.

'You fix a ribbon on your baby?'

'Yeah. Red, with some gold stuff in it.'

'Mine's yellow.'

'I wonder, do they take them off?'

'Don't say it.'

They have to step back for a white couple coming out with a baby in one of the shell-like plastic baskets; the Centre must give them away. The baby has pale straw-coloured hair. The woman is carrying him, and as they go round the van, Maylene hears her say, 'That's *weather*, darling. This is *cold weather*. Oh you'll get to love it, you'll have a little sled—Oh, Charles, isn't he adorable? Just *exactly* what we dreamed of.'

The man halts to look. 'Yeah, yeah,' he says happily. 'Sure is. . .we better get him in the car before we freeze his little nuts off.'

'Charles!' she giggles.

A weary looking older white woman comes walking slowly around the corner from the main door. She halts by the van's driver's side and starts fumbling with keys. Then she sees them.

'Oh—I'm so s-sorry—' And then she's crying openly, leaning her head on the van. Uncertainly, the girls go around to her.

'Oh, I'm sorry. . .D-don't mind me, it's j-just a mistake, it's all a terrible mistake.' She's crying so hard, silently, that her body shakes the van.

'Ma'am, you shouldn't drive like this,' says Maylene's new acquaintance, whose name is Neola. 'Is there something we can do for you?'

'N-no.' The woman's head swings from side to side, despairingly. 'A mistake—look at me! My periods stopped four years ago. I thought I was through with all that, I thought there wasn't any danger, and we didn't take any—and then the doctor took another test and told me the baby was defective. *Bad* defective. And it would cost like thirty thousand dollars so it could even walk. We don't have any thirty thousand dollars, all we have is just the money for our girl's college. And so I decided to have an abortion, but they said that was illegal now. I had to *h-have* it. And it tore me all up inside, when you're older, you're not flexible like a girl.' She lifts her head and stares at them despairingly, adding in a low voice, 'When you looked at her from a certain angle she didn't look defective, you know. Just for a second she'd look really pretty. Like she might have been if I hadn't been so *old*. Oh-h-h. . .oh dear, I didn't mean to dump my troubles on you, you probably have enough. When I was in the hospital first there was a little girl who'd been raped by four men including her own father—and they wouldn't help her. I heard later she tried somewhere illegal and died. *That's* trouble, I shouldn't boo-hoo.'

She looks around disorientedly, then at the keys in her hand.

'My dears, I have to take this junk-pile out. Where can you stand? You're watching the door, right?'

'Yeah. Oh, we'll find a place.'

'Easier said. It's colder'n a bitch.' Hearing her own words she laughs jeeringly.

But there just is no shelter. The cars beyond the van are all knee-high cars, except one truck at the far end.

'We'll go down there.'

'Where you can't see the door. Oh, *dear*.' The woman looks across the mid-lane to the row of cars opposite. 'Could you see the door from there, I wonder?'

Suddenly they all jump as a horn taps melodiously right opposite. A car door opens, and a formidably chic, young, pale-skinned black woman leans out.

'You watching for your kids?' Her accent is markedly 'white'.

'Yes.' Maylene is intimidated by this spectacular creature.

'So am I. I was going to ask if you want to sit in here with me where it's warm. You can see perfectly.'

'Oh, yes thank you.'

'Well that solves the problem,' says the white mother of the defective child, getting laboriously into the van.

She drives away, and Maylene and her new acquaintance climb timidly into the warm velour interior of the fanciest car they've ever been in.

The light-skinned woman says, 'Only one problem. If I see someone with my son I'm going to follow them. That's why I have the car facing out. You may have to get out in kind of a hurry—but there'll be time. I won't kidnap you.'

'Follow them?' Maylene asks, surprised.

'Yes. I want to see who they are and where and how they live. Oh, I'm not going to make trouble or anything. They'll never know I know—but I want to keep track as long as I can.'

'Oh, I wish I'd thought of that,' said Maylene wistfully. 'But of course I don't have a car.'

'Hmm. . .' The strange young woman is evidently turning this over in her mind, trying to figure some way to help, but there seems no way. 'A taxi, maybe?'

Maylene laughs. The stranger picks up her real leather purse. 'Look—'

'Oh, I couldn't, I just couldn't,' Maylene protests.

Reluctantly, the young woman puts the purse away. 'Did you bring your baby in?'

'Yes. . .and she's, uh, breast-fed—'

'Oh, well,' the other says relievedly, 'I hate to tell you, but she won't be coming out today. They wean them first.'

'Have you been waiting long?' asks Neola.

'Six hours. I don't know why. It's crazy, but I have this hunch. . .'

'Did you put a ribbon or something so you can be sure?'

'Yes. A big blue headband.'

'Mine's red and gold, and hers is yellow,' said Neola. 'We were wondering, do they take them off?'

The girl sighs. 'Yes. That's another trouble. I guess they leave them on if they're going to show them right away, but they probably come off tonight. The first day must be the only time you really have a chance, unless you get close enough to see its face. I s'pose that's all my hunch is, really—just a last chance.'

There's a silence in the warm car. Several couples come out with baskets, but none of the babies wears a bow.

'God, you hear some stories,' the pale woman says reflectively.

'Yeah.'

'Are you one of the tragic ones? Don't mind my asking, I'm kind of a reporter. I'm going to do a piece on this, believe it.'

'No,' says Maylene sadly, 'I just couldn't feed us both. I'm a K-Mart Company trainee, and they take so much out of the pay they said we'd get.'

'Me too,' says Neola. 'Only I'm at an airline, learning computerised reservations. They say, when you get good and are due for your full salary, they fire you and hire other trainees because it's cheaper and the new girls are almost as good because they try so hard, see?'

'Sweethearts,' the reporter girl says acidly. She pulls out a notebook and asks them for some facts and numbers. Maylene notices that her attention never totally leaves that door.

'Why did you have to give up your baby?' she asks daringly when the strange girl puts her pad away.

'I didn't exactly *have* to. I wanted to because I hate his damned father. I thought he was my *friend*, see, not to marry, but like a real deep friendship that would last. . .and he's great, politically.' She notices their blank expressions. 'I mean, he seemed to be all for women, and ERA, and real equality, etcetera, etcetera. Yak-yak. One afternoon I happened to pick up the extension while he was chatting with a mate, and I learned a whole lot in a big hurry. Among other points his advice was, always keep your women pregnant: "a little bit pregnant". Notice that "women", too. Plural. He wasn't just talking macho, he meant it, he was giving real advice to a pal on how to live. Anyway I went home and soaked a couple of pillows crying. And then I tried the abortion route, I guess you know all about that. . .' She sighs. 'I'd imagined we could sort of raise the baby together, you know—Oh, I didn't expect him to do housework, we weren't living together. But I thought he'd be—like—*there*. Now it seems he has kids all over town he's never seen. The great revolutionary. Keep'em barefoot and pregnant.' She laughs the strangest, hardest laugh Maylene has ever heard.

'Oh,' say the other two girls together, not understanding much except the pain.

'But you could keep your baby?' Maylene asks.

'Correction. *His* baby. *His* little pregnancy. You know how he did it? He punches pinholes in his condoms. And I thought he was so nice and considerate, wearing them. Because my doctor says the pill is bad for my heart. Pinholes! And I think once he pinholed some girl's diaphragm. No, I don't want the pinhole baby, thank you.'

Maylene can sort of not quite almost understand.

At that moment the front seat fairly leaps under them as the strange girl jerks upright to see better.

'It's him! It's him! They've got my baby!'

Across the street, a light tan couple are laughing over a white baby basket out of which sticks a little head with a big blue bow.

The girl is quietly turning the motor on.

'Listen kids, I'm sorry but this is as far as we go. Oh God, they're getting into that Mercedes. Look, here's what you do. Go straight *in* that side door and look around hard and fast at the babies on show. Then sit down as if you're expecting somebody. Make up a name, say anything—Mrs Howard Jellicoe. Tell'em she told you to wait. Get it? They'll let you stay long enough to be sure if your babies are going to be shown tonight. If not—I hate to say it—I'm afraid you've had it. It's getting late. Of course, you could always try tracking them legally, claim there's an inheritance or something.'

The girls are out now. She pulls the brake off. Down the row, a silver-coloured car is quietly backing out towards them.

'Goodbye, kids. Good luck. Remember, walk straight in!'

The silver car is pulling out of the far exit. Their temporary benefactrix accelerates smoothly after it.

'You know,' says Neola, 'I don't think she hates that baby so bad.'

Maylene nods. Their own plight strikes home on a blast of icy wind.

'I'm scared,' Maylene says.

'So'm I. But we're together, the worst they can do is tell us to leave. We aren't breaking any law. Come on now. Come on.'

They go up to the Adoptions door and enter. The same mice Maylene had seen hours ago are still frisking on the walls. In her panic, she forgets all about Mrs Howard Jellicoe. But Nurse Tilley, guessing their trouble and knowing how cold it is outside, lets them stay quite a long while, and even look through the window to the back.

The long lines of cribs bewilder and discourage them. Just as they're about to turn away, they see a nurse pick up something from the floor by the cribs—a full plastic bag.

'That poor man from the plant must have dropped this,' they hear her say, holding it up. 'But whatever *is* it?'

One of the doctor-looking men comes over and looks.

'Pigtails!' He snorts. 'Piggy-wigs' tails!' He shakes his head and goes away.

'Yech,' says the nurse, going to a side door.

After one last despairing look, Maylene and Neola turn away. It's clear that no red or yellow ribbons are waiting to be shown this night.

* * *